Stone Society Book 2

Faith Gibson

All rights reserved. In accordance with the U.S. Copyright Act of 1976, the scanning, uploading, and electronic sharing of any part of this book without the permission of the publisher is unlawful piracy and theft of the author's intellectual property. Thank you for your support of the author's rights.

This book is a work of fiction. Names, characters, places, and incidents are the product of the author's imagination or are used fictitiously. Any resemblance to actual events, locations, or persons, living or dead, is coincidental.

The author acknowledges the copyrighted or trademarked status and trademark owners of the wordmarks mentioned in this work of fiction.

Copyright © 2015 by Faith Gibson

Published by Faith Gibson

Editor: Jagged Rose Wordsmithing

First e-book edition: February 2015

First print edition: February 2015

Cover design by KPG, photos from Shutterstock and Natalya Sidorova / 123RF

ISBN: 978-0692369333

This book is intended for mature audiences only.

Dedication

Kendall – Without your dedication, the series wouldn't be off to such a stellar start. Thank you for all you do, and just basically being my sunshine.

The man – Thank you for each and every woohoo when I sell a book. I love you, babe.

Acknowledgements

My writing posse: Kendall, Jen, and Nikki – we did it. Again.

My beta readers: Alex B, Sharon B, Candy R, Tanya R, and Shannon P.

KPG – Another stellar cover. Your talent just grows.

All the ladies at TaSTy WordGasms, thank you for blogging, pimping, Gregor's Cover Reveal and Release, and just basic stellarness.

Pam Brooks – the ultimate Rock chick. Thank you for the shout outs, my rock and roll hoochie koo.

Ashley Westphall-Carr – I like having a shadow. Thank you for following me around.

JAG – you are there every single day, rooting me on. Dude.

Prologue

2044

A sleek, black Harley pulled up to an open gas pump. Gregor Stone eyeballed the bike, comparing it to the one he was currently filling up. His was a couple of years newer, but the other one had more chrome. Sharp. The driver pulled their helmet off and hung it over the mirror on the handlebar. Long red hair cascaded down the back of the rider, as a black leather boot swung over the seat. A blue jean clad ass sashayed into the store. *Fuck me.*

Gregor put the nozzle in the holder and waited. "Please see cashier for receipt." He strode inside the store, stepping up behind the redhead. While he was waiting his turn, Red pulled several bills out of her pocket to prepay, and one floated to the floor. Sandalwood and leather filled his nostrils, making him lightheaded. Red bent over to retrieve the wayward cash, and her divine ass landed firmly in Gregor's crotch. A groan escaped his throat as the biker stood up and glanced over her shoulder. "If you're gonna ride, Stud, make sure you pull my hair."

With a wink, she turned around and paid the cashier then strolled out the door, not looking back. Gregor just stared, mouth agape. His body was humming.

"She's feisty, that one," the cashier said with a chuckle.

"I need my receipt, Peg. When are you going to add paper to the pumps?" Gregor's eyes never left the redhead as she put high octane into her ride.

"Now, Warden, if I put paper out there, you wouldn't have a reason to come in and see me. Here you go." Gregor turned to the woman behind the counter. If

1

Peggy was a day younger than sixty, he'd put the paper out there himself.

"Thanks, Beautiful." Gregor leaned across the counter and kissed her cheek.

By the time he was done flirting with his old friend, the back end of that hot piece was rolling out of the lot.

What the hell is wrong with me? Tessa Blackmore rode her bike hard. She felt fine until she stopped to get gas and bumped into the warden, literally. Gregor Stone. What an ass. Too bad his nice backside was attached to the rest of him. Fucking full-blood. Gods, she ached all over. Just how fast can the flu come on? Pretty damn fast.

She parked behind her house, not bothering to garage her Harley, then climbed off and made her way into the kitchen. She stripped out of her clothes and headed to the shower. The ache was so much more than the flu. Pain shot through her hands, and her gums felt like they were going to explode. She dropped to her knees and grabbed her head. "Agggggg! NO, this is impossible!" Tessa had helped several of her kind through the change, so she knew what to expect. "He CANNOT be my MATE!" She yelled to the cosmos.

Tessa's job within the family was to watch over the offspring of human women and full-blood Gargoyle shifters, helping them through their transitions. Half-bloods didn't come into their powers until they met their mate. This was an unknown fact within her community. She stumbled on the information when she found her Uncle Jonas' journal. A journal that was now in her possession, locked in her safe. He didn't know Tessa knew nor that she had the journal.

Her fangs elongated nipping her lip. "Shit!" She reached up to wipe the blood and nicked her chin with a claw. "Dammit!" This was easier when she was watching someone else go through it. She held her hands out in front of her. *Imagine going in for a manicure with these suckers.* Laughing at her sick joke, she poked her mouth again. Concentrating, she thought about her human hands, and her claws retracted. She did the same with her fangs.

Collapsing on the floor, she was really glad she didn't get wings.

One

The first time Tessa had been followed, she found it exhilarating. The second and third, annoying. This time it was just downright pissing her off. Once again, a Mustang got on her tail and began a chase through the side streets and back roads of New Atlanta. Once again, she lost her pursuer. When she felt the coast was clear, she looped back around the way she had been traveling and headed to her cousin's house. Isabelle refused to answer her calls. Ever since Tessa told her the truth about who and what they are, the doctor had been keeping to herself.

Tessa hadn't seen her cousin since she accompanied Isabelle to the Penitentiary. The Pen's previous doctor was killed in a riot, and for some reason the warden felt Isabelle would make a good prison doctor. If he knew about her background, that would make sense. Isabelle was the daughter of Jonas Montague, the famous scientist and doctor who created the first cloned human. Being the largest prison in the south that contained the Unholy, they needed a doctor who was capable of dealing with non-humans.

Isabelle was a half-blood Gargoyle shapeshifter who hadn't yet gone through the change herself. She had, however, watched one of her older brothers go through his transition recently. Tessa needed to visit Dane and see how he was faring now that he was back at work as a detective with the New Atlanta Police Force. Being a half-blood shifter would give him an advantage when hunting the bad guys.

When Isabelle had been approached by Gregor Stone about the position at the Pen, Tessa knew in her heart her cousin would take the job. Her feelings were hurt, her pride wounded. Tessa really couldn't blame her, though. If she

4

were the one with the medical degree and her father chose to share his secrets with her rebel cousin, she, too, would feel slighted. Arriving at Isabelle's home, she drove her Harley around back. Isabelle's car wasn't in the drive, but she could have parked in the garage.

She shut the bike off, put the kickstand down, pulled her helmet off, and hung it over the handlebar. Tessa threw her leg over the bike and walked to the backdoor. She knocked then used her key to let herself in. "Isabelle," she shouted to her cousin. She stopped in the kitchen when she noticed a stack of papers on the table. Leafing through what appeared to be a new-hire packet, Tessa figured Isabelle had indeed accepted the job. "This might not be a bad thing," she muttered to herself.

Tessa's cloned brother, Tamian, was sitting in the Pen. When she visited the massive structure with Isabelle, she had seen him, mind spoke with him, told him she would get him out of there. For some ungodly reason, he thought he belonged in there. She knew better. She had looked after her brother over the years, and there was no better person on this planet. He was a giver, and she was going to get him out.

Tessa didn't know if all cloned siblings could hear each other's thoughts. She needed to teach Tam how to shield his from her when he was on the outside. There were just some things you really didn't want to know about your brother.

Now that Isabelle was working as the Pen's resident physician, Tessa could visit and scope the layout of the place. She knew breaking her brother out was going to be difficult, but she was up for the challenge. As long as she could avoid the warden, all would be well.

Fucking Gregor Stone. Why couldn't she have mated with a nice young Irishman? A nice *human* Irishman? But *no*, she must have pissed off the fates somewhere along the way for them to stick her with the hardass who ran the prison.

Isabelle Sarantos had been at her new job less than a week and was already wondering if she had made a mistake. For the last three days she worked non-stop to clean out her office. The previous doctor had been a slob. Now, she could finally see the surface of the desk. She sorted the abandoned paperwork into stacks. Some were inmate notes, some were random scribblings, and others were items that would more than likely end up in the trash.

She decided to take a break from sorting and started shuffling through the files. The first thing she did was put them in alphabetical order. Since these files were open and on the desk, the inmates could need immediate care. The phone on her desk rang causing her to jump. She hesitantly picked it up, "Hello?"

"Doctor Sarantos, there's a call for you on line one." The male voice disconnected. Who would be calling her here? She pressed the "line 1" button. "Dr. Sarantos speaking."

"So you took the job. I guess I should have known you would." Tessa must have invaded her home again. The papers detailing her new position were on the kitchen table, and the snoop would no doubt have read them.

"What do you want, Tessa? And please stop breaking into my home. As a matter of fact, leave the key on your way out."

"I don't need a key to get in the door, but that's beside the point. When were you going to tell me, or were you? It's going to be difficult to watch over you there."

"I have done well on my own all these years dear cousin. I have a feeling I can manage without you a few more. Besides, the warden is here. I can think of a lot worse men to look out for me." Isabelle heard Tessa choking. "Are you all right?"

"Fine. Freaking fine. You might want to watch him, and I don't mean stare at his ass. I *do* mean be leery of the man. He's been known to have a bad temper."

"How do you know so much about Gregor?" On the other end of the phone, Tessa coughed again. "What is wrong with you? Are you coming down with something?"

"You know we don't get sick, and now it's *Gregor*? What happened to Warden or Mr. Stone? You aren't actually interested in him, are you?" Tessa asked, not sounding like herself. She sounded...jealous.

"No, I'm not interested, but he is hot. The way his pants stretch over his tight ass. Yum."

"Yum? Did you just say yum? Who are you, and what have you done with my cousin?"

"I can appreciate a nice male physique. I was married to someone built just like him you know." Isabelle tried really hard not to think of Alexi. She had fallen quickly for the Greek god, and theirs had been a whirlwind romance. She had been young when she met him, and he talked her into moving to Greece to practice medicine there.

On one hand, she had been scared out of her wits. After seven years of studying, she deserved a nice long vacation; but still, she was too young to pick up and move to a foreign land. On the other hand, she really had nobody at home she needed to get back to. Once she started college, her foster family was out of her life, and she was basically alone. Having Alexi and his family was a huge incentive to stay. She mistakenly read their acceptance as love. What they were really after was her knowledge of her father's findings.

"Belle, did I lose you? Are you there?" She was brought out of the past by the one relative who stayed in touch over the years.

"I'm here. Now, why did you call, or are you just being nosy about Gregor?"

"I couldn't care less about him. Just so you are aware, he's a full-blood. You need to keep that in mind. And no, I don't need anything; I was just confirming that you did indeed turn your back on the family when we need you most."

"I will not have this conversation with you again. Don't call me at work; it's unprofessional and unnecessary." Isabelle hung up on Tessa. God she was so frustrating. "I turned *my* back?" As far as Isabelle was concerned the family turned their back on her a long time ago. She had sixteen brothers and sisters she hadn't known about until Dane, *and* she was a shifter. How in the holy hell do you let your child go their whole life not knowing what and who they are? Somehow she was going to find all of her siblings.

Gregor Stone is a full-blood? Why did Tessa wait until now to spring that on her? *Crap. Is he related to Nikolas Stone? That would make sense. Sort of.*

Returning to the inmate files, she read through several, noticing a pattern in the diagnosis and treatment. Holy crap! What the previous doctor had been doing was not only dangerous, but unethical. She opened another file, and what she read had her head spinning. *Oh my god.* She picked up her cell phone and dialed her cousin. Hopefully Tessa was still snooping at her house.

Two

Tessa had been in Isabelle's house several times but had never taken the opportunity to really look around. It was more than likely smaller than most doctors' homes, but Isabelle had never been pretentious or extravagant. She was a beautiful woman who never played to her looks. She dressed modestly and kept her home just as humble. She drove a gas-saving hybrid and had a recycle bin in the garage. Yep, her cousin was a do-gooder.

The one thing that stood out the most to Tessa was the lack of personal items, namely photos. There were no pictures anywhere in Isabelle's home. None on the walls, on the mantle over the fireplace, or in her bedroom. Not even a wedding photo. Even though the marriage to Alexi ended in tragedy, she should still have at least one picture of their life together. Maybe it was too painful to remember the happier times. Tessa's own home was filled with photos, but most of those were of places, not faces. She had the pleasure of traveling all over the world, checking in on her cousins. She did take photos of them, but from afar. Those photos were on a thumb drive she kept secure in a hidden safe.

Tessa was just starting her position as watcher for the family when Isabelle moved to Greece. Since Isabelle was so young, the family had Tessa watching the older siblings. Tessa still checked in on her cousin when she could. Jonas and Caroline had taken great pains in hiding the truth from Isabelle. When she was little, they lived a life of solitude, keeping Isabelle away from the public eye. If she wasn't around anyone, she couldn't spill the secret that Jonas was alive. As a precaution, he continued to wear disguises daily around his daughter. She was allowed to go visit Tessa and Elizabeth every so often. When Isabelle got old enough to notice her mother and Elizabeth were not aging, Caroline left. Jonas placed Isabelle with a couple in

Tennessee, explaining that his health was fading. Rico and Maria Sanchez cared for Isabelle until she graduated high school. Caroline watched over her daughter from across the street.

Jonas had taken Tessa under his wing when she was a teenager. Even though they spent a great deal of time together when she was a little girl, she didn't truly begin learning from him until she was older. He confided in her, telling her she was special to him since he successfully cloned her. She and her brother, Tamian, were his greatest accomplishment. Tessa felt bad for Isabelle. She should be the one sitting by Jonas, learning about the shifters and the cloning process. When she asked her uncle about it, he told her Isabelle had her own place in the world. She needed to learn independence, something Tessa had in spades.

Both Tessa and Tamian were sworn to secrecy regarding Jonas being alive, and Tessa's contact with her cousin waned with time and distance. Jonas hadn't felt Isabelle was mature enough to handle the knowledge of the shifters nor the responsibility that came with being a watcher. Tessa was an old soul, and even though she acted immature at times, she was mature in the ways that mattered. It helped having Jonas in her life. He raised Tamian until he was a teenager when he and Tessa swapped places. Even though Tam went to live with Elizabeth, he still visited Jonas often so they could spend time together. Once Tessa was old enough to travel, she left her family behind and started her own journey.

Tamian. Her brother was sitting in the Pen for some bogus rap, and she needed to figure out why. She had watched the news report when he was arrested at Lion Hart Dojo; some bullshit about him going berserk and attacking not only the owner, Geoffrey Hartley, but two others as well. Why had they called him Timothy? An alias, she presumed. Tamian St. Claire was the most calm, rational person on this planet. Jonas and Elizabeth felt it would be safest if she and Tamian kept their distance from each other, but with their bond being so deep, they usually ended up in the same area. They weren't twins, but the connection she felt with him had to be just as intense, if not more so. He was created from her DNA after all. He just happened to get the goodness gene from their mother.

When she went with Belle to the Pen, she had seen her brother. He told her he belonged in there. Something about that wasn't right, and she was going to get to the bottom of it. Belle taking the job was going to make her quest a little bit easier. She would only tell Isabelle about Tamian as a last ditch effort. Until then, she would just have to make herself a frequent visitor at the facility. She needed to observe and figure out Stone's schedule. There was no sense in bumping into him if it wasn't absolutely necessary. Once had been enough.

Tamian's identity had remained constant for the most part. He wasn't being stalked by Gordon Flanagan. Tessa, however, changed her identity often. It was amazing how easily you could become another person with a few strokes of the computer keys. She had different names for every city she visited. The man who thought of himself as her father was a monster and was hell bent on finding her. It was his life's mission to tear the world apart until he found his child. He had never come close, until recently.

Flanagan was convinced his twin brother, Magnus, had been instrumental in Elizabeth's disappearance with Tessa. When Flanagan got too close to finding either her or Elizabeth, the family would send in a decoy, trying to lure the man out. Taking Gordon Flanagan down was proving to be next to impossible. Over the years he created his own army of monsters who were dubbed the Unholy. These inhuman creatures were the worst of the worst, and they kept him sheltered and protected at all times, at all costs.

When The World Council Delegation had recently been held in New Atlanta, a decoy, Conrad, had gone in, trying to flush Gordon out of hiding. Unfortunately it backfired.

Flanagan managed to kidnap twelve Delegates, one of those being "Magnus", and the end result was a horrendous death for the man. Had her cousin been a full shifter, he could have protected himself. Since he hadn't gone through his transition, he was merely a human. Tessa felt responsible even though she shouldn't. Normally, only the cousins who had already gone through their transitions knew of the family. Somehow Conrad had found out and insisted on volunteering. Everyone in the family knew the risk of being undercover, as well as the possibility of coming face to face with Gordon. Tessa argued if Flanagan somehow found out his brother was dead, he would stop coming after him. They countered that if he thought Magnus was dead, he would turn up his efforts in finding Elizabeth. Wasn't that his ultimate goal anyway?

Tessa was supposed to be flying to Louisiana in a few days to check on one of the cousins who had yet to change. Normally she would be looking forward to such a trip. Instead, she had a bad feeling in her gut about leaving. Whether it was Isabelle, Tamian, or someone else, she wasn't sure. She just knew she was needed here.

She locked the back door behind her and straddled her bike. She still had a couple of days before she left, and she was going to make the most of them. Just before she cranked the engine, Tessa's phone vibrated in her back pocket. She pulled it out and looked at the caller ID: Belle. Surely she had butt dialed her, because her cousin only called when she needed something. She'd made it perfectly clear she didn't need Tessa anymore.

"Belle?" She answered just in case.

"You're not going to believe what I found. My god, Tessa. The man experimented on the inmates."

"Who, the doctor?"

"Yes, and he knew about us and the Gargoyles. It's all here in his notes. He was secretly extracting blood from Unholy and injecting it in the inmates to see what effects it would have. Where would he get Unholy blood?"

"Isabelle, don't mention this to anyone, especially Gregor. I'm on my way." She disconnected her phone and buckled her helmet in place while letting her bike warm up. *Sonofabitch.* Tessa had overheard about Dr. Henshaw being killed in a riot. The guards should be careful who they gossiped around. What if the doctor had been in the middle of the riot on purpose? The man was either really brave or really stupid. Tessa voted on the latter. Wasting no time, she headed to the Pen, praying the whole way Gregor would not be hanging around Belle's office.

Dane walked into the precinct for the first time since his transition had taken place. It was almost sensory overload. Several people welcomed him back and asked if he was feeling better, but for the most part, it was business as usual. He walked by the dispatcher's desk and said good morning. Kim replied, "Good morning, Dane. There's a guy named Jasper waiting for you." She pointed to a tall redheaded man sitting in a visitor's chair, drinking a cup of coffee.

"Thanks, Kim."

"Jasper?" Dane held out his hand as the guy stood. As they shook, something passed between them. Some sort of recognition on a molecular level. Dane searched Jasper's face to see if he felt it.

Jasper was laughing and pointing. "Dude, fangs." He grinned and took another sip of his coffee.

Dane touched his hand to his mouth only to cut his finger on a sharp canine. "Fuck." Maybe he should have taken more time off. He thought he had all this phasing shit under control.

"You okay? Seriously, phasing in public? Tsk tsk." Jasper obviously thought it was funny. Dane did not. Wait, why was this Jasper not freaking, and how did he know the terminology?

"Why don't we go to the back?" Dane concentrated, and his fangs retracted. He headed to the back of the precinct where they could speak privately. When Jasper followed him into a conference room, he shut the door. "How do you know about phasing?"

Jasper, grinning, answered truthfully. "Because I'm one of you. But seriously, why are you showing fang in public?"

Dane was confused. Was this guy one of his brothers Caroline had mentioned? "Because I am still getting the hang of this shit. I thought I had it under control, but then when we shook hands... I don't know, something happened."

"You look older than most newbies. I transitioned when I was about sixteen."

"That's uh, interesting. I'm Dane Abbott, but I guess you already know that. Chief Kane is taking a few days off. For now, I'm in charge, and we need to have our early morning brief."

"Yeah, I've met Kaya. She's pretty cool."

"You've met her? When?" Dane didn't like the fact that Jasper was already familiar with Kaya.

"When she was abducted. That was some bad shit that went down. I'm just glad Rafael got to her in time."

"She told me a little about him." Actually, she was pretty vague about the guy.

"Yeah, he's a great leader," Jasper said with admiration in his voice.

Now Dane was really confused. Jasper was another shifter, *and* he knew Stone. Did that mean... *Shit*. He had a

14

department to get going. He would have to worry about Rafael Stone later.

Three

Gregor was already thinking about going out for a beer. Most days he didn't mind being behind his desk or patrolling the halls at the Pen. Ever since his initial meeting with the new doctor, he had been feeling out of sorts. Now that Rafael had found his mate, Gregor couldn't think of anything else. Until a few weeks ago, he and his brothers lived their lives without any expectation of finding the one person they were meant to bond with for life. The few female Gargoyles who were still living were already mated.

The King had found his mate in the police chief, a human. Why the fates had now decided to let them bond with humans was a mystery, like the fates themselves. All the Clan could figure was because their own females were nearly extinct. If the Goyles could mate with humans, there was hope for them all. Hope was one of those feelings Gregor hadn't felt in a long time. He spent his days watching over the prison, making sure the evil they captured stayed put. He spent his nights patrolling New Atlanta, helping his brothers in taking down the Unholy. The Stone Society ruled the shifter community with his older brother as King. They rarely interfered in the human matters. Kaya Kane, Rafael's mate, was an excellent leader of the human law enforcement.

When the recent murders fell in the Society's lap, they had no choice but to get involved. Vincent Alexander was arrested for targeting Rafe and the family. They were still trying to find out why he had attempted to take Kaya out in the process. It was possible she was just at the wrong place at the wrong time. Both Rafael and their cousin Julian had shielded her from a sniper rifle. The second time Rafael had phased fully, wrapping her in his wings. He was left with no choice but to confide in her with the knowledge of what he and his family were: primordial shapeshifters.

Gregor's desk phone rang. "Stone."

"Sir, this is Whitley at the guard shack. There's a Tessa Blackmore here to see the doctor. I thought the doctor was deceased."

Ah, the elusive redhead. Nikolas had the pleasure of meeting Isabelle's cousin when he inquired into Jonas Montague's journals. He said she was a real firecracker. Tessa had accompanied Isabelle for her interview, but Gregor hadn't seen her anywhere. "We have hired Dr. Henshaw's replacement. Dr. Isabelle Sarantos started earlier today, before you came on duty. Tessa is Isabelle's cousin. Please add her name to the list of approved visitors."

"Yes sir."

Gregor hung up the phone then dialed Isabelle's extension.

"Dr. Sarantos."

"Isabelle, it's Gregor. You have a visitor."

"I apologize. I will not allow my personal life to interfere with my job, but I need to speak with Tessa regarding my clinic."

"No need to apologize. You are welcome to have visitors any time Isabelle, as long as it doesn't interfere with the inmates."

"Thank you. I will meet her at the back door." They disconnected. Gregor had to play nice. The main reason for hiring the doctor was to get close to her and find out if she knew anything about her father's missing journals, or even better, human bonding. Nikolas was of the opinion this Tessa knew just as much as her cousin did. Not only did they know about the journals, but they both knew Jonas Montague was a shifter and that he was indeed alive and well, hiding out somewhere.

Gregor stayed in his office, out of the way. He wanted to observe the women together, and his Goyle hearing would allow him to eavesdrop. He rolled his chair over so he could see out his door, through the outer waiting

17

area. Isabelle passed by. The rumble of a motorcycle echoed outside. A few minutes later the sound of female voices passed by his door headed toward Isabelle's office. A wave of lightheadedness hit him. *What the fuck?* He rose from his desk and waited until the sound of their shoes was farther down the hallway.

He silently headed in their direction. Luckily, the supply closet was next to Isabelle's office. He could hide in there and listen. He was just about there when his cellphone rang. *Shit.* He reversed directions so they wouldn't hear his conversation. He slid the phone open but didn't speak until he was once again in the privacy of his office. "Stone."

"Something amiss?" His brother Dante, the city's medical examiner, had some type of ESP. He could gauge moods by just the tone of voice.

"I was just about to eavesdrop on the doctor and her cousin. What's up?"

"I happened to run into several Unholy this afternoon. Why they were out in the daytime is beyond me, but luckily for me, they were. I got to have a little fun, and now I am bringing them to you. I wanted to make sure you were still there."

"Yeah, I'm here. How far out are you?" Knowing his brother, not far.

"I'm pulling up to the gate now. I will see you in a few," Dante informed him.

Gregor headed toward the Basement. Isabelle and Tessa would have to wait. If it weren't for the special restraints Julian created, it would be a battle to apprehend and detain the Unholy. Instead, the restraints did their job, and less than an hour later, the Unholy were in their cages. Dante followed Gregor to his office. They quietly passed by Isabelle's office in case Tessa was still there. Gregor turned when Dante's footsteps slowed down then stopped. His brother had one hand on the wall, head hanging down.

Dante shook his head then continued on. When they arrived at Gregor's office, he asked, "Are you okay?"

"Yeah, fine. I'm sorry I interrupted. The Unholy could wait; the women, maybe not. That would have been the perfect opportunity to listen in." Dante was back to his usual frowning self.

"I probably should have, but honestly, I'm not so sure I'm ready for that."

"What do you mean?" Dante took the empty chair opposite Gregor's desk and leaned back on two legs.

"That's the second time I've been disoriented, and both times were when this Tessa was around. At first I thought it was Isabelle, but I've been around her enough now that I am either immune to her or she isn't the one."

"The one, as in your mate?" Dante sat his chair down and leaned his forearms on his legs.

"Yes. No. I don't know, I mean I haven't been around her long enough to really tell."

"Well, it's too late tonight. What do you say we hit The Tavern? We haven't been out in a long time. It isn't either of our nights to patrol. Who knows, maybe you'll see a nice young blonde to take your mind off the redhead."

Gregor considered it. "Why not? Let me run home and shower, and I'll meet you there."

"Sounds good. I need to take the van back to the morgue anyway. I'll see you in a couple of hours. By the way, what is that smell?"

"What smell?"

Dante shook his head, "Never mind." They both stood and walked out the door. Dante turned right, headed back toward the entrance to the Basement. Gregor went left, headed to his Hummer.

Tessa couldn't believe Dr. Henshaw had been secretly trying to create more Unholy. It was a good thing for her the idiot had been caught in the mayhem. If he were still alive, Belle wouldn't be working at the prison, and she wouldn't have access to her brother. She read over the files with her cousin, making notes and giving suggestions. She knew more about the cloning process than most scientists, having learned from the best. While Henshaw wouldn't truly have been creating clones, he could have succeeded in turning normal, if somewhat psychotic, men into monsters. The same way Gordon had created his army.

After about an hour, Tessa told Belle she had to go. She wanted to read Dr. Henshaw's notes, but right now she wanted to look for her brother more. She left Isabelle's office and headed down the hallway. She thought with it being so late there would be fewer guards for her to run into. *Tamian?* She reached out with her mind. Her extra-sharp hearing allowed her to gauge when guards were in the vicinity. She would stop and listen then continue when the coast was clear.

Tamian? Either her brother was on a different level or he was asleep. Loud footsteps halted her progress. When the noise lessened, she peered around the corner just in time to see the retreating back of a tall, fit guard. She admired his backside as he stopped at an unmarked door. He slid a keycard in the slot, waited for the light to turn green, and then went through. *Shit. I need to get my hands on one of those.* She tried Tamian one more time, to no avail.

Retracing her steps, she quietly walked past Belle's door toward the exit. Voices coming from Gregor's office piqued her curiosity, so she paused and listened in on the conversation. "Why not? Let me run home and shower and I'll meet you there."

Oh crap. She had to get out of there. Now. She took a chance and rushed past the open doorway, not stopping until she got outside. There were only a couple of vehicles in the parking lot. One of those surely belonged to Gregor. If she cranked her bike now, he would hear it and know she was just leaving. She toed the gear shift up into neutral and pushed her bike as fast as she could, which was pretty fast considering her shifter strength and speed. When she was out of sight from the back of the building, she hopped on, cranked the engine, and threw her helmet on. She eased on the throttle, making as little noise as possible on the tricked out bike.

She didn't breathe until she got past the guard shack. The sentry lifted the security barrier before she got there, so she just rolled on through. She gave him a two finger salute and grinned. Tessa wanted to forget about wardens, clones, and her brother being locked up, and she knew just the place. Even though she was going to a biker bar, she decided to go home and clean up a little first. Maybe add a little silver to her mostly black attire. It was still early, and anyone she knew would get there later as well.

Tessa didn't normally fuss too much with her looks. Her long, red hair was naturally wavy. Her shifter skin required no makeup. Not wanting to look too plain, she did swipe on a little mascara and some lip gloss. She swapped her plain black belt for one with a blingy Harley buckle and added silver hoops to her ears. The woman in the mirror was as close to dolled up as Tessa ever got. If she couldn't go somewhere dressed in jeans, she would rather not go. Tessa once again straddled her bike. She hit the back roads and headed in the direction of her favorite hangout in New Atlanta. It was a local biker joint where she could toss back a few beers and shoot some pool. It was just the place to forget her worries for a few hours.

Four

Gregor was sitting at a high top close to the pool tables when Dante walked into The Tavern. New Atlanta's bar scene was as lucrative as ever. People came from out of town just for the thrilling nightlife. There were bars and clubs for every walk of life, but Gregor and Dante weren't into the busy dance scene. The Tavern was a hole-in-the-wall biker bar complete with a couple of shitty pool tables, a dart board that had seen better days, and cheap beer. The women who came there were after one thing: a one-night stand with a roughneck. Neither he nor Dante were in search of a hook-up, but that didn't mean they didn't enjoy looking. A hot woman was a hot woman.

Dante sat down, and a cute little blonde waitress bounced over to their table. "Hello, fellas. What can I get you?"

Gregor glanced at her nametag. "Hello, Candy. I'll have a Budweiser."

Dante added his order, "A double-shot of Jack, neat." Candy told them she'd be right back and flitted off.

Dante was quiet, staring off into space. Normally he was a chatterbox, full of useless knowledge about bodies and autopsies and strange things he saw in the morgue. "Hey, what's up?" Gregor was worried about his brother.

Dante took a minute before answering. "I'm not sure how I feel about this human bonding, to be honest. I know Rafael is all for it, but what if it doesn't work out? What if we meet our mate, and they are nothing more than human? We have watched Sin go through the heartache of experiencing his wife die. Twice. Is it really worth it? What if they do get pregnant but can't handle a shifter fetus?"

Their conversation was interrupted by Candy bringing their drinks. She leaned across Gregor, brushing his arm with her breast, handing Dante his drink. "Can I get you fellas anything else right now? Are you hungry?"

"No." Gregor didn't bother with the young girls feelings. He would leave a good tip, but he wasn't going to encourage her advances. Over the years so many women had tried in vain to get the nod from both of them. Neither had risen to the occasion. Dante's tastes were much more eclectic, and when he did reach out for female comfort, it was never close to home. Gregor kept a few women on speed dial in case his rougher side needed to be exercised.

"I have to agree with Rafael on this. I don't think the fates would give us a mate, human or not, who couldn't handle what we are. I am hoping to get closer to the good doctor, gain her trust, and subtly ask about her father's journals. I still haven't come up with a plan on just how to approach the subject though. Oh, fuck me." Gregor almost doubled over.

"What is it?" Dante placed a hand on Gregor's arm.

"I'm not sure, but it's the same sick feeling I was talking about earlier." He searched the bar, not seeing any familiar faces. Dante glanced around with him, not that he would know who to look for. Just when he was about to give up, a sexy voice infiltrated the room.

"Yo, Gavin, set 'em up!" A redheaded biker chick came strutting though the bar. Tight jeans topped black riding boots. A Harley tank top was tucked into said jeans, a leather jacket thrown over one shoulder. A black belt with a shiny silver Bar and Shield buckle wrapped around her waist. Red hair swung in time with her hips.

"Holy shit, that's her."

Dante couldn't take his eyes off the show. "Her who? Tessa?"

23

"No, the chick from the gas station." Gregor would never forget that ass as long as he lived. Her smirky lips and those green eyes were a punch to the gut. "Fuck me."

"I don't recall you mentioning a *chick* from a gas station. Would you care to enlighten a brother?"

"A few years back, I stopped to get gas. She pulled in at the next pump over. Same bike as mine only chromed the fuck out. She must have twenty grand in chrome alone. Anyway, there was no receipt paper in the machine, so I went inside to get one. She dropped a dollar on the floor and when she bent over to get it, her ass ended up in my crotch. I swear to the gods, I thought I was going to pass out right then and there." Gregor couldn't take his eyes off the woman who was waiting for the man he assumed was Gavin to rack the balls on the pool table.

"Why don't you go talk to her?"

"And say what, 'Remember me, the guy you shoved your ass into'? No, I'll just watch from here. If my reaction to her from this far is any indication, I don't think I could stand to be any closer."

"What if she's your mate? Do you not want to find out?" Dante had finally lost interest and returned his gaze to Gregor.

"I'm not sure I do. But she can't be. I mean, I've had these same feelings a couple of times at the Pen, and I know she hasn't been in there. I'll just enjoy the view from here."

Tessa hadn't been to The Tavern in forever. She was always too busy watching monitors and checking on her cousins. Tonight she decided she was going to let loose. She strolled into the bar, saying hello to familiar faces. When she saw her old buddy Gavin at a pool table, she yelled at him to set up a game. She wouldn't play for money. Tonight was about relaxing, drinking a little, and shootin' the shit with whoever happened along.

As she crossed to the far side of the room she yelled at the bartender, "Yo, Jimmy, hit me up." She always ordered a Budweiser with a tequila shot. If she didn't have things to do tomorrow, she might have ordered a double shot. She loved this bar. She could dress like she normally did, maybe embellish with a little more silver here and there, and feel right at home. She had been to some of the swankier clubs in the city, but they just weren't her style. Techno-pop music blaring through speakers as a strobe light flashed around a room did nothing for her other than give her a headache. Here she could drop a few bucks in the jukebox, play whatever rock song she wanted, and kick someone's ass at pool, all while just being herself.

Gavin didn't wait for her to reach the table. He met her half-way across the room and picked her up in a bear hug. "Put me down ya big oaf!" She squeaked out.

He dropped Tessa to her feet and yelled over the music, "Trixie girl, where you been so long?"

"Staying away from riff raff like you! Are you ready to get your ass handed to you?" She cocked an eyebrow and issued the challenge. Tessa never gave a real name no matter how often she visited an establishment or how well she pretended to get to know people. Tamian and her mother were the only ones who called her by her given name: Andrea. She hated the name because Gordon had picked it out. Why her mother insisted on calling her that was a mystery. Elizabeth hated Gordon more than Tessa did. Tamian probably used the name because no one else outside the family did. It could also be since his middle name was Andrew, he felt it kept them connected.

Tessa used a different name in every city she visited, and sometimes it became difficult keeping them all straight.

She tried to stick with names that were similar, at least ones starting with a T. In her heart she would always be Tessa.

She grabbed a cue off the wall and rolled it on the table to make sure it was straight. She chalked the end and pointed it at her old friend. "I'm feeling generous, I'll let you break." She grinned her devious smile, the one Gavin knew meant trouble.

"I don't need your charity, Sweet Cheeks. Ladies first."

Tessa barked out a laugh. "I don't see a lady, but thanks." She placed the cue ball close to the rail and lined up the stick, pulling it back a few times then letting it fly. One solid and one stripe went in. She studied the table, looking at not only the first shot, but several after. She was that good. "Nine ball, side pocket." She always called her shots so when she took someone's money, they knew she wasn't lucky but skilled. After a couple of combos and a bank shot, she was on the eight ball. As she did with the others, she sank the black ball in the designated pocket. Grinning at Gavin, she said, "Rack'em."

Jimmy brought her drinks and put them on the table nearest her. She picked up the tequila first and threw the fiery liquid down her throat, slamming the glass on the table. Gavin set up the next game while she took a few pulls on her beer. Even before she drank the tequila she was feeling warm. There was a hum present in her body that shouldn't be there. She took a look around the bar, checking out the other patrons. She just about choked when her gaze landed on Gregor Stone. *What in the fuck?* She should have eavesdropped a little longer, and she might have overheard his plan to come there tonight.

Gavin pulled her attention back to the game. "You in this one, Sweet Cheeks, or you gonna stare at the warden all night?"

Tessa glared at the man. "Shut it. I was *not* looking at him. You want to put some money where your mouth

26

is?" She knew he would. Gavin couldn't stand losing to her, but he definitely couldn't resist a bet, no matter the odds.

"You're on." He pulled his wallet out of his back pocket and slapped a hundred down on the table. "That enough for you?"

Tessa grinned. "It's a start." She busted the balls and commenced to running the table. When Gavin was down three hundred bucks he finally gave up. Tessa surveyed the room. "Any other takers?"

"Yeah, I'll take you." Gregor was waving a hundred at her.

Five

The unease in Gregor's gut would not lessen. When Gavin picked Trixie up and swung her around, Gregor's beast fought to be turned loose. Dante convinced him there was no better way to find out if she was the cause of his discontent than to get closer. When she asked for another challenger, he took the opening. He rose from his stool and walked toward the pool table. She was glaring at him for some reason. "My money not good enough for you, Red?"

"Green's green. Rack 'em." She turned her back on him and downed the rest of her beer. When she sat the bottle on the table she yelled to the bartender, "Jimmy, hit me."

"You come here a lot?" He hadn't been here in a while, but he did frequent the place enough to have remembered her.

"When I'm in town, which isn't often. You gonna rack the balls or gossip all night?" Her sassy mouth reminded him of their run-in at the convenience store.

"Are you in a hurry?" He arranged the balls in the rack and set them on the dot. He carefully lifted the rack and hung it out of the way.

"I just don't like idle chatter." Trixie walked to the end of the table where he was still standing. "Do you mind?" He would have to move before she could break.

Gregor's knees weakened. "Don't mind at all." He backed up so she could get into position. As he did, he inhaled deeply. That was a stupid move. The scent of leather and sandalwood washed over him just as it had a few years ago. He nonchalantly placed his hand on the table to keep his balance. *Fuck me.*

"Excuse me." Trixie obviously wanted him out of her way. He did move but only far enough for her to barely get

28

a shot off. When she missed she scowled at him. "You could give a girl a little room, you know."

"And why would I want to do that, Red?" He flashed what he hoped was a sexy smile.

Instead of smiling back she continued to frown at him. "Because just maybe you're creeping me the fuck out."

Creeping her out? What the hell? He never had a problem with women before. "I guess you play for the other team then." He took a look at the table and counted the balls since he had been watching her instead of the game. Seven stripes scattered nicely. He called his first shot and sank it with the cue ball lined up perfectly for the next one.

"Why the hell would you say that?" She was blocking his way.

"Excuse me." When she didn't budge, he nudged her with his knee. "You could give a guy a little room, you know."

"Answer the fucking question, Stone."

Ah, she knew who he was. Ninety percent of New Atlanta probably knew who he was, too. He didn't hide from the television cameras when reporters came to the Pen. "So you know who I am, huh?"

She continued to stand her ground. "Of course I do, but you didn't answer my fucking question."

"Such language. And coming from such a pretty mouth. Would you please move? Or would you like for me to move you?" He would love to move her. Closer.

"I'm not moving anywhere until you answer my question." The hand not holding a pool stick was propped on her hip. Taking a big chance, he grabbed her around the waist and kissed her. Her immediate protests turned into groans, as she opened her mouth and searched for his tongue. He was just beginning to enjoy the taste of beer and tequila when she bit him.

"Ouch, you brat! What was that for?"

29

"Don't ever put your hands on me again." She threw her pool cue on the table and retreated to the bar area. She grabbed the beer Jimmy brought to her and downed it in one go. Who could do that? Most men couldn't even chug a beer without letting up.

"You're just afraid to lose, Red," Gregor yelled over the music blaring from the jukebox.

She slapped some bills into Jimmy's hand then stormed out of the bar. *Well hell. That didn't go as planned.*

Son of a motherfucker. Tessa knew when Gregor finally got his hands on her she would be in trouble, but she didn't realize the bond would be as strong as it was. She was ready to climb his rock hard body and fuck him right there in front of Jimmy, Gavin, and everyone else. What possessed him to kiss her? Dammit! She never lost her cool. But holy Mother of Zeus, his mouth on hers caused her body to all but melt into a puddle. Her back still zinged where he'd placed his hand. Her lips were tingling, and she couldn't breathe.

She pulled a pack of cigarettes out of her saddlebag and lit one. Leaning against her bike, she took a deep pull off her smoke, trying to calm herself. She should have left the instant she saw him. Now her chances of getting Tamian out of the Pen were slim. She would have to be extra diligent going to see Belle. Fuck! She screwed up. Tamian needed her, and whether or not Isabelle admitted it, she needed her too. Tessa pulled on her helmet and cranked her bike. She needed the wind in her face to clear her mind. She had a feeling nothing would clear her body. No, Gregor Stone had just imprinted himself on her, and she debated leaving the city tonight. Fucking full-blood.

Tessa took one last drag and blew a line of smoke out from between her lips. She snuffed the cigarette out on the sole of her boot then shoved the butt into the pocket of her jeans. Not bothering with back roads, Tessa headed straight for the interstate. New Atlanta traffic was always busy, but this late on a weeknight shouldn't be too bad. She needed to open the throttle and let her bike run free. Trying to get her mind off Gregor, she thought about her cousins. She really should call and check in with Dane. It had been a couple weeks since he transitioned, and now he was back at work with the police department. If she got pulled over for speeding, she could ask him to take care of it. What's the use in having relatives in high places if you didn't access the perks of their positions? It was either that or hack the system and fix the ticket herself.

She rode until she was almost out of gas. Ironically, she pulled into the same gas station where her troubles all started. If the store wasn't so close to her house, she would never set foot in the place again. She cut the engine and dropped the kickstand. She didn't bother removing her helmet. It was late, and she was not in the mood to chit chat. She went in the store and dropped a ten on the counter. "Fill-up on three." Chester picked up the money and said to her retreating back, "Good seeing you too, Trixie."

She was really starting to hate that name. She had used it as a joke, but somehow it stuck. Still, it was better than Andrea. She filled the tank then headed home. She had a trip to plan, and that meant getting another watcher on Isabelle duty.

Tessa was the youngest watcher for the family. There were a couple of others, but they had families and didn't travel as often. She knew Ezekiel was already in New Mexico, so she called Sam. Samuel Brooks was a cousin who lived in New York. He was a half-blood whose mate was a human. They had a daughter, Sophia, who worked in New Atlanta at the library. So far she wasn't showing any traits of being a shifter, but they were still keeping an eye on her. Sam was training Sophia to become a watcher herself.

Tessa called Sam's number. The answering machine picked up after a few rings, so she left a message for him to call her back. She called his cell and got the same thing. Even if he were asleep, he or his wife, Monica, would pick up the phone. She thought about calling Sophia but decided to wait. Tessa had met Sophia, and she really liked the girl. She reminded her of a bohemian, free-spirited gypsy who was usually giggling about something. While they may not have much in common, the girl was smart and knew quite a bit about shifters and their history. Full-bloods included.

While Jonas and Caroline were opposed to the full-bloods finding out about their half-blooded relatives, they, along with Tessa's parents, thought it prudent all offspring be taught their history. Tessa's father was Xavier Montagnon. He was from the original line of shifters and was a full-blooded Elder. If anyone had reason to hide his human mate and offspring, it would be him. Xavier worshiped Elizabeth and doted on Tessa. Tamian wasn't as close with their father since he had spent most of his youth with Jonas. While technically Xavier wasn't Tamian's father, he claimed him as if he were.

Tessa's phone rang. She frowned when she saw who it was. "Hello?"

"We need to talk. Something has happened, and we need to strategize."

"I was just about to schedule my trip back to New Orleans. I will arrange to fly there first."

"I can't wait to see you."

"You too." The line disconnected. Tessa opened her computer and booked her flights. This was going to be a long trip.

Six

Gregor stood off to the side of the room observing Rafael with Kaya. Just a couple of weeks ago all the brothers had little optimism in finding their mates. Now, hope was back. In the beginning, Kaya had been reluctant to let Rafael into her personal life, mostly because Rafael was a murder suspect. As soon as he had been cleared, she accepted his love and the bond. She seemed right at home in the manor. The only drawback Gregor could see was the fact she was a veteran cop and put her life on the line every day. Rafael was not happy about this, but he would not command her to quit. That was no way to start their relationship.

Laughter coming from the kitchen grabbed Gregor's attention. "You should have seen him, he was as surprised as I was." Jasper, a cousin who had recently relocated from the west coast, was telling a tale. When he first arrived, the man would barely speak. Now he fit right in with the rest of them.

"Who are you talking about?" Gregor clapped him on the shoulder as he walked by.

"Dane Abbott, Kaya's detective. We shook hands, and his fangs popped out."

All conversation ceased as everyone turned to Jasper. Kaya dropped her coffee cup, the hot liquid splashing on her jean-clad legs. "What did you say?" She gripped Rafael's arm for support. Priscilla, the housekeeper, grabbed a towel, mopping up the spilled coffee. "Please, Priscilla, I will clean up the mess. I'm the one who made it." Kaya pulled at the older woman, trying to get her off the floor.

"Priscilla, we'll clean this up. Please continue with breakfast." Rafael asked everyone to make their way to the dining room. Once everyone was seated, he turned to Jasper. "Are you saying Dane Abbott is a shifter?"

"Well, yeah, but I think he's a newbie. He had no control over his phase."

Kaya asked, "What's a newbie?"

Rafael explained it to her. "Someone who has just started their transitions. Mason is a newbie, but he had control of his phasing after the first day. Jas, how did he explain it?"

"He didn't really, just said he was still getting the hang of it and wanted to know how I knew about phasing. I told him because I was one of his kind. He then mentioned Kaya being out for a few days, and I told him I had met Kaya and thought she was really nice. He wanted to know when I met her, and I said when she was kidnapped."

"Did you tell him I'm a shifter?" Rafael sounded a little irritated.

"No, he said he had a brief to conduct, and he dropped the subject. Seriously though, he's too old to be a newbie."

"Kaya, when Dane was missing, where did he say he had been?" Rafael threaded his fingers through hers while he spoke to his Queen. If they were in the same room, Rafael was usually touching her.

"He said he was in the hospital, or a private clinic to be more precise."

"This doesn't make any sense. If he were one of ours, we would know about it. Jasper, get close to Dane and find out as much as you can. If he won't open up, then I will think of something else. Kaya, don't let on that you know anything just yet. If he didn't tell you the truth before, I doubt he will now. We need to find out all we can about Dane."

"Gregor, any word from our inmate?" They were hoping to get information voluntarily out of Vincent Alexander.

Gregor shook his head, "Not yet. He must have been a chain smoker, because all he writes is 'cigarette'. The doctor prescribed the patch for him, but I've watched him through the window. After a few minutes he pulls it off and throws it on the floor. As far as any information, nothing. I'm going to give it a few more days." He didn't have to finish his statement. If after a few more days they still didn't have any information on Gordon Flanagan, Gregor would get tough with him. Try to make him communicate.

After breakfast was over, the men all went their separate ways. Gregor hung back, asking to speak with Rafe.

"What is it my brother?" Rafael asked Kaya to excuse them as they walked outside to the patio.

"I think I've found my mate. There's something strange about it though. Dante and I went out last night, and I saw a redhead who bumped into me a few years ago. Back then, I didn't think anything about the reaction my body had to hers. Knowing about the possibility of mating with humans has me taking a closer look. Last night, I thought I was going to pass out. Just being close to her had my head in a fog. I wanted to see if I could get a reaction from her so I kissed her. Rafe, I thought she was going to fuck me right there in the bar. Until she bit me. The brat bit me." Gregor was laughing now even though it hadn't been funny the night before.

"Then what happened?"

"She told me I creeped her out, threw her pool stick down, and stormed out of the place." Gregor didn't laugh at that. He wasn't a desperate man who hit on random women. The women came to him. "At first I was confused, because I had these feelings at work. Then I remembered what Nikolas said about Tessa being a redhead and riding a motorcycle. It took me a while, but I think I've finally put two and two together. Rafe, I need to see a picture of Tessa."

"I'm sure Nik or Julian can provide you with one. Go to the lab before you go to the Pen. Gregor, if Tessa is your mate, this could be good for us." Tessa had knowledge about Jonas Montague that the men needed.

Gregor shook his head sadly. "I hate to say this, but I don't think I'm going to get the fairy tale romance you and Kaya have, Brother. Red obviously doesn't like me, and I pretty much can't handle being around her. No, for whatever reasons, the fates have decided to play a joke on me."

"You don't know that. I felt the same way at first when I met Kaya, but let me tell you something. When you get the beast under control, it will be like nothing you ever imagined."

"I hope you're right. Now, go be with your woman. I'll talk to you later." Gregor pulled Rafe in, clapped him on the back with a quick hug, and released him. "Be well, my brother."

"And you as well."

Gregor wasn't concerned about his beast. He didn't think this woman would let him close enough to need to contain his inner hunger. For whatever reason, she didn't like him. If he didn't know this, he would think she was the perfect woman. She was a feisty redhead who rode a motorcycle and shot pool with the best of them. She had a smart mouth, and she cursed too much. While that might turn some men off, Gregor found it appealing. She was a tough broad, and that cranked his motor.

When he arrived at the lab, Gregor parked his Hummer between Julian's Corvette and Nik's Audi. The sports cars were cool but Gregor preferred the more rugged vehicle. While he did have a few muscle cars tucked away in his garage, if he needed speed, he would hop on his motorcycle and ride the wind.

Once inside, he found both his cousins at their computers, fingers tapping away at their keyboards. It never ceased to amaze him how geeky they both were. If geeky meant being the best at what they did, who was he to judge?

36

"Gregor, what brings you here?" Julian asked while continuing to type.

"I need to see a picture of Tessa Blackmore." He really didn't want to get into the mate discussion again, but he knew they wouldn't let this go with no explanation.

Nikolas stopped typing and asked, "Didn't you say she had visited the Pen? How do you not know what she looks like?"

"Yes she visits. It's just that every time she has, I've been busy with something else, you know like putting Unholy in the Basement."

"Here you go." Julian pointed to his computer monitor. "Oh shit, I know that look. It's the same one Nik has when he returns from the library."

Gregor grimaced when he noticed Nik's expression. "I hope I don't have *that* look." His cousin was not happy.

Julian inclined his head in his brother's direction. "Nikolas' mate has been M.I.A. the last few days. Tessa's *your* mate, isn't she?"

"I'm not sure, but yeah, I think she is." Why would Tessa tell everyone at The Tavern her name was Trixie?

"If you've never seen her face, how do you know?" Nikolas asked, frowning.

"Oh, I've seen her face, I just didn't know it was Tessa. About three years ago she bumped into me at a gas station. Then last night she came into the bar where Dante and I were having a drink. I thought I was going to black out. You know the feeling, Nik." His cousin nodded. "I challenged her to a game of pool to get closer to her. That in itself was a mistake. After a few minutes of barely containing myself, I couldn't take it any longer. I kissed her. I'm pretty sure she's the one."

"That's great news, right? Not only do you have Isabelle working for you, but now you can possibly get the information we need from her cousin." Nikolas had spent many hours poring over the family journals, searching for information on bonding with humans.

"We'll see." Gregor didn't want to admit to his cousins that the woman who was potentially his mate couldn't stand him.

"I need to get to work. I'll catch you two later."

Gregor's mind tried to sort through everything he knew so far about the spitfire. If Tessa was Trixie, he would make sure the next time she came to see Isabelle he was ready for her.

Merrick tracked the redhead through the passenger window of his Mustang. He glanced at the picture in his hand then back at the woman. Greta Powell, age 33. He put the photo back in the manila file folder and tucked it between his seat and console. Was she a dog lover? Most women were. He pulled up alongside her. "Excuse me, ma'am, have you seen a white poodle? My dog decided to run away, and I can't find her anywhere."

The pretty woman stopped and bent over, taking in Merrick's features. He didn't look like a stone-cold killer, did he? He flashed his straight white teeth and his dimpled grin. "Hi. Please tell me you've seen her. She's kinda old, and I'm really afraid for her."

"I'm sorry, I haven't." Greta was eyeballing Merrick's physique. He probably should have on long sleeves with the weather being cool, but the way she was checking out the swirling tattoos wrapping around his bulging biceps could work to his favor.

"Would you help me search? Please?" Greta studied his face and nodded. He unlocked the door and like a mouse to the proverbial cheese, she slid into the trap. "I really appreciate this. I'll drive slow and you call for her."

"What's her name?" Greta must not watch the news, or she would know she fit the profile of the most recent murder victims.

"Gretel." He couldn't resist.

"What did you say?" It was obviously similar enough to Greta to alarm her.

"Gretel, as in Hansel and Gretel. You know, where the kids are shoved in the oven by the witch? My mother just loved that story."

"Yeah, I know the one. I just..." Greta turned toward the window and started calling for the missing dog. Driving slow gave Merrick the opportunity to check out his latest catch. She was just like the rest: red hair, slight build, beautiful face. He might have to have a little fun with this one before he snuffed the life out of her.

Seven

Isabelle was ready to give the warden her list of things she needed for the clinic. The medicine cabinet was stocked with items that at first glance didn't make sense. After she read the notes Dr. Henshaw had scribbled in various files, they made perfect sense. She hated to think ill of the dead, but the man had been crazy. If she didn't know better, she would think he had been on Gordon Flanagan's payroll instead of the Pen's.

Tessa told her to keep this information to herself, to not tell Gregor. What if Gregor already knew? She didn't know the warden at all. No, until she had no doubt she could trust him, she would not divulge that she was aware of what Henshaw had been up to. Isabelle still hadn't made it through every inmate's file. There were so many, and the ones she had looked at required more than just a cursory glance. The inmates who were truly in need of medication were the ones who were being neglected.

She didn't care that they were criminals; they were human. Isabelle had taken an oath, and that oath didn't allow her to discriminate. She wanted to check on those prisoners who had been used as guinea pigs. She also couldn't stop thinking of the albino. Something about him spoke to her, told her there was more to the man than just what was on the surface. The one thing she did know was he needed nicotine. The patch she was giving him obviously wasn't strong enough, so she ordered a higher dose. She also ordered the medication that would help alleviate his cravings. If he was going to be stuck in a cell the rest of his life, he would not see a cigarette ever again.

Isabelle gathered her papers and headed to Gregor's office. She would probably need to explain some of the medications. At her clinic, she ordered her own supplies. She needed to find out the protocol for the Pen and also find out who besides her could order prescription drugs. Stopping just outside his office door, she listened to make sure Gregor wasn't on the phone. When she didn't hear talking, she knocked. "Come in." She should find his deep voice sexy. Instead, it was just another sound to her.

"Good morning, Sir. I have the list of supplies and medications I need."

"I told you, Isabelle. There's no need to call me Sir. Let's see what you have."

She handed the long list to him and waited while he read over everything. He didn't flinch at the list of medications. "Do you want to order the meds yourself, or did you want us to get them?"

"I wanted to ask you what protocol is in that regard. With Dr. Henshaw being deceased, I didn't know if you had someone else to order the medicine. I will be glad to place the order."

"I have a cousin who is a doctor and he could order them, but since you are running the clinic now, I don't see a reason you shouldn't do the ordering yourself."

"Can I ask you a question?" Isabelle still didn't know why they had singled her out for the job. Gregor nodded so she continued. "Why didn't you ask your cousin to take this job, why me?"

Gregor didn't hesitate. "My cousin happens to be the city's medical examiner. He loves what he does and would never consider leaving his position. Your name came up when we researched local doctors who specialized in infectious disease. While you will not be dealing with Unholy, your background made you a frontrunner. There are several inmates who have become ill while serving their time, and Dr. Henshaw was having a difficult time with a diagnosis. If he were still alive, I would have probably reached out to you anyway. When you go through the inmate records, I want you to concentrate on the open cases

41

he was working on. Hopefully you will be able to discover what he could not."

This made Isabelle feel much better. Of course he could be lying, but then again, if he was telling the truth, it would make her job much easier. Maybe soon she would be able to confide in him.

Tessa paced across her living room. Her fifth phone call to Sam had gone straight to voicemail just like the first four. She hated to call Sophia, but she was getting desperate. She thumbed through her contacts and found the girl's number.

"Hello?"

"Sophia, this is Tessa. How are you?"

"Hey, Tessa. Honestly, I'm not doing too good. I was just about to call you. Have you spoken to my father?"

"No, I haven't. I take it you haven't spoken to your mother either?"

"No, it's like they've both disappeared. Tessa, this isn't like them. Either of them. They would never leave and not tell me."

"You're right. Shit. I have to take off to Louisiana, and I wanted to see if he could keep an eye on Isabelle. I don't know how long I'm going to be gone. I realize this is really shitty timing. I'm pretty sure she'll be okay, but you never know."

"Of course. The clinic is close to the library, so I can check in on her during breaks."

"Uh, actually she has a new job. She started working at the penitentiary a few days ago."

"Why would she do that? She has her own practice."

"Somehow she stumbled onto Dane, and I had to tell her the truth. While she was watching him transition, she came face to face with her mother. Talk about a shock; seeing Caroline after all these years, and the woman still looks to be in her thirties. She also found out Jonas is still alive and that I have spent time with both her parents over the years. Isabelle feels betrayed, and she wants nothing to do with any of us. Taking the job at the Pen was more an act of rebellion than anything."

"I guess I would feel the same way. Of course I'll check in on her. You go ahead on your trip and don't worry about Isabelle. Just promise me you'll keep an eye and ear open for my parents. I'm really worried about them, Tessa."

"I'm going to make a few phone calls as soon as I hang up. We'll find your parents."

"Thanks. I need to head to the library now."

"Speaking of the library, did you ever find out how Jonas' journal ended up there? Nikolas Stone getting his hands on the first diary is not what we need."

"Um, it had a fiction jacket on it. Someone must have planted it there. I will ask around and see what I can find out. I'm running late, I'll talk to you soon."

"Later." Tessa hung up. She had a nagging feeling in her gut that something bad was going on with Sam and Monica. And that damn journal. Somebody must have put it in the library on purpose. Her first thought had been Sophia since the girl worked there, but what motive would she have?

Tessa placed several phone calls, but nobody had heard from Sam. He had not been sent out of the country and should be at home. Since Elizabeth also lived in New York, she was going to personally check on him. Elizabeth and Xavier never moved around. That was not the norm for the Gargoyle community. It was hard to explain why you never aged. Xavier had more money than the gods and had set Elizabeth up in a fortress. An extravagant, multi-million

43

dollar fortress on a thousand acres. The area above their property was a no-fly zone. How Xavier had managed that was anyone's guess.

While Tessa roamed the world looking after her cousins, Elizabeth stayed put, rarely leaving her home. Xavier did not take chances with his mate. He would kill Gordon Flanagan with his bare hands should the man ever find Elizabeth's location. Technically, Elizabeth was still married to Gordon, but there was no way she could file for divorce without him finding her. Staying married on paper was the lesser of two evils.

No, until Gordon was dead, Elizabeth was stuck with that particular burden. Using half-bloods as decoys to lure the man into the open had so far proved fruitless. He sent his army to do his dirty work. Even though he was getting on in age, he was still proving to be a pain in the ass. The recent murders of the delegates had put a halt to their plans in locating him. Human casualties were just not acceptable.

Before Tessa left the state, she needed to make one more trip to the Pen. She wanted to tell Isabelle she was leaving, but more than that, she wanted to see Tamian.

Eight

Rafael's time with Kaya had passed too quickly. When she said she would give him a week he didn't realize most of his time would be spent taking care of Clan business. Now that she was ready to go back to work, he had free time. "Bella Mia, please take one more day. I am not ready to let you go."

His beautiful mate smiled up at him, her blonde hair fanned out over the pillows on their bed. She had a satisfied look on her face, one he had put there. "You're very tempting, but one more day will turn into another one more day. I am already behind in filing reports, and I don't like that reporter knowing about murders before I do. Besides, I need to keep an eye on Dane. I can't believe he's a shifter. I've worked with him for years, and he's never let on he's anything but human."

"If I hadn't told you that I'm a shifter, you would never have known. Unless we phase in front of someone, our secret is safe. I hope Jasper can get to the bottom of what's going on. If Dane is a newbie, that opens up a whole new set of questions. I want you to be careful around him."

"Like I said, I've worked with him for years, and there's no one I trust more to have my back." Kaya must have seen the hurt look in his eye because she quickly amended her statement. "Except for you. I trust you with my life, my King." She soothed the hurt away with her lips on his chest and her hand on his cock.

Rafael knew better than to ask Kaya to quit her job. Until she was pregnant with their child, she would continue working. For now, he didn't want to talk about her job or Dane. If he only had one more day with her, he was going to spend it in bed. By the time he was finished with his Queen, she would be able to think of nothing other than the way he made her feel. He pressed his lips to hers, softly. His beast was momentarily sated, therefore he could give her some tender loving. It wouldn't take long before his needs turned rough again, so while he could, he was going to be gentle.

Dane was pouring over paperwork when Jasper walked into his office. Actually it was Kaya's office, but while she was on leave, he was taking advantage of the quiet space. "Hey Abbott, how you doing?" Jasper leaned against the door frame, arms crossed over his chest. When Jasper confided he was a shifter, Dane wanted to ask him a thousand and one questions. When he was going through his initial transition, Tessa had told him there were others. She just didn't tell him he would be working with one.

"I'm good. I was just going over the results from the coroner's office." If he could get his mind on business, he might possibly make it through the day without talking about shifting. "The DNA results from the victim at the warehouse match those from the hotel room, but we still can't confirm the body was that of Magnus Flanagan. We've searched every database there is, and there is no record of Magnus Flanagan anywhere. I'm betting he had someone wipe his identity so his brother couldn't find him."

"If this victim isn't Flanagan, why would he pretend to be? He would have to have known the danger, unless he was trying to draw the man out. Who would be crazy enough to do that? From what I've read, Gordon Flanagan is the vilest man to ever walk this earth."

"That's what we're trying to find out. He's not old, but he isn't getting any younger. He has made it his life's mission to find that which was stolen from him. My guess is he's getting desperate and when people get desperate, bad things happen. I'd say twelve dead bodies is just the beginning of what he has planned."

"If only Vincent Alexander would talk, maybe we could find out where Flanagan is hiding out."

Dane thought for a second, "How do you know about Alexander? He was put in the Pen before you got here." He observed Jasper's face. For what, he wasn't sure. Something told him there was more to his new partner than what was visible on the surface. Not that he thought Jasper was hiding anything, he was just different somehow.

Jasper closed the door and took the seat across from Dane. "I've been in town a while. I was just waiting for my application to be approved. During that time, I kept up with the goings on in the city. But back to my original question, how are you? Are you getting your phasing under control?"

Dane really needed to talk to Tessa. She and Caroline didn't tell him not to talk about himself but then again, they didn't tell him to broadcast what he is either. Before he could answer, the desk phone rang. He held up one finger to Jasper and answered, "Abbott. Yeah, I'll be right there." Speak of the devil, Tessa was there to see him.

"I have a visitor. We'll need to finish this conversation later. For now, I need you to see if you can locate Elizabeth Flanagan. I know it's like finding a needle in a haystack, but that's what the chief wants us to do." Dane rose from his chair and made his way to the front of the precinct.

Dane couldn't miss the looks Tessa was getting from his fellow officers. She was a good-looking woman even if she was wearing a funky jacket. Before he knew they were related, he thought she was hot. Now he could still appreciate her attractiveness, just in a platonic way. "Tessa, what brings you here?"

Her smile hadn't changed. It was the same every time he saw her: bright with a little smirk. "Is there somewhere private we can go?"

"Yeah, we can go to my office." He led her back to Kaya's office and shut the door. She held her finger to her

47

lips and pulled something out of her backpack. She sat a small black box on the desk and flipped a switch. "Now we can talk without anyone hearing us. Not that anyone here could actually hear us, but you can never be too careful."

Dane pointed at the gizmo on the desk. "Where did you get that?" He knew hi-tech items existed, he had just never seen one up close.

"From your father. Now, how are you? I'm sorry I haven't been by sooner, but I've been keeping an eye on Isabelle."

"My father? Oh, Montague. It's going to take some time to get used to the fact he's my biological father and that I'm, well, this." He swept his hand down his body. "Listen, I'm glad you stopped by. We have a new detective who just started, Jasper Jenkins. Is he one of my brothers? Caroline didn't tell me the names of my siblings other than Isabelle."

"Why would you think he's your brother? Did something happen?"

"You could say that. When I first met him and shook his hand, my fangs dropped. He just laughed. When I asked why he wasn't freaked out, he said he was one of us."

Tessa's face paled. "Dane, he is not one of us, as in half-bloods. He must be a Gargoyle and new to the city. Shit. There's so much you need to know, and I don't have time to go into all of it. I've got a missing watcher *and* I have to head out to Louisiana in the morning. I need to find out about this Jasper and why he would just offer up that he's a shifter, unless he hasn't met them all and thinks you're a full-blood."

"Isn't that a good thing? I mean, if he's a shifter, I can learn from him." Dane was getting more confused.

Tessa was shaking her head. "Gargoyles don't know about us, Dane. We have kept ourselves secret all these years. Your father was ostracized from the Originals for mating with your human mother. If they find out about us, we don't know what the repercussions will be. I'm sorry I

48

can stay longer, but I really have to go. I need to see your sister before I head out of town. But listen, be careful. Don't give away any information about us to this Jasper. If he asks questions, just be vague."

Dane knew that was going to be as impossible as finding Elizabeth Flanagan. "I'll try, but Tessa, he's a detective. He's smart *and* he's a shifter."

"Just do your best. I will be back as soon as I can, and we'll talk more about it then." She walked up to Dane and wrapped her arms around him in a sisterly hug.

The door to the office opened, and Jasper stuck his head in. "Sorry to interrupt, but we have another murder. I'll just let you two get back to whatever you were doing." He closed the door.

Dane sighed, but Tessa laughed. "How long do you think it'll take before this is all over the precinct?"

"Not long, you're too cute." Dane grinned at his cousin. They said their goodbyes, and Dane prepared mentally to go to the crime scene. No matter how many dead bodies he saw, it never got easier.

Nine

Tessa left the police station and rode to the prison. If she was lucky she would have a chance to talk to Isabelle then sneak around and find Tamian. She needed to get her hands on Belle's electronic entrance card so she could visit other levels. If she was unlucky, she'd run into Gregor. She spent all day going over various scenarios of getting caught and getting away. She needed more Intel on the layout of the Pen before she attempted breaking her brother out.

Tessa had spent the last thirteen years honing her skills. Her cover as an archaeologist enabled her to travel the world and keep an eye on her cousins. Even though she was a watcher, her job sometimes came with danger. Not all of the cousins were in semi-safe locations such as New Atlanta. When the near apocalypse happened thirty-three years earlier, countries fell apart, causing them to revert to less than civil behavior. Why her family didn't have the shifters move to safer cities was a mystery. It was a question she asked every time she was in her father's presence, and his answer was always the same: for their safety. Xavier obviously hadn't visited the cities where they lived, or he would know the cousins were far from safe.

Tessa slowed her bike as she neared the guard shack, but the man just waved her on through. Hmm. That was unexpected. She drove around to the back of the building and parked by Belle's car. The same few vehicles were in the lot as were yesterday with the exception of a van, so that meant Gregor was more than likely in the building. Shit. Hopefully she could call Belle and bypass having to deal with the warden. She pulled her cell out of her pocket just as the back door opened. Luckily it was just one of the guards. She walked through the door without being questioned.

She probably should have called her cousin first, but if Belle was in a mood she might not want to see her. Tessa

50

slipped quietly down the now familiar hallways. She paused at Gregor's door, listening for any proof of her mate. He would talk quietly, then he would pause. Good, he was on the phone. Curiosity got the better of her so she listened closely. "We went out to a bar last night. No, it was rather boring. There was a pretty blonde who caught my eye. Yeah, you know I'm a sucker for blondes." Tessa was fuming. A *blonde*? What the fuck happened after she left The Tavern? Did he not know she was his mate? *Fuck you, Stone.* She continued on past his door to Isabelle's office.

She didn't bother knocking; she just barged in and closed the door. Isabelle looked up at her, eyebrows raised. "You know, you really shouldn't just show up here without calling. What if I wasn't here? Would you just go through my office like you go through my home?"

Tessa pulled the same black box out of her backpack that she had in Dane's office. She flipped the switch and set it on the corner of the desk. Isabelle pointed at it, "What is that, and *what* are you wearing?"

"This is a device that allows us to speak freely without being overheard. I don't want the warden's super hearing to be a problem. Have you found out any more about what Henshaw was up to?" Tessa didn't explain the odd looking jacket she was wearing.

Isabelle shook her head. "No, but I don't believe Gregor is in on it." Tessa cringed every time her cousin called Gregor by his name. She couldn't have the man, but she didn't want her cousin to harbor any feelings for him either.

"And why's that? You didn't mention any of this to him, did you?" She really hoped Isabelle was being smart.

"Of course not. He actually brought up the fact that Dr. Henshaw was having trouble diagnosing some of the inmates, and he wanted me to pay careful attention to those files. If he was in on it, he sure made himself seem innocent."

51

"Innocent my ass. I'm telling you, do not trust him."

"What do you have against Gregor other than him being a full-blood?"

Tessa was not having this conversation now. "Isn't that enough? Anyway, the reason I'm here is to tell you I'm going out of town for a while. I have to check on one of your siblings. She's a few years older, and I haven't visited her in a while. I've called one of the other watchers, Sophia, and she's on standby should you need anything. Here's her number. She's a little younger, but she has been training for a few years." Tessa handed Isabelle a slip of paper with the information scribbled on it.

Isabelle crossed her arms over her breasts. "Do you know all my siblings? Who are you going to see, and where does she live? I would like to start meeting my family."

"Yes, I know all your siblings, but they have no idea who I am. I am going to see Lillian who lives in Louisiana. I understand how you feel, and as soon as I get back, I will give you the lowdown on who your siblings are and where they all live. Right now, I don't have time," Tessa explained.

"I still don't see why you feel like I need a babysitter. I've seen Dane change, so I know what to expect. And I don't go anywhere but here and home. If I were going to run into my mate, I think I'd have done it by now, don't you?"

"You go to the grocery store, the gas station, the post office, the library. You could run into him or her any of those places, including here." Tessa threw the *her* in there just to get a rise out of her cousin. She knew Isabelle had experimented with girls in college.

"What do you mean *her*? I don't like women, and if my mate happens to be a woman, she's just out of luck."

"I'm just saying your mate could be anyone, and you could be in their presence at any time and not realize it. Now, I have to go pack. My plane leaves early in the morning, and I need some sleep. Take care of yourself, and if you need anything, don't hesitate to call Sophia." Tessa packed the black box in her backpack and started to slide it over her arms. On second thought, leaving the backpack would give her an excuse to visit again. She didn't wait for Isabelle to say goodbye. Tessa slipped out the door and headed away from Gregor's office. Tessa used her bond with Tamian to search for him silently. When she got no response, she found the nearest door leading to the stairwells.

Isabelle would kill her if she found out her keycard was missing, but it was the only way she would be able to look for Tamian. She was pretty sure the steps going up led to the main cell blocks, but something in her gut told her to go down. At the bottom of the steps was another door requiring her to use the access card. She paused before swiping it, listening for guards. When she heard none, she swiped the plastic and was grateful the buzzer made little sound. She hesitated again, searching for guards. When she found none, she continued on her way. She had entered solitary confinement. Tamian surely wouldn't be down here because his crime didn't warrant it. Still, Tessa peered in the windows of the steel doors on the first level. It wasn't bedtime yet, but most of the men were lying on their beds. Luck was on her side when she located her brother. *Tamian. Tam, wake up.*

Her brother opened his eyes and jumped off the bed. *"Andi, what are you doing down here?"*

"I told you I was going to get you out of here." That ever present pull between them tugged at her brain.

"And I told you I'm in here for a reason. Listen to me. I put myself here. I'm undercover. You have got to stop this craziness before you get caught. How did you get down here anyway?"

"That doesn't matter. What does matter is you. Are you okay? Why would you put yourself in this hell hole?"

53

"I'm trying to get Intel on Gordon. There are men in here who were in his army. I'm listening to see if I pick up any information that can help us find him."

"So you just went and got yourself locked up? How did you manage solitary if you were arrested for assault?"

"The warden was in on it. Gregor and his cousin, the owner of the gym, asked me to do this. Don't you see? It's perfect."

"You do know they're full-bloods, don't you?" Tessa couldn't believe he put himself in here with the enemy.

"Yeah, but they're the good guys."

"How do you know that? Better yet, just how long have you been in New Atlanta?"

"I've been here a while. Someone has to watch the watcher." Tamian winked at her.

Tessa listened for a moment. She was out of time, someone was behind her. "Tam, I have to go. Promise me you'll take care of yourself in here."

"I promise." Tamian placed his hand on the glass. "I love you, sis."

"And I love you." She placed her hand on the window briefly before taking off at a quiet jog. She hoped like hell there was another staircase leading back up to the main floor. She opened a door and was thankful the stairs did indeed lead up. She took off running up the stairs only to find the door to the main floor wouldn't open. Why would Isabelle not have access to the main floor? She couldn't stop now, she continued up until she found a door she could open. The one she finally found unlocked led to the roof. *Well shit.*

Ten

Gregor was alerted the moment Tessa pulled up to the guard shack. Less than a minute later the rumble of her Harley sounded outside the building. It had been her bike he heard the day before. Now that he had kissed her, she was imbedded in his senses. He knew the minute she entered the building. He wanted nothing more than to confront her and demand answers, but at the last minute a plan sprang to his mind. As soon as she was within earshot, he pretended to be on a phone call. *Let's just see how creepy I am now, Brat.*

Her footsteps stopped just outside his door. At the mention of a blonde, the sharp intake of breath was loud and Tessa's pulse sped up. Yep, she was pissed. Gregor laughed out loud as she stomped off toward Isabelle's office. After giving her a few steps head start, he followed her. It was rather easy considering her mind was on his words. She didn't bother knocking on Isabelle's door; she just barged right on in and shut the door behind her. No problem, he would just listen from the supply closet. He slipped into the small room and waited.

Isabelle told her cousin, "You know, you really shouldn't just show up here without calling. What if I wasn't here? Would you just go through my office like you go through my home?" Then nothing. Silence. *What the hell?* He stuck his ear to the wall, but he still heard nothing. That was odd. Even if they were whispering he would be able to detect it. After about twenty minutes the door opened, and Tessa told Isabelle, "Don't hesitate to call Sophia."

Gregor listened for Tessa's footsteps to pass by. When they went the other way, he quietly opened the closet door and followed. Where was she going? She had been there enough to know the way out of the building. She stopped at the door to the stairs that led to the first floor.

She couldn't get through there; she didn't have access. Tessa surprised him when she pulled a keycard out of her back pocket and swiped it over the sensor, peering around the corner before entering the doorway that led to solitary confinement. What the fuck was she doing?

Gregor grabbed the door Tessa entered just before it closed and gave her time to get to the bottom of the steps. He quietly called to the guards on duty using the radio. Almost all of the men who worked in the prison were shifters, so he knew they would hear his whispered command. "There is a redheaded woman wandering the halls. I want you all to back off and allow her passage. Do not follow and do not let her see you. I want to see where she goes." Gregor followed her, staying far enough behind that she couldn't hear him. Nikolas thought it was possible she and Isabelle both had shifter blood. If that were true, her hearing could be enhanced as well. He took extra precautions, just in case.

He stopped at the door to the first floor and listened. He could tell by her footsteps she was stopping at each cell. Was she searching for someone? Why else would she be down here? The mating bond called to him. It had been ever since she walked into the building. Now that she was on the first level around the criminals, his beast was clawing to get out. It recognized his mate and the fact that she was around dangerous men.

When he got close enough to see her without being seen himself, he noticed she was standing outside St. Claire's cell. She was staring in, but she wasn't saying anything. She stood quietly for a few minutes then whispered, "And I love you."

Gregor's heart shredded. Why would he think a woman as gorgeous as Tessa wouldn't have a man in her life? But St. Claire? Geoffrey assured him that Tamian had no family in the area. What if she was his girlfriend and he had lied to Frey? Tessa's footsteps alerted him that she was now jogging. This time he directed his command to the guard in the control room. "Quickly, override the system so the only door her key card will work on is the one leading to the roof. I am going to trap our little trespasser." He followed quietly up the steps, hearing her softly swear when she was denied access to the door leading to the exit. He grinned inwardly. Had it dawned on her yet that she was screwed?

Tessa stepped out into the brisk October night air, holding the door until it quietly clicked shut behind her. She stepped over to the ledge, gauging the height.

The door opened behind her. She turned to see Gregor with his gun drawn and aimed at her. The ledge was only a few steps away.

"Stop." Gregor wasn't moving. He was probably feeling the bond and trying to keep it in check. She was most definitely being drawn to him. If she had been paying attention, she would have known it was him she was connecting with and not Tamian. She peered over the edge then grinned at the warden.

"Don't make me shoot you, Red."

"You won't shoot me." She couldn't help goading the Gargoyle.

"And why's that?" He cocked the hammer.

She shrugged. "Because I'm a girl?" She crept closer to the edge of the roof.

"You're out of your pretty little head." At least he didn't shoot her. Yet.

"You think I'm pretty?" She had been called cute her whole life. She really liked pretty.

"You know you are, now come over here. Don't make me have to drag you down the stairs."

Tessa momentarily imagined Gregor grabbing a handful of her hair and dragging her, caveman style, down the steps. Why did that turn her on? Oh, maybe because he was her mate, and anything he said to her would cause her body to want his.

"You want me? Come and get me." She freefell into nothing, opening the wings of her flight jacket. This was crazy, even for her. The building wasn't exactly high enough for her to fly from. She just had to make sure she dropped slow enough that she didn't break any bones upon impact. Landing would probably hurt like a bitch. Mate or not, he was going to be pissed.

When Jonas found out Tessa was BASE jumping, he equipped her with the best and most technologically advanced suits there were. He even designed a jacket that could be worn without the pants for shorter distances. At that moment, she was glad she had put it on instead of her leather jacket she normally rode in.

If Gregor wanted her, he would have to phase and come get her. She didn't think he would risk that. The ground came up quickly, and she tucked and rolled. She continued rolling a few feet before she finally stopped. It wasn't the graceful landing she had hoped for, but at least she was unharmed for the most part. Gregor cursed at the same time he phased and flew right for her. *Holy shit.*

She didn't have time to move before he was on her. "Holy hell, are you okay? Talk to me, Red." He was on his knees beside her, his beautiful wings unfurled. When Tessa grinned at him, Gregor lost it. "What in the FUCK did you think you were doing? You could have been killed!" Yep, pissed.

Tessa figured her best option was to just keep quiet. What could she say, really? She was caught, red-handed. Gregor's wings disappeared behind his back, but his fangs were still out. His uniform shirt was shredded. He didn't wait for her to answer. He grabbed her and threw her over his shoulder. Definitely pissed. This was awkward since her flight jacket was bulky, but obviously it didn't bother him.

She beat on his back with her fists, "Put me down you overgrown beast." He did not put her down. He took her, kicking and hitting, into the prison. Several guards backed against the wall, allowing them to pass. When they got to his office, he put her on her feet.

"Sit." He pointed to a chair. She did not sit. What she did do was calm herself so her own fangs and claws would not make a showing.

Eleven

Gregor was furious. What the hell was Tessa thinking jumping off the roof? She could have been killed. Okay, maybe not killed, but hurt. Badly. And he phased. With no thought to anything other than her safety, his wings opened of their own volition, and he dove after her. Gods, was that how Rafael felt when Vincent Alexander took a shot at Kaya? His heart stopped momentarily as his mate jumped off the roof. Had he realized she was wearing a flight jacket, he probably could have kept his emotions in check. Seeing her plummet to the ground filled him with an emotion he had never known in his five hundred and sixty-seven years. Fear.

Gregor picked up the phone and dialed Isabelle's number. "Can you come to my office immediately? We have a situation." He didn't wait for her to respond, he just slammed the receiver down on the base. Tessa was removing her jacket when he yelled, "Do you want to tell me why you think you have a right to walk around this prison, to floors that are secure for a very good reason, and then try to run from me?"

He waited for an answer that wasn't coming. Isabelle ran into the office and stopped short when she saw Tessa. "What are you doing? I thought you had to go home and pack."

Gregor needed answers. Did Isabelle not know about Tessa's plan to find Tamian? "Isabelle, it seems your cousin, Trixie, decided to take a walk around the prison, to the first floor no less. Did I not make it clear the first level was off limits? And why would you think it's okay for her to go down there unescorted if I told you it was unsafe for you?"

Isabelle sputtered and her face reddened. "Warden, I assure you I have no idea what my cousin is up to. And her name is Tessa, not Trixie. Tessa, what were you doing on the first level? How did you even get down there?"

Tessa pulled the key card from her back pocket. "Here, this is yours." She handed the security badge to her cousin, unapologetically.

"What the hell? You've done some screwed up stuff but stealing my security card? Are you trying to get me fired?" Gregor could tell that Isabelle was furious with her cousin.

"Yes, *Tessa*, please tell us what you were doing on the first level, and why were you at Tamian St. Claire's cell?"

Gregor would have missed it if he hadn't been a shifter. There was something that passed quickly between the two ladies.

Tessa glared at him but she did not answer. "Isabelle, I put my trust in you when I hired you. I hope you don't allow the antics of your younger cousin to cost you your job. I want answers and nobody is leaving here until I get them."

Isabelle gasped and by the look on her face, he had said the wrong thing. "Why do you think I'm older than she is?" She asked Gregor while pointing at Tessa.

"Because, you're so much more mature. *She's* a brat." Gregor sneered at Tessa.

"Wait a fucking minute! Just because I don't have a stick up my ass all the time does not make me a brat." Tessa jabbed her fists on her hips, leaving Isabelle with her mouth hanging open.

"Mr. Stone, I do apologize for my cousin's behavior. She's rather sensitive."

"Pot, kettle," Tessa muttered under her breath.

This was getting them nowhere. "Miss Blackmore, I want to know what you were doing on the first level and I want to know now." Tessa looked to Isabelle who was not offering any help. Before she could say anything, Isabelle grabbed her stomach.

"Oh god." She doubled over and groaned. "Oh shit, Tessa. Tell me this is just a stomach bug."

Gregor didn't understand what was happening. One minute he was questioning Tessa, the next, Isabelle was lying on the floor.

"What's wrong with her?"

"Just help me get her to her car. I need to get her home." Tessa grabbed her stuff off the floor. "Isabelle, where are your keys?"

"In my office. Oh god, Tessa. It hurts."

"Shh, I know. Just hang on." Tessa turned to Gregor, "Please. I need to get her keys and get her home. Help me?"

"Of course. Go get her stuff, and I'll meet you outside." He lifted a writhing Isabelle off the floor. Tessa frowned at the sight of him holding her cousin. She did *not* like seeing another woman in Gregor's arms.

Barely a few seconds passed before Tessa was there. "What are you doing?" Gregor was putting Belle in his Hummer instead of her own car.

"I'll drive, you sit in the back with her." He opened the back door to his vehicle and gently laid the doctor down.

Tessa climbed in the backseat with her cousin. "You're a pain in the ass."

Gregor started the engine. "I'm trying to help, and you're calling me names. Now, I need an address." He studied his mate in the rearview mirror. She was doing her best to soothe Isabelle. When she told him where Isabelle lived, he spoke the address into his GPS that, after calculating, told him which way to go. It was hard to keep his eyes on the road when Tessa sat so close behind. His heart warred between the feeling of kissing her and watching her jump from the roof. Two totally distinct emotions, neither one less powerful.

62

Isabelle was moaning and struggling. He split his attention between the road and Tessa. They arrived at Isabelle's home, and Tessa told him to pull around back. He opened the door and she slid out, grabbing her cousin in her arms. Tessa carried Isabelle as if she weighed nothing. "Here, let me take her."

"No!" Tessa pushed past him and walked up the back steps.

"Tessa, I can walk. Put me down. And why are we here? Why didn't you take me..." A pain-filled moan cut off the rest of her sentence, and Tessa continued toward the house.

"Shit." Tessa stopped moving.

"What's wrong?" He had no idea why she wouldn't allow him to help her with her cousin, unless she was jealous. He knew the mating bond could cause extreme possessiveness. She was shifting her load, attempting to pull the keys from her pocket without dropping the other woman.

"Tessa, don't be obtuse. Let me help you." He held his hands out expecting her to hand over her cousin. Instead, she surprised him when she told him, "Get the keys. They're in my right pocket."

She thrust her hip toward him, and he slid his fingers in the tight pocket. If Isabelle didn't need immediate help, he would put his hand somewhere besides her hip. He grabbed the keys and unlocked the door. The alarm system beeped. "432867." She told him the code as she continued on into Isabelle's bedroom.

He stood in the bedroom door as his employee thrashed about, and his mate attempted to alleviate her discomfort. Tessa turned and instructed him, "I'd prefer if you leave. I'm pretty sure she won't want you to watch."

"Watch what? Tessa, what's happening?" He was helpless, not knowing what to do to assist her.

"She's going through the change." Tessa turned in a circle, searching for something. "Can you turn the thermostat down? It should be in the hallway."

Gregor found the thermostat just outside the bedroom. "How far?" He asked pressing the buttons on the box.

"Try fifty for now. She's burning up." Gregor returned to the bedroom to see Tessa placing a wet washcloth to Isabelle's forehead.

"What change?" Gregor asked as he stood by, once again helpless.

"The transition. You know when a shifter changes for the first time?"

"How do you know?"

"Turn around. I need to get her down to her underwear." Tessa didn't wait for him to comply. She undressed her cousin who was calm for the moment. "I just know."

Gregor was floored. Nikolas had said it was possible they had shifter blood, but he didn't really believe it. Until now. "She's one of us?"

"No, she isn't one of *you*." Why did she sound so appalled?

"Then what is she?" There was no other explanation. She had to be a shifter. He glanced behind him, taking care to keep his eyes on Tessa.

She was searching for something in his eyes. Just when he thought she wasn't going to answer, she told him, "She's a half-blood. Her mother is human."

Holy hell, it was true. It was possible for humans to mate with Gargoyles. This was the best news he had ever heard.

Tessa did her best to soothe her cousin. She got up and rewet the washcloth then wiped the doctor's brow as sweat beaded as soon as it was wiped away.

"But why is she changing so late in life? Why now?" Being part human must have something to do with the change. Is that why Dane Abbott had just gone through his?

"Because sometime in the past few days, she has been in contact with her mate."

"What does that have to do with it? Wait, are you telling me that half-bloods don't transition until they meet their mate? What if they never meet them?"

"Then they remain human."

"So the doctor has met her mate." Gregor puffed up.

"Get your fat head out of the clouds, big guy. It's not you."

Gregor knew that, he just couldn't resist taunting her. "How do you know it's not me?"

"Do you get any special feelings when you're around Belle?" She wouldn't look at him. Tessa didn't honestly want to know the answer to the question. She was a pain in his ass, but did he really want to hurt her?

"What kind of feelings?"

"Special, out of the ordinary emotions you don't get around any other woman. Like the ones you get when I'm around."

"You mean repulsed?" Shit, that just slipped out. No, his comment didn't hurt her feelings, it pissed her off.

"Fuck you, Stone," she muttered under her breath. Yeah, she knew she was his mate, so why did she dislike him so much?

Twelve

Gregor kept his eyes on Tessa as she rose from the bed and walked past him without so much as a glance. He followed her into the kitchen where she filled a bowl with ice then added water to it. She sat the bowl on the counter, not letting go of the edges. Gregor leaned his backside against the counter, standing as close as he could without touching her.

Tessa, still holding onto the bowl sighed. "Look, this is going to be a long couple of days. I'd appreciate it if you'd give us some privacy. This isn't pretty to watch, and I know she won't want an audience."

Gregor could understand that. Even though it had been over five hundred years since his first transition, he remembered the initial pain. He knew the female Gargoyles didn't get wings, so it would only make sense the half-bloods wouldn't either.

"Do you want me to bring your bike to you? You have no transportation, and I don't like the idea of you being stuck here with no wheels."

"Nobody rides Lita but me," she scowled at him. Did she not realize he had the same bike?

"You do know I have a bike just like yours, don't you?"

"No, yours is not *just like mine*. She has been modified."

He had an adrenaline junky for a mate. Perfect. "So instead of trusting her to me, you'd rather be stuck here?"

He crossed his arms over his chest waiting for an answer.

"I thought I repulsed you. Why would you care if I'm stuck here without wheels?"

"I think you know that you don't actually repulse me, Red." Gregor now regretted his earlier statement, even if he had been joking.

She pulled a key out of her left pocket and held it out. "If you put one scratch on my bike…"

"You'll what?" He couldn't help but smirk down at her. He might not be as tall as his brothers, but he was a hulk compared to her small frame. He took the key from her hand, wrapping his fingers around hers, not letting go. He would take advantage of every chance to touch her, even if it drove him insane. The mate pull obviously didn't affect her as it did him. She just continued to frown.

"I'll be careful, but Tessa, if you need me, just call. I'll be here for you." He couldn't resist. Gregor reached out and ran his index finger down her face. Her eyes closed, and he could smell her arousal. So she *was* affected. Before she had a chance to pull away, he kissed her softly on the forehead.

He left the women alone and headed back to the Pen. As soon as he arrived, Gregor headed downstairs. Tessa was his, and he needed to make that clear. He stopped at the albino's cell and glanced in. He was awake and staring at the ceiling. Gregor stepped to the next cell and unlocked the door. Tamian sat up quickly. "What is it, is everything okay?"

Gregor held his finger to his lips and motioned for Tamian to follow him. He didn't want the albino to hear anything that had to do with Tessa. When they were in the stairwell, he said, "Everything's fine. Why wouldn't it be?" He wasn't sure how to approach the subject without sounding like a jealous fool. "I just wanted you to know that I caught your girlfriend. She won't be visiting again anytime soon."

"Oh shit, Andi! Is she all right? I told her not to come back, that I'm here on purpose."

67

Gregor was confused. "Andi? You mean Tessa, the redhead that was just down here?"

"That's what she calls herself, but yeah, that's her. And she's not my girlfriend. Listen, I don't know how she got down here, but when I explained to her I put myself in here, she assured me she wouldn't come back. That's good, right?"

"She's not your girlfriend?" But she told him she loved him. What else could she be? "Your wife? I was under the impression you didn't have any family here in New Atlanta."

"What? No, man. Andi's my sister. Is she okay? I know she can be a little hard to handle sometimes, but she has good intentions. How did she even get in here?"

Gregor's heart lightened by about ten pounds when Tamian confirmed Tessa was his sister. "She was here visiting her cousin, Isabelle. I guess that makes her your cousin, too. We hired her on as the doctor after Henshaw was cut down by the Unholy. Tamian, I just watched Isabelle begin her transition." He didn't elaborate. If Tamian was a shifter, he would know what that meant.

"Andi's with her, right? She's the best at seeing someone through their change." The man was seriously concerned. Frey had been right; Tamian St. Claire was a good guy.

"Yeah, I just drove them both to Isabelle's house. Andi, *Tessa* asked me to leave." It had taken everything in him to leave her there, knowing she was his. Feeling it was one thing. Knowing she felt it, too, was something totally different. She knew she belonged to him.

"Do you know why your sister dislikes me so much?" He hated to sound like a teenage girl, but dammit, he wanted to know.

Tamian clapped him on the shoulder. "Because you're a full-blood."

Gregor shook his head. He didn't understand what being a Gargoyle had to do with it since Tessa herself was a shifter. "I think we need to go to my office and talk." He led Tamian up the stairs. Gregor shut the door, and they were both seated.

"Tessa mentioned Isabelle is a half-blood, that she has a human mother. I need you to fill me in on everything you know, St. Claire." With the news that humans and Gargoyles could mate, Gregor's hopes for the future of the Clan rose one-hundred percent. He needed confirmation to give Rafael and Kaya.

Tamian shifted in his seat. "I would prefer Tessa be the one to tell you."

"Why's that? And why was Tessa just standing at your cell door not speaking?"

Tamian seemed nervous. What was he hiding? Gregor needed some answers so he asked him, "You obviously know what I am, so why shouldn't I know about you and Tessa?"

"Ours is a different story, one I do believe you should be told. But man, it's her story to tell you. Her place as your mate."

"How do you know she's my mate?"

Tamian stood and paced the small area. "Let's just say I know all about my sister, more than I want to know. Can we talk about something else? Like Vincent Alexander?"

This got Gregor's attention. "What about him? Has he spoken?"

"Oh, you could say that. The man is off his rocker as far as I'm concerned. To answer your question, yeah, he's talked. More like rambled. One minute he's coherent, then the next, it's as if his brain is scrambled. I do know he needs a fuckin' cigarette. Jesus H, he won't shut up about that godsdamn patch. Anyway, I'm pretty sure he was working for Flanagan, because he mentions him often. He's also mentioned the name Merrick a couple of times. But I'm gonna tell ya, the thing that scares me the most about him is the fact that he knows who Isabelle is. He called her Izzy."

"How would he know Isabelle? Unless he heard us talking outside his cell..." Gregor hadn't considered Tamian could be a shifter. "If you can hear him through the walls that means you're either a Gargoyle or a half-blood who has gone through your transition. I'm going to bet since you're Tessa's brother, you're a half-blood. Tessa told me the transition for you happens when you find your mate. Why isn't yours here with you in New Atlanta? Or is she?"

Tamian stopped pacing. "Gregor, I really don't feel comfortable having this conversation until you've spoken to Andi. I'm not trying to hide anything, not really. She has the whole story, and if I give you bits and pieces, it could throw a wrench in the family's plans."

Gregor stood up and faced Tamian. "You're not giving me anything. There's so much I need to know, but for now, tell me the truth about the bonding. Humans and Gargoyles, are they successfully having children? With no complications? Please, Tamian, my King just found his mate, and she's a human. I would love to give them some good news."

Tamian sighed. "That much I will tell you; yes, it's possible." He scrubbed his hand down his face. "Man, Andi's gonna kick my ass eight ways to Sunday. I think I'll stay in lock-up a while."

Gregor laughed. "She's a handful, I'll give you that. But why... never mind. I will just have to convince her she wants me."

Tamian laughed, "Yeah, good luck with that."

"Back to Vincent, tell me everything he's said. Motherfucker, I knew he could talk."

Both men sat back down, and Gregor took notes of everything the albino had said so far. After they were finished, Gregor escorted Tamian back to his cell then looked in on Vincent. The shifter was on the floor doing push-ups. Gregor counted to a thousand and shook his head. After the day he'd had, Gregor was ready for a drink. Or ten. First he had to call Rafael and give him and his Queen the good news.

Greta's green eyes were staring at Merrick. He really should close her lids, but he loved the look of surprise on her face. How easy it had been to get her into his bed. Well, a bed. There was no way he would risk fucking a mark in his own home. He took her to one of the apartments recently vacated by Vincent Alexander. Fucking Alexander. Merrick knew he was a wild card when he enlisted his help with kidnapping the delegates. The albino had been brilliant in abducting twelve grown men from their hotel rooms with no one the wiser. For some reason, he became obsessed with the pretty blonde police chief, and now he was rotting in a cell at the Pen. Gordon had warned Merrick that the albino had a few screws loose, but he took the chance anyway.

Merrick almost felt sorry for Vincent. When he was a young man, Vincent had been tortured to the point of death just so Gordon Flanagan could build his army of Unholy. Too bad Flanagan hadn't hired smarter scientists. Where Vincent was a shifter, the Unholy were unpredictable monsters. Working for Flanagan put him in their crosshairs every once in a while, but Merrick was smart enough to give them a wide berth as much as possible. He only knew the story of how the Unholy came to be because Flanagan still employed those same scientists. They bragged to anyone who would listen about how they successfully created the creatures.

Merrick returned his attention to the beautiful girl in his arms. "Greta, Greta, Greta." Merrick had rather enjoyed

71

the sex. When he squeezed her neck while pounding his cock into her core, she had really let loose. Until she figured out the autoerotic asphyxiation was turning into murder. He pushed her red hair back from her face just before he watched her body slip silently over the bridge railing.

Thirteen

Trevor flipped the three deadbolts on his door. He went to his spare bedroom and shut that door and locked it as well. In the closet, he removed the loose paneling that camouflaged a hole in the back wall. Behind the paneling was a safe. Spinning the tumblers, he entered the code that only one other person in the world had access to: his brother, Travis. He opened the safe, pulled out a leather-bound journal and shut the door.

When Travis was born, the doctors found a defect in his heart. His parents quickly made the decision to clone him. Trevor hadn't been born, he had been created. Concocted in a laboratory to be back-up parts for his older brother. Imagine finding this out when you were a small child. The knowledge that you had been created, just in case, could possibly give you a complex.

Luckily, the doctors were able to repair Travis' heart and Trevor's wasn't needed. Travis loved his little brother and took every opportunity to show it. When Travis found out the reason his parents cloned him, he distanced himself from them. Their mother argued that they did it for his sake, but he was repulsed. The bond he and Trevor held went deeper than anything he could ever feel for them.

Trevor started the journal as a project in school. He met a few other cloned children, and they formed a secret group. They sat together at lunch, met on the playground during recess, and even had sleepovers on the weekend. As they got older, their group expanded as more and more clones joined them. Trevor added each and every name to the journal, documenting characteristics they all had in common.

By the time he was in college, Trevor's journal was full, and he had to start a new one. He refused to keep the information stored on a computer. Call him paranoid, but with men like Gordon Flanagan free to hunt the clones while searching for his child, he vowed to keep the information safe. Eventually, Trevor entered the information on a spreadsheet which he transferred to a flash drive. He never left the data on the computer. It was immediately wiped clean. The flash drive was also stored in the safe.

Now, sitting in his spare bedroom with the latest journal opened in front of him, he scanned the list of clones. The name of the latest body brought into the morgue had seemed familiar. Flipping back a couple of pages, he found it. Sonya Bell, thirty-two, red hair, green eyes. She was the second body brought in within the last three weeks that fit the same description. His boss, Dante, had to tell him their hair and eye color because clones had one thing in common: almost all of them were color blind.

The M.E. had pondered at the similarities, thinking it was time to inform the Chief that she more than likely had a serial killer on her hands. Trevor knew what Dante didn't. Both of the victims had more than just physical traits in common; they were also clones.

He closed the journal and rubbed his eyes. He had to decide whether or not to confide in his boss.

"You should have seen her; she grinned at me then jumped off the fucking roof." Gregor paced Dante's office while he told him about Tessa. "She fucking grinned. Now I know how Rafael feels about Kaya. I'm telling you, I had no choice; I shifted and dove after her. I have never felt fear in my life until that moment."

"Tell me about the sick feeling you get." Dante sat behind his desk, arms crossed over his chest.

"It's like Rafe described it, sort of like vertigo. Your world turns on its axis, but you're trying to remain upright.

The more I'm near her, the worse it gets. I feel the need to constantly touch her."

Dante closed his eyes. Gregor was just about to ask what was wrong when the office door flew open. "Dante I have to tell…"

Trevor stopped talking when he realized Gregor was in the room. "Hello, Warden."

"Trevor, what do you need to tell me?" Dante encouraged him to continue.

Trevor looked between the two men and remained silent.

"I will leave and let you two speak." Gregor knew Trevor was not a fan of his.

"Hang on. Trevor, is this a personal matter or business?" Dante would tell Gregor anyway if it was business.

"Business. Personal. Both. Mostly business."

"Then you can speak freely in front of Gregor."

"Okay…" He still hesitated, obviously not wanting to talk with Gregor in the room. "It's our latest bodies. When I read their names something clicked. They don't just look alike. They're both clones." Trevor chewed on his thumbnail while he studied the two men.

"How do you know this?" Dante asked his assistant.

"Would you let it go if I said I just do?"

Dante frowned at Trevor. "What do you think? You can't come in here claiming to have knowledge of the victims and leave it at that. How do you know?"

Trevor sighed and stared up at the ceiling. "Because I keep a database of most of the clones in and around New Atlanta."

It was Gregor's turn to question Trevor, "Why would you keep that information?"

"Because…" Trevor whispered, "Because I'm a clone."

"But that still doesn't explain why you would keep a database of the other clones." Dante stood and put his hands on Trevor's shoulders. "Look at me." He waited until Trevor met his eyes. "I don't care that you're a clone. You are smart, and you're a great assistant. But I would like to know why you keep tabs on the others."

Trevor relented. "It was something I started a long time ago. When I was in school, we all sort of hung out together. When we found each other, we automatically became friends. The older we got, the larger our group. I was the keeper of the information, you know, names, addresses, phone numbers. That way we could always stay in touch when we went off to different colleges. We were one big family. Others were assigned to keep their own lists and send them to me to add to the main one. It just grew."

"How many names are on your list now?"

"About two thousand."

"Two thousand? Holy hell. If there are that many names, how did you know our victims were on your list? I know you're smart, but two out of two thousand is like a needle in a haystack." Gregor hadn't realized there were that many clones in the world, much less in New Atlanta.

"I have a very good memory. This is information I have been storing for years."

"Was it just their names that triggered the fact that they were clones?" Dante asked him.

"No, they were both redheads with green eyes. When we get victims with similar features, I automatically try to link the murders together. Another thing I find odd is that someone who looks like our victims visited Dane recently. Remember when I went to check on him a couple of weeks ago?" Dante nodded. "A woman who looked like these two was coming down the hall from his apartment."

Gregor asked, "Was she a redhead, too?"

"I have no idea. I'm color blind." Trevor murmured.

Gregor held up his hand. "Hang on. How old are the victims?" Surely it was a coincidence that they were redheads.

"Early thirties."

Gregor didn't have a good feeling about this. At all. "I want to see the bodies."

Dante asked, "What are you thinking, Brother?"

He didn't miss the look Trevor gave them both. Trevor had worked with Dante for several years, but he still didn't know they were related. "I'm thinking I hope they don't resemble Tessa."

Dante was leading the way to the morgue when his phone rang. "You two go ahead, I'll catch up."

Trevor led Gregor into the holding room. He opened both doors and rolled out the tables that housed the victims. Gregor was going to be sick. These women could be Tessa's sisters. "Fuck me."

"We have another one. Body dumped over St. George's Bridge," Dante informed them as he entered the room. "Gregor, what is it?"

"They look so much like Tessa they could pass for her sisters. Did you get any information on the latest victim?" Dante just nodded.

"Godsdamnit. Tessa isn't a clone so this has to be a coincidence." Gregor needed more information before he went off the rails, but there was no way he was going to let her out of his sight if these murders continued.

Dante put a hand on his shoulder and squeezed. "I have to go. You need to call Rafael and tell him what you told me earlier. Don't think about this until we have more information. You're probably right that this is a coincidence."

Gregor knew Dante was just placating him. "Yeah, call me when you know something definitive."

Gregor needed some air. He left the morgue, got in his Hummer, and rolled the window down. What he really wanted to do was to fly, and taking Tessa's bike to her would give him the opportunity. He drove to the Pen, traded his Hummer for her bike, and rode it to Isabelle's. Even though he wanted to see Tessa, he needed to go see Rafael and fill him in on the half-bloods. Tessa looked out the window as he cut the motor. He inclined his head in her direction. With a hint of hesitation, Gregor walked into the darkness and took to the skies.

Fourteen

Gregor walked into a fairly quiet manor. Priscilla was in the kitchen singing to herself as she iced a cake. The King liked his sweets, and Priscilla indulged him. It was a good thing Gargoyles had such high metabolisms or they would all be overweight.

"Gregor, you're just in time for a piece." She put the last dab of icing on and smiled at the finished product.

"I'd love a slice later. Right now, I need to talk to Rafe. I know this is his last night with Kaya, but he is going to want to hear what I have to say." Gregor walked by the cake, swiped a finger through the icing, and stuck it in his mouth. His eyes nearly rolled back in his head, it was so good. She swatted at him like she would a small child.

"Priscilla, you have outdone yourself." He gave the older woman a kiss on the cheek. She had been like a mother to him and his brothers for the last thirty years. His own mother was back in Italy. After their father was slain in an attempt on the throne, she left America. She said it was too painful to be around her sons.

"Did I hear my name uttered in vain?" Rafael was standing in the doorway, grinning at his brother. His beautiful woman was standing at his side, face flushed. Gregor could smell the sex on them both. He didn't blame them for staying in bed until the absolute last moment. He would do the same if he were in his brother's shoes.

"You did. Kaya, you're looking well. I have some news that you both will want to hear. I also have some you probably won't. Can we sit?"

Had it been just the men, Rafael would have led them to the patio. Gregor wasn't surprised when he took them to the billiards room instead where it was warmer.

"Quite a lot has happened today. So here's the condensed version: I found my mate. I was right, it's Tessa.

She snuck down to level one and talked to her brother, Tamian St. Claire. I followed her, and then she jumped off the roof. I phased and went after her. I took her to my office and called Isabelle, but before I could get to the bottom of anything, Isabelle began shifting. She is a half-blood. The half-bloods are children of human mothers and Gargoyle fathers. That is the good news.

"The bad news is that while Kaya has been taking some time off, there have been more murders. Dante got a call right before I left the morgue. I'm sure Jasper will have more information when he gets home, but the odd thing is that the victims are apparently clones. If Trevor is correct, this one will be as well. The really bad news is they all look just like Tessa."

Both Rafael and Kaya were staring at Gregor like he needed an exorcist. "What do you mean she jumped off the roof?" Rafael asked at the same time Kaya asked, "How does Trevor know the victims are clones?"

"I know it's a lot, so let me start with Tessa. Obviously, she is some type of adrenaline junkie. She came into the Pen prepared. She was wearing a flight jacket, so when I say she jumped off the roof, she pretty much flew. At the time, I didn't know she was prepared. With no thought, I phased and went after her. I already knew she was my mate, but that sealed the deal. I now understand what you meant when you said you had no choice but to phase." Rafael nodded. His wings had immediately wrapped around Kaya when she was shot at a third time.

"I took her to my office to figure out why she was sneaking below to talk to St. Claire. Only they weren't talking. They were just standing there, staring at each other. I still haven't figured that one out yet, but I have an idea. While I was questioning Tessa, Isabelle doubled over in pain. I drove both women to Isabelle's home, and that's when Tessa told me Isabelle was going through her transition. It seems that with the half-bloods, they don't change until they meet their mate. So, somewhere along the way, Isabelle has had contact with hers. We just don't know who it is yet.

"I wanted to get more information, but Tessa basically kicked me out. Oh, and she hates me. Anyway, I went back to make it clear to St. Claire that Tessa is mine, and he let me know just as quickly that he's her brother. He didn't want to elaborate on anything, saying it was Tessa's place as my mate to tell me. He did confirm that human women can have Gargoyle babies and live to tell about it. Tamian has his own story, one I need to get out of him. He said Vincent Alexander can talk and has been doing quite a bit of it, some coherent, some not.

"Vincent also knows Isabelle somehow. He has mentioned Flanagan's name as well as someone named Merrick. Tamian is going to continue listening in on the albino to see if he says anything useful. I wanted you to have some privacy on your last night together, but after I visited Dante, I needed to come see you. I have a theory. Rafe, the women in the morgue could be Tessa's sisters. They all have red hair and green eyes and are approximately the same age."

Jasper came into the room and confirmed Gregor's prior suspicion. "I'm afraid the latest victim fits the same bill. We don't have an identity yet, but I'm sure someone will call her in as missing soon. She had the same handprint around her throat as the other women."

Rafael asked Gregor, "So what's your theory?"

"I think Tessa is Flanagan's daughter."

Kaya asked, "What makes you say that?"

"Like I said, it's just a theory, but think about it. Both Tessa and Isabelle know Montague, and Isabelle is his daughter which should make Tessa his niece. She is the right age. St. Claire is her brother. I've not read a lot about clones, but I have heard there is some sort of psychic connection. That could be why Tessa was just standing at his door. They were speaking to each other with just their minds."

"That's crazy," Kaya said.

"Yes, and you didn't believe in shapeshifters a couple of weeks ago either." Rafael took her hand in his and squeezed.

"I am just theorizing here, but it adds up." Gregor walked to the mini fridge and pulled out a beer. "Anyone else?"

Jasper held up his hand. "I'll take one. What I don't get is how does Flanagan know what Tessa looks like? Didn't she disappear when she was a baby?"

"Yes, but her mother has red hair. Flanagan has red hair and believes he is the father. We know since she's a shifter he can't be the father unless he's a Gargoyle, which I don't believe he is. He is assuming she will look like Elizabeth did at her age."

They all pondered Gregor's theory until Kaya asked, "Jasper, how did it go at work today with Dane?" She would be returning tomorrow, so it only made sense she would want a heads up.

"I tried to get him to open up, but he pretty much avoided me all day. Kept himself holed up in your office with some redhead."

"Redhead? Was it Tessa?" Gregor's jealousy was rearing its green head.

"I didn't get a good look at the woman. She was in his arms with her back to me." Jasper took a drink of his beer.

"It could be that reporter. I think he likes her, Gregor." Kaya was trying to spare his feelings, but it wasn't working.

"Doesn't matter. What does matter is we find out who's killing these women and put a stop to it. I will get Dante to call you when he has examined the latest victim. I need to check on Isabelle. She is my employee after all."

Rafael grinned, "Sure. It has nothing to do with the fact that Tessa is helping her."

If Kaya hadn't been in the room, Gregor would have told Rafe to go fuck himself. Having a Queen around was going to take some getting used to.

Rafael pulled Kaya onto his lap. "You said Tessa hates you. Any particular reason why?"

"I asked Tamian. He said it's because I'm a full-blood. I need to find out why the prejudice. It's not like we knew about the half-bloods. But if that was Tessa at the precinct today, she may have told Dane to keep tight-lipped around you, Jasper."

"How do I handle Dane? Do I tell him I know the truth, or do I wait and let him approach me?" Kaya asked Rafael.

"Now that we have this latest information, it will probably make both your lives easier if you tell him you know. Trying to hide a secret as big as being a shifter is a tall order." Rafael pushed Kaya's hair over her shoulder as he spoke to her. Gregor wanted that with Tessa. Wanted the closeness, the intimacy.

"Do I tell him about you, the Clan? Since he's one of you now, aren't you his King, too?"

Rafael nuzzled Kaya's neck. "Yes, I am his King, their King. For now, say as little to Dane about that as possible. We have to find out as much about the half-bloods as we can and why they have been hiding all these years. Gregor, I need you to get closer to the women. Surely you can get one of them to talk to you. If you went to Isabelle's home, then you accomplished something Nikolas could not. He went back to the place where he had followed the women after their initial conversation, but the place was locked up tight. He would have needed to break in to get inside."

Gregor asked, "Didn't he say the house he went to was close to the University?" Rafael nodded. "The house I went to is on the south side of the city. It definitely wasn't closed up; it was homey and lived in. Isabelle did ask why Tessa took her home instead of somewhere else, though. That is just another mystery to solve, but it will have to wait. Jasper, how close are you to finding your own place to live?" The manor was large enough that he wouldn't be getting in the way, but Gregor could imagine Rafael didn't want any distractions now that he had found his mate.

Jasper finished off his beer then answered, "Sixx called me earlier, something about a glitch in my accounts. As soon as he gets that figured out, and I have my new identity, I'll be moving out. I found a place pretty close to yours. My property isn't as heavily wooded, but it's still private."

"Did Sixx say what kind of glitch? Julian called earlier and was concerned about the missing data in your file. Jasper, I have to ask you, and I need you to answer honestly; did you mess with your records for some reason? When you transferred out here from the west coast, your employment had been tampered with." Rafael wasn't accusing Jasper, he just needed answers.

Jasper didn't hesitate to respond, "Sixx didn't say, and no, Sir. I'm not stupid, but I'm definitely not smart enough to hack into files. What about it was tampered with?"

"The dates you were a fireman. Those had been erased."

"Oh, shit. Shit, shit, shit. Rafe, I might know who did it. Can Julian go back far enough into my computer and trace the dates and times?"

"I'm sure he can. What are you getting at?" Rafael set Kaya off his lap and stood up.

"I was, I had…" Jasper was nervous.

"Jasper, it's okay. If this has anything to do with what you and I talked about already, you can speak freely in front of Kaya and Gregor. They both know."

"They do?" Jasper was shocked. The look on his face made that apparent.

"Yes, we do. And we don't care." Gregor gripped his shoulder, showing his sincerity.

"I had a boyfriend, Craig. He was also a firefighter, but he was in the closet. He told everyone we were roommates, not lovers. He was super smart, and I caught him on my laptop more than once."

"Call Julian and give him all the information you can. Hopefully this will tell us who hacked our system and why." Rafael held his hand out to Kaya who took it and stood beside the King.

Jasper left the room to make the call, and Gregor's cell phone rang.

"Stone. Hey, Brother. Where are you? Absolutely. I'll be right there."

Rafael had the look in his eye that Gregor knew all too well. When it came to the Unholy, all the Gargoyles lived for the fight. Knowing he'd overheard the conversation just now, he shook his head at his brother. "Oh, no. You are not going patrolling. You stay here with your woman."

"I didn't say a word." Rafael grinned before practically dragging Kaya back to their bedroom.

Gregor went in search of Jasper. They needed as many Goyles fighting as they could get.

Fifteen

Isabelle practiced releasing and retracting her fangs without cutting her lip while Tessa was on the phone. Sophia had been relieved that Tessa was there to help her cousin through the change. Transitioning was something Sophia knew little about. Her parents were still missing, and Tessa told her to concentrate on them. Elizabeth had called earlier to let her know she couldn't find Sam either, and she was going to take over the search herself. Tessa called the airline and changed her flight. Belle was phasing easily, so Tessa should be able to take off a day later than planned.

"Why did you bring me here instead of taking me to the house where you took Dane?"

"I didn't think you would want to be around Caroline. Was I wrong?"

"No, you weren't wrong. There's something I don't understand. Dane came to me with flu-like symptoms. It took him over 24 hours to begin his transition. Why did mine come on immediately?" Isabelle had been quiet for most of the day. She had dealt with the pain like a champion. At first, she wanted to take the pain pills she had prescribed for her brother, but Tessa told her it was something she needed to deal with. Unmedicated. After the pain from the initial phase subsided, Belle had stopped complaining. Tessa was proud of her cousin. Knowing first-hand how badly it hurt, she told her how well she had managed.

"Everyone's is different. It could be that he had no direct contact with his mate. They could have been in close proximity, just enough to cause the initial reaction. He also could have truly been sick before he began his transition." Tessa's own transition came on like a bat out of hell as soon

86

as she touched Gregor. "Where have you been other than work and home?"

Isabelle didn't hesitate, "Nowhere. I have driven to the Pen and back home. That's it."

"Then your mate has to be someone you work with. Or, heaven forbid, an inmate. Have you been around any inmates at all?"

"No, I haven't. I have been going over files and doing inventory..." She faded off.

"What? What are you thinking?" Tessa didn't like the worried look on her face.

"How close do you have to get to someone for them to be your mate? Do you have to touch them?" Both her fangs and claws were showing now.

"Belle, calm down. What's wrong? Have you been close to any of the inmates? Is that what has you worried?"

Her cousin was pacing the room now, blood trickling down her chin where her fangs were cutting into her bottom lip. Tessa stood and grabbed her by the arms. "Stop it. Right now, stop. Look at me. Breathe. You have to get yourself under control. There will be instances where you get upset in public, and you have to be able to keep your fangs and claws in check. Now, close your eyes and breathe."

Isabelle's eyes closed and tears rolled down her cheeks. "I don't want my mate to be a murderer," she whispered. Tessa wrapped her in a hug, something she had never done before. Tessa wasn't the nurturing type, but her cousin needed the comfort.

"Shh, it's okay. It's probably one of the guards. I don't think the fates would have someone like you mated to a criminal."

Isabelle pulled back and wiped her face with her clawless hands. "Do you think it could be Gregor?" Tessa hated the hopeful look. She ran her hands down Belle's arms then backed off.

"No, I know for a fact he isn't your mate."

"How do you know? Unless… Oh my god. He's your mate, isn't he? That's how you know for sure."

Tessa didn't say anything. That was all the confirmation she needed. "Why didn't you tell me? And why do you act like you hate the man if he's your mate? You're supposed to be living happily ever after, aren't you?"

"It doesn't always work that way, especially when there's a Gargoyle involved. I don't want to talk about him right now. Let's concentrate on getting you rested. I still have a trip to take." Tessa didn't want to think about Gregor and living happily ever after. It just wasn't in the cards for them.

Isabelle let it go. "Okay, I'm going to take a shower."

Tessa waited until the water was running before she stepped out the backdoor onto the porch. Breathing in deep, she allowed the cool air to seep into her lungs. What she really wanted was a double shot of tequila and a cigarette. She only smoked when she drank, but right now she needed to keep a clear head, so she didn't allow herself either. She leaned against the porch railing and raised her face to the moon. It was waning, just like her heart.

The fight had not done as much good as Gregor wanted. He relished flying, fighting, feeling alive. It hadn't been his night to patrol, but the Unholy had decided they needed to create chaos and a lot of it. As he and Jasper flew to meet up with the others, he couldn't get Tessa off of his mind. He needed the wind under his wings, the cool air ripping through his lungs. When they arrived at the address Julian had given, Gregor was amazed at the sight below. The last time this many Unholy were out in the streets, they were fighting each other to cause a diversion. Kaya had been abducted by Vincent Alexander and the Gargoyles were busy fighting the monsters instead of protecting their future Queen.

Gregor didn't hesitate. He dove right into the middle of the mayhem, claws out and slashing. The Unholy were an unpredictable lot. He couldn't figure out why they remained hidden for months at a time and then all of a sudden they infiltrated the city streets fighting among themselves. The humans had smartened up over the last thirty years and stayed out of their way for the most part. The Pen still had plenty of room for those who were dumb enough to get caught by the Gargoyles.

Now, several hours and a shit ton of locked up Unholy later, Gregor attempted to relax. Never had his heart felt so conflicted. He had found his mate, yet she didn't want him. Didn't even like him. All because he was a Gargoyle. That in itself didn't make sense. She was half Gargoyle. There was more to the story than just a prejudice, and he needed to find out what. If she could give him a good reason they shouldn't be together, he would deal with it. What he would not deal with was a half-ass excuse.

Sitting on the deck of his cabin, he opened another beer. The moon was barely visible behind a cloud as he gazed into the sky. Gregor's home was a large, three-story structure constructed of logs and stone. While he insisted on calling it a cabin, Julian reminded him it was a lodge. Gregor was one of the few Gargoyles who lived alone with no servants. His home was nestled in the woods on one hundred acres. Rafael had designed the home for him, but Gregor had built it himself with the help of Dante. Where Rafael and Sin had stuck together since they were small, he and Dante felt a closeness to each other. Not only were they close in age, but they held a special bond that wasn't there with the others.

He loved all his brothers and cousins. Being Clan meant they had each other's backs, always. He and Dante had formed a connection in early childhood that had never wavered. If one ever left New Atlanta, the other would surely follow. His thoughts drifted back to Tessa. He wanted to check on her, check on Isabelle. He knew the transition was rough on males; he just had to wonder how it was on females. He had never witnessed one of the female Gargoyles going through the change.

Tamian said Tessa was the best one to help her. He stood in awe as his tough-as-nails mate had tenderly cared for her cousin as gently as she would a child. Did Tessa want children? Hell, did she already have kids? Could that be why she didn't want anything to do with him? Isabelle had been married before. If her husband hadn't died in a boating accident, it was possible they would still be together. Then what? Would she leave her husband for her mate? Fucking hell, this was getting more complicated as he sat there. He needed answers. Since Tamian wouldn't give them to him, he was just going to have to get them straight from the source.

"Hello?" Tessa sounded out of breath when she answered his call.

"Hey, Red. I'm just calling to check on our patient."

"*My* patient is doing just fine. How the hell did you get this number?" Tessa was huffing on the other end of the line.

"Isabelle has you listed as her emergency contact. Did I interrupt? You sound as if you're in the middle of something."

"Mr. Stone, what I'm doing is none of your concern, and yes, you did interrupt something. If you don't have any more questions, I'll just be going." Damn, she was feisty. Why did that turn him on?

"Actually, I do have another one. Will you go to dinner with me tomorrow night?"

"I will not be here tomorrow night, so no." Damn, feisty *and* rude. So why was his dick stirring to life? He liked sex rough, and sometimes mixed with a little pain, but rudeness? Maybe he was more of a masochist than he thought.

"Okay, the next night then. We need to talk."

Tessa sighed, stopping whatever she had been doing that caused her to sound out of breath. "I won't be here the next night, either. I'm going out of town."

"Then when you return. How long will you be gone?" He knew he sounded desperate, he just didn't care. This woman was his mate, and if he didn't get close to her, he would never get the chance to bond with her.

"I have no idea, Mr. Stone. One, two weeks possibly. So don't wait up." The line went dead.

There was no way Gregor was going to be able to wait one day to see Tessa, much less one week. Two? Where the fuck was she going? He had to see her. He didn't care if she didn't want to see him. Now that he knew she was his mate, the urge to be around her was getting worse, not better. He still needed to take Isabelle's car to her, so this would be a good excuse.

With it being so late, he could drop off Isabelle's car then fly back for his bike. He had already grabbed her car keys before he left her house, ensuring he'd have an excuse to return. The thought of seeing Tessa had his dick twitching. Decision made, he headed to the garage. He lifted his helmet from its perch atop the handlebars and straddled his bike.

The drive to the Pen was quick since he lived so close. Once there, he wedged himself into the toy car and headed to the doctor's home. Luck was on his side; Tessa's bike was still in the driveway. He parked in front of the garage and turned the motor off. Even though he wasn't as tall as his brothers, the compact was still a tight fit for someone of his stature. He had to wrangle himself out. He should have come up with a plan, something suave to say to make Tessa want him, but that just wasn't his style. Other than Frey, he was the biggest roughneck of the family.

The backdoor opened, and Tessa was stalking toward him. "What are you doing here?"

The ever present scowl on her face didn't mar her beauty. Her green eyes were shining. "Since you are leaving town, I didn't want Isabelle to be stranded." He dangled the keys in front of her, hoping she'd take the bait. Tessa stepped closer and when she was in arm's reach, he snagged her body, twisting her so that her back was to his front. He wrapped both arms around her, caging her in so she couldn't move. She wiggled furiously, "Let me go. What the fuck do you think you're doing, Stone?"

"I'm holding you captive so I can talk to you. You have a tendency to walk away from me." She kept wiggling her ass. Did she not realize she was grinding into his dick? Oh, the things he wanted to do to her ass.

Gregor wanted so badly to strip Tessa naked, feel her skin to skin. Standing in the middle of Isabelle's driveway was not the place for it. Tessa leaned back into him, her ass nestled against his hard cock. He let out a groan and she froze.

Sixteen

Gregor's breath was hot in Tessa's ear. "I just wanted to bring Isabelle's car to her and to tell you to be careful. Watch that ass while you're gone."

When he groaned, Tessa realized her attempt to get away was turning him on. Feeling his erection against her ass gave her all kinds of dirty thoughts. "What do you care about my ass?"

"I would hate to see something happen to it. It's a mighty fine ass, and it's mine, Tessa. Just like you, that fine ass is all mine."

She was panting. He had her panting like a fucking dog. "What...what are you planning on doing with *your* ass?" She knew what she imagined him doing with it.

He pulled her back even tighter to his body, his erection rubbing against her jeans. She couldn't help the shudder that flowed through her or the juices that were soaking her thong. He licked the rim of her ear then grabbed her hoop between his teeth and pulled. "First, I'm going to spank it. I'm going to spank that pretty ass until it's pink. Then, I'm going to eat it. I'm going to eat you out from your pussy to your tight pucker, until you beg me not to stop." He scraped his fangs down the side of her neck. Another shiver took up residence in her nerve endings. "And just when you think I'm going to let you come, I'm going to flip you over to your stomach and put you on your knees so your pretty, pink ass is waiting for my dick. I'll stretch your hole with my fingers, and when you're ready, I'm going to ease my hard cock into your tight little ass. *My* ass."

If Gregor hadn't been holding her so tightly, her legs probably would have given out. The promise of him doing what he just described had Tessa ready to get naked. Gregor's thoughts about her ass were right in line with hers. She had to get away from him, out of his arms. Hell, out of

93

the fucking country. She had to go. She wiggled her ass against his erection, hoping it was tormenting him. "That's never going to happen. I told you not to touch me again. When I get loose from here…"

Gregor interrupted her, "You're going to what, Red? You know what I am and what I'm capable of. Sure, you might be a shifter, too, but you are a female." Now he was just pissing her off. The wet between her legs was still there, but the urge to fuck him was quickly dwindling.

"Boy, you sure know how to entice a woman. Go all fucking caveman. Why don't you beat on your chest while you're at it, grab my hair, put me in my place."

"I'll grab your hair all right, but you'll enjoy it." Gregor fisted her hair and pulled her head back so he could see her face. She glared at him, hoping he would let her go. Instead he kissed her. Hard. She kept her lips closed for all of five seconds, but the mate pull was too strong. She opened her mouth to him, allowing his tongue entrance. She didn't want to want him. She wanted to push him away and run for her life. Her body had other ideas.

Gods could the man kiss. He kept his mouth firmly against hers. His tongue, however, was softly caressing her own. She had no doubt he could make her come by kissing alone. When they both needed air, Gregor finally turned her loose. "I want answers, Red. I *need* answers. And according to your brother, you're the only one who can give them to me."

She whirled around, "My brother? What the fuck did he tell you?" She was going to kill Tamian if he had told Gregor anything.

"Not enough. Look, I don't know what you have against Gargoyles, seeing you are half Goyle yourself. Why don't you explain that to me?"

"Tessa?" Isabelle chose that moment to come outside. Saved by the Belle. Tessa laughed at her own joke.

"What's so funny? Oh, hello, Mr. Stone, I didn't realize you were here." Isabelle's eyes got wide, realizing she had interrupted something. "Uh, I'll just go back inside now. Good to see you." She turned, but Gregor stopped her.

"Isabelle, don't be silly. I just came to bring your car and find out how you're feeling. How *are* you feeling?" If Gregor was affected by their kiss, he was doing a bang-up job of hiding it. Tessa glanced at his crotch. His shirt was hanging in front of his groin area, but she would bet any amount of money his dick was throbbing as hard as her pussy was.

The two of them chatted, and Isabelle finally said goodbye, hoping to return to work in a couple of days.

"As you can see, she is fine. Thank you for bringing her car. Now, you should go."

"Are you really going out of town?" Gregor adjusted his cock and stuck his hands in his pockets. She wanted to adjust his dick for him. With her mouth.

"Yes, I really am. Now if you'll excuse me..." He was on her again before she could finish. Dammit he was quick.

"Listen to me." He had one arm wrapped around her waist, holding her body to his. His erection was evident between them. He lifted her chin with the other hand so she had no choice but to look at him. "I want you to be careful. There are women being murdered, and they all happen to look just like you."

Tessa gasped. "What? How do you know this?"

"Because, Red. I know someone who works in the morgue; there are three dead women who could pass for your sister. I'm not telling you this to scare you. I'm telling you this so you'll watch your back. I don't want anything to happen to you. You might not like me, and while I don't understand that, I'm willing to wait until you do." Gregor placed his lips next to her ear. "I like you, and I have nothing but time." He ran his tongue along the rim of her ear before softly placing a kiss on her cheek. He released her and walked off. She immediately wanted him back. Damn her traitorous body.

Gregor removed his shirt and tied it around his waist. He continued walking until he was out of her sight. She waited. She kept her ears open and her eyes glued to the night sky. There. There above her was the most beautiful sight she had ever seen: her mate with his wings unfurled, soaring higher and higher until even she couldn't see him. Her heart skipped a couple of beats. Yep, she was fucked.

When Tessa walked back inside, Isabelle was on the telephone, whispering, "Okay, I will see you soon."

"Who are you going to see soon?" Was Belle hiding a boyfriend?

"Nobody. You should go home. I appreciate your help through the transition, but I'm fine now. Really. I just want to be alone and do some reading. I need to rest. Don't you have a trip to pack for?"   Isabelle was nervous and Tessa had a feeling it was because she caught her on the phone.

"Yeah, sure. I wouldn't mind sleeping in my own bed tonight. Just take it easy and keep practicing. You are going to have to be able to control yourself completely before you go back to work. You will be around the inmates soon; being a beautiful woman, they are going to come on to you, saying crude things. You need to be able to handle that."

Isabelle was just staring at her.

"What?"

"You called me beautiful. Nobody has ever called me beautiful." By the sadness on her face, Isabelle was being honest.

"You're joking, right? Alexi must have told you how stunning you are. Have you not looked in the mirror lately? Okay, maybe not lately. Right now you look like shit. What I mean is, you look tired. But Belle, you are beautiful. You have a natural beauty that most women pay good money

96

for. You don't need hair color, or makeup, or Botox, or any of that stuff. Seriously, take a good, long look at yourself. Enough with the mushy stuff, I'm outta here. I'll be in New Orleans for a while. You have Sophia's number if you need anything." Tessa didn't have her leather jacket since she had worn her flight jacket to the Pen. She'd have to tough it out. Grabbing her key and helmet, she left her cousin sitting with her mouth agape.

Her first order of business was to find out who Isabelle had been talking to. If it weren't a big deal, she wouldn't have been so secretive. Tessa arrived home and pulled her boots off. She went to her office and fired up the computer. While she was waiting on it to boot up, she grabbed a beer out of the fridge. Damn Gregor Stone, acting like he cared what happened to her. Shit, bodies were turning up who looked like her. She needed to check into that, too.

Tessa sat down and hacked into Isabelle's phone account. She might not have gone to college, but the skills she had accumulated over the years were priceless. "Here we go. Enrico Sanchez, New Columbia, Tennessee." So Isabelle was still in touch with her caretakers. Tessa really couldn't blame her. They had been more family to Isabelle than her own.

With that little mystery solved, Tessa finished her beer, gathered as much information as was available on the dead victims, which, so far, wasn't much, and called it a night. Normally, she did some sort of cardio before she went to bed, but she had taken care of that at Isabelle's. She had a long day ahead of her tomorrow and needed a good night's sleep.

Flanagan was going to have to give Merrick a raise after this latest victim. He dabbed Neosporin on the scratches to his face. Bitch had been a fighter; he'd give her that. He scraped under her fingernails, hoping to remove all evidence, but one could never be certain. His DNA was on record since he had served in the military. Maybe it was time for a new identity in a new location.

Gordon Flanagan had recruited Merrick when he received a dishonorable discharge from the Army for cruel and unusual punishment. He had enlisted so he could torture the fucking enemy with permission. Who knew the government had limits on torture? Flanagan lured him in with the promise of free rein on the torture and the possibility of immeasurable wealth. So far, he had immensely enjoyed his role in Flanagan's organization. Fucking and killing were his two favorite past times. When you put them together, the high was better than any drug. The money was good, but he could measure it. His bank account needed a boost, and Gordon was going to give it to him.

When he first started working for Flanagan, he overheard a conversation that was not meant for his ears. Gordon was scooping up as many ex-military as possible to add to his own army, one in which the men would be turned into super-soldiers. Where the scientists had totally fucked up with Vincent's DNA and the Unholy, they were convinced the new formula would react the way they wanted it to.

Merrick hadn't come up with a plan quick enough to escape the long grasp that was Gordon Flanagan, and he had become the first test subject. The scientists injected him with the serum and sure enough, the formula worked. He was the first soldier in their new regime. Merrick was faster and stronger, but he still wasn't as strong as the Unholy. Those bastards were just motherfucking crazy. But then again, so was Flanagan.

Seventeen

Gregor hated the unknown. He was 567 years old. Before last week, he'd never thought about the future. Until now. Until Tessa, he lived his life day to day, taking things as they came. He and Dante were happy in their jobs. Both had moved to New Atlanta soon after the bombings to help Rafael put the city back together. It wouldn't be long before they would need to change locations and take on new identities. Thirty years was a long time to look a certain age.

Because of Tessa, he thought about tomorrow, about what happened next. He was bound and determined to understand why she was so dead set against him just because he was a Gargoyle. Fuck, her own father was a Goyle. Maybe that was the problem. It was possible she hated her old man and had been abused. He would ask her when she returned from... he didn't even know where she was going. Not that it was any of his business. He wanted it to be his business. He hated not knowing if she had someone else in her life. He hated not knowing what she was doing right this very second. He wished with every fiber of his being that she was sitting beside him on his deck enjoying the sunrise peeking through the tall pines.

Gregor was used to the solitude that his cabin in the woods offered him. He relished being alone with nature, with himself. The family of deer at the edge of the tree line gave him the same sense of tranquility that Rafael's garden bestowed on him. Until Tessa. Now the tranquility was replaced with longing. The peace replaced with sorrow. The contentment replaced with loneliness. How could this be? How could one woman turn his whole life upside down in a matter of days? Hell, it hadn't even been days. If he thought about it, it had been less than 48 hours. She had him scribbling poetry for fuck's sake. If he could not convince her to give him a chance, give *them* a chance, he was well and truly fucked.

At least today wasn't Saturday. He never appreciated having to go to the Pen more than he did this very moment. Working would take his mind off his mate and everything he didn't know about her. He drank the last of his coffee and headed to the shower. Gregor cranked the water to cold, but his cock still ached to be touched. He would never be able to wear his shirt tucked in again. He constantly sported a hard-as-nails erection and a set of blue balls he figured would not be going away any time soon. Not unless he could get one little redhead on board. Or on his cock. *Fuck.* Just thinking of those green eyes and that sassy tongue had him stroking himself. He leaned a forearm against the cool tile wall and studied his hand as it groped his length.

Jacking off was not Gregor's favorite way of relieving tension. Of course he enjoyed the release, but he would rather his hands be fisted in long red hair or massaging a pair of tits while he was getting his dick sucked. Masturbating had lost its allure a long time ago. Getting frustrated, he pictured Tessa in the middle of his bed on all fours as he slid his cock in and out of her pretty, wet pussy. Close. Oh gods, he was so close to coming. He placed one foot on the bench at the back of the shower. Reaching between his legs, he slid a finger in his hole, searching for the spot he knew would do the trick. As soon as he hit his prostate, his orgasm sped through his balls and out his dick. He hissed Tessa's name as he stroked his cock until the last tremor was gone.

Gregor hurried and bathed, doing his best to think of anything other than Tessa, before his dick decided it wanted more. While he dried off and put on his work clothes, his heart was warring with his head. His heart wanted him to call Julian and have him hack the airlines to see where Tessa was going. His head told him that was

100

invading her privacy, and he should leave it alone. His heart told his head to shut the fuck up. He called his cousin.

"Gregor, what can I do for you so early in the morning?" Julian yawned into the phone.

"I need to you to find out where Tessa is flying to." Gregor poured coffee into a travel mug.

"You mean you want me to hack into the airline system?" The keys of Julian's keyboard were already being tapped. Not only did Julian have a computer room at the lab that would rival any government's, but his home was equipped just as well.

"Yes, that's exactly what I mean." Gregor pulled his boots on and laced them.

"I do not see any passenger named Tessa Blackmore listed. She's probably using an alias. What was the name she used when you met her, Trixie?" Julian chuckled. "Nope, no Trixie's either. Any suggestions?"

Gregor thought back to his conversation with Tamian. "Try Andi."

"No Andi Blackmore, or Andrea Blackmore. Ah, here we go. Well what do you know? We have one Andi Stone flying first class to New York."

Gregor was glad he wasn't drinking coffee at that particular moment or he'd probably have choked. "That can't be right; she would never use my last name."

"I'm telling you, Brother, that's the only Andi listed. It may not even be her. Are you sure she's flying today? Commercial? She could have a hot Gargoyle flying her somewhere." Julian was chuckling on the other end of the line.

"Jules, have you been smoking pot? It's a little early to be cracking jokes. Especially ones that aren't funny." Gregor's heart was tapping out a beat in his chest that had nothing to do with the caffeine he was drinking. It was spelling out hope. Hope that Tessa was thinking about him. "That really can't be right. She would require identification in that name. Maybe she isn't leaving until tomorrow. You know what? Don't worry about it. I don't need to know where she's going anyway. Thanks Jules." He hung up and sat down on a bar stool.

Tessa's identification would have to have been made long before now. Their very first encounter at the gas station had been what, three years ago? Holy fuck! What if she had been using his name all this time? Of course, it could be as a joke. No, he wouldn't get his hopes up. He would wait until she returned from New York or wherever the hell she was going and talk to her.

Gregor grabbed his travel mug, moved through the covered walkway that led to his garage, and climbed in the Hummer. As he settled in and buckled up, he thought about Tessa and her bike. Did she have a vehicle she drove in the winter? What kind of car would his mate drive? He really couldn't see her in a hybrid like her cousin drove. No, Tessa was an adrenaline junkie. She probably drove a sports car.

As he drove to work he wondered about his mate. She was going out of town, but for what? To see a lover? For a job? He knew so little about Tessa. At least when Rafael found Kaya, he knew what she did for a living. Tamian was tight-lipped when it came to his sister. Maybe he could get the information out of Isabelle. He would give her today to rest up, but then he was calling her.

Kaya walked into the precinct to the shouts and applause of her team. She hadn't been gone all that long, but she knew her being abducted by a lunatic had gotten around the precinct. She held her hands up and waited for the chatter to die down. "Thank you all. It's good to be back, and I'm ready to get down to business. Let's head to the meeting room and get our morning brief out of the way."

She continued on to her office where she stowed her purse and set her laptop on the docking station.

From behind her, Kaya heard Dane say, "Welcome back."

She checked her emotions before she looked her lead detective in the eye. "Dane, thank you for taking over while I was out. I will let you lead the brief this morning since I am not completely up to speed." He didn't appear any different. She must have been studying his features too intently.

"What is it? Kaya, why are you staring at me like that?"

She had to keep cool until after the meeting. Then they would talk. "I guess I just missed you. Now, let's go. Don't want to keep the team waiting." She smiled and squeezed past him out the door.

Jasper was already sitting in the conference room with the others. They had decided over breakfast that Kaya would talk to Dane alone. He looked at her now and gave a slight nod. Kaya stood at the front of the room with Dane standing beside her. "Good morning. I want to thank Abbott for taking up the slack while I was out. I also want to say welcome to our newest detective. Jasper, welcome to New Atlanta. Since Dane is more familiar with the current caseload, I'm going to let him have the floor."

Kaya stepped out of the way, and Dane took over. "We have another victim in The Redhead Murders. For lack of a better name, that is what we will be giving the press when we issue a statement. Greta Powell, age 33, was reported missing this morning by her roommate. The photo she produced matched the victim found last night. The roommate has already been to the morgue where she identified the body as that of Miss Powell. The M.E. confirmed earlier that all three women died from asphyxiation. He is going to run DNA testing on the victims. They look so much alike they could pass for sisters; he wants to rule that out as a possibility. Regardless of whether or not they are related, we want to issue a press statement to the public so other women out there who fit the profile will remain diligent."

Dane handed out assignments, and the team left to get busy with their day. Jasper didn't hang around, and Kaya told Dane, "Let's go to my office. We need to talk."

Eighteen

Kaya shut the door and motioned for Dane to sit. "Great job in there. Maybe one day you will be Chief." She smiled at him, but the frown on his face removed her smile. "What?"

"Are you planning on going somewhere?" Dane was not the same flirty, carefree man she had known for years.

"Of course not. But if I were, would that bother you?"

His frown only deepened. "Yeah. Yeah it would. You're the best Chief this department has seen in a long time. And I have no desire to take your place. Too much responsibility. What's going on?"

"What do you mean?" The wheels were turning behind those blue eyes, and she knew he was thinking way too hard about things.

"I mean, you're different. You were abducted by a crazy man. Instead of seeming traumatized, or at least stressed, you're... I don't know, happy. In all the years we've worked together, I've never seen you so calm."

"I am happy. Happy to be alive. You're different, too. Instead of the happy-go-lucky man, you haven't smiled one time since I've been back. What changed?"

"This wouldn't have anything to do with Rafael Stone would it?" Dane ignored her question. She wasn't going to let him turn this around on her just yet. She wanted to get him to open up without her coming right out and telling him she knew.

"We're talking about you. You seem tense. You know you can tell me anything, right? No matter what it is. When I was kidnapped, I saw some things that opened my eyes. I also realized there are people behind the scenes helping us do our jobs."

Dane studied Kaya's face, chewing on his bottom lip. "You know, don't you?"

This wasn't exactly the opening she was hoping for. "Yes. I know what you are. I know what Jasper is, too."

"Yeah, well, it wasn't nice of you to spring him on me like that."

"I had no idea you were a shifter nor that you had gone through your transition. If I had, I would have handled things differently. Since I didn't..." She let him think about it.

Dane stood but had nowhere to go in the small office. "He acts like this is no big deal. It's all new to me, and I can't even talk about it."

"Why can't you talk about it? As far as Jasper's concerned, he's been a Gargoyle his whole life. He's a full-blood, so to him it isn't a big deal. When you've lived five hundred years, it won't be a big deal to you either."

"How do you know all of this? Does it have to do with Stone?" Dane pinned her with a look that said he expected the truth.

"Yes, it has everything to do with Rafael. Now that you're a shifter, you will meet him, too. But not as a suspect being interrogated by a detective. You will be introduced to your King."

"King? What the hell are you talking about? Tes... nobody told me about having a King." Dane was getting agitated. Kaya was afraid his fangs were going to drop.

"There's a lot you don't know about your kind, but there's plenty of time for that. I know you are still getting used to your new body. I think you should..." There was a knock on the door and Jasper stuck his head in. "Sorry to interrupt my Qu...Chief, but we have another redhead. The call just came in."

"Dane, go check it out, and take Jasper with you. Don't forget, it really is good to talk about this." Kaya

106

inclined her head toward Jasper. "Call me when you have more information."

"You're not coming with us?" Dane had his hands on his hips. If he didn't look so stressed, she might have laughed.

"No. I have very capable detectives for field work," Kaya told him.

He huffed at her then followed Jasper out the door.

Kaya and Rafael had talked at length about how much she should tell Dane. She finally convinced him that telling Dane the whole truth, like ripping a Band-Aid off, would be better than dribbling tidbits of information to him. He was already struggling with the lack of knowledge. She really hoped he opened up to Jasper. Rafael had given both she and Jasper carte blanche in speaking to Dane about their kind. In turn, they hoped Dane could give them at least some information about the half-bloods.

The silence hung thickly in the air during the ride to the crime scene. Jasper wanted Dane to talk freely with him, especially now that Kaya had admitted knowing the truth. His new partner was obviously not ready for a heart-to-heart.

Dante and CSU were already at the scene when they arrived. Dane, being the senior detective, took lead. "Dante, what do we have?"

Dante nodded his hello to both men then answered, "Same as the others. Female, red hair, green eyes, approximately thirty years of age. COD appears to be strangulation as there is bruising on her neck."

Both men waited on further instructions from Dane, but he seemed to be lost in thought. Jasper clapped him on the shoulder. "Dude, you okay?"

"It's these victims. They look quite a bit like someone I know."

"Tessa," Dante and Jasper responded at the same time.

Dane narrowed his eyes at them. "Oh my god, you're one, too?" He was staring at Dante when he asked. Dante looked at Jasper who just shrugged. It wasn't up to him whether or not Dante admitted he was a Goyle. Rafael had held a video conference call, filling the Clan in on Dane's becoming a shifter and the redhead murders. He and Kaya agreed to keep each other informed of all happenings so they all could work together.

"So how many of us are there?" Dane asked, hands on his hips. Jasper was getting used to the gesture. Even though it looked funny for a big, strong man to stand like a put-upon woman, he really couldn't blame him. If he had just transitioned, not knowing what had been hidden in his core his whole life, he might be agitated as well.

Dante held out his hands, palms up. "Tens of thousands? We would have to ask Nikolas since he is the keeper of the archives. There actually may be more than that since we don't know how many half-bloods there are. Do you know how many of you there are?"

Dane shook his head. "No, not really. I only know that I have sixteen brothers and sisters. I don't even know all their names. Only one."

"And that is?" Jasper was fishing.

"I think we should get back to the crime scene. We can talk about less important stuff later." Dane walked off to where the body of the latest victim was being bagged for transport to the morgue.

"The fact he has sixteen siblings bodes well for Rafael and Kaya," Dante told Jasper.

"I was hoping he would spill about Tessa. It's going to suck if his girlfriend turns out to be Gregor's mate. Maybe I can get him to open up a little more on the ride back to the station." Jasper left Dante to do his M.E. stuff, and he went to observe Dane. Having never actually been a police officer, there was a lot to learn.

Jasper walked up right as one of the CSU mentioned a possible break. A couple of her fingernails were broken off. If they were lucky, there would be DNA evidence on her hands they could use in all databases available to them. Once the body was loaded up, Dane told Jasper there was nothing more for them there. They headed back to the office.

"Since we have more than one body that resembles your friend, are we going to treat this as a serial killing?" Jasper asked, still learning protocol within the department.

"That's the Chief's call, but yeah. I'm sure she will. We need to get the profile together of the killer and get it on the news. These women need to be careful. We don't know who this guy is or why he's killing the look-alikes."

"What if it's to draw your friend out? Or maybe they are searching for her and don't know exactly what she looks like. Then again, maybe this bastard just randomly chose redheads because they remind him of his mother and she abused him as a child." Jasper was throwing theories out, hoping to offer something useful to the case and to see if Tessa meant something to Dane.

Dane scowled at Jasper, "Or maybe it's because they look just like Tessa. And before you try to get inside my head, she's not my friend. She's my cousin."

Excellent. Gregor's not going to have to kick his ass. The rest of the ride back to the office was made in silence.

Gabriel smiled as Rebekah squeezed his hand tightly. She loved walking through the woods during the fall. She could stand and admire the changing colors of the leaves for hours. Gabriel could admire Rebekah for hours. The way the sunlight glinted off her honey blonde hair beckoned for him to touch it. The silky

strands slid through his fingers as she rambled on and on about the trees and the weather. "Did you hear what I said?" She was grinning at him, her beautiful smile as bright as the sun shining down on them.

"I'm sorry, my love. I was admiring your beauty." Gabriel cupped her soft face in his hands and placed his lips on hers. Rebekah moaned into his mouth, and he drew her closer, wrapping his arms around her.

When they came up for air, Rebekah placed a hand on his cheek and whispered, "You are the beautiful one."

Gabriel grinned at his fiancée. "Men are not beautiful." He once again touched his mouth to hers, but she pulled back quickly. "Ouch! What the?" She was backing up and pointing at him. When she found her voice, she screamed. Gabriel looked behind them; a Gargoyle stood in the clearing, fully phased.

"Rebekah, it's okay. I'll protect you." Gabriel turned to place himself between the albino looking monster and his woman, but the Gargoyle was gone. He turned back to face Rebekah who was still screaming and held up his hands. "It's okay. He's gone." Gabriel noticed the claws at the end of his pale fingers. "No, Rebekah, I'm not...I won't..." Rebekah was running away from him. He had to stop her, to explain. Using his shifter speed he caught her easily.

His hands gripped her slender arms that were now covered in ribbons of blood. His claws cut through her skin, marring the perfect canvas. "Oh gods, no. Rebekah, I am so sorry, I'm so sorry."

"REBEKAH, I'M SORRY!" Vincent flew off of his prison bed, wings unfurled, chest heaving. *Rebekah.* Who was the girl in his dream? Why was she so familiar? He needed a cigarette. Fuck the patch. He banged on his cell door. He continued hitting the metal door with his fist until a guard stood at the window. This was the same guard who came to his door every time he beckoned. He held up the same worn message: cigarette. By now, he knew the guard wouldn't give him a smoke, but he would at least get a patch. The small scrap of material wouldn't help for long but it would take the edge off. The guard opened the slot and slid the small square through to him. He grabbed it, pulling the paper backing off and slapped it on his arm.

If the guard was surprised at seeing an inmate with fangs and wings, he didn't show it on his face. This guard, Deacon, didn't walk away. He waited until Vincent was under control. "Are you ready to talk now? I have a feeling if you give the warden the information he wants, he'll get you a whole carton of cigarettes. Think about that." Deacon walked off, and Vincent considered it. If he didn't give them the information he had on Flanagan, he would rot in this hell hole. Alone. If he did talk, he would still be held prisoner, but maybe he would be taken out of solitary. He could have a cigarette. Maybe he could feel the sunlight on his face.

The warden and some of the guards came and talked to the prisoner in the next cell over. Why were they so nice to him? The warden even let him out of his cell every once in a while. Maybe he gave the warden information he wanted, and he got to go out in the sunlight. Vincent was cold. So cold. He just needed the sun on his face for a few minutes. Sunlight. Rebekah.

Nineteen

Tessa's plane landed at LaGuardia as scheduled. While it wasn't the closest airport to her destination, she preferred the larger, busier hub where she had a greater chance of being lost in the crowd. She wove her way through the throngs of passengers rushing to make their flights on time. Since she wouldn't be staying, she had no luggage to wait for at the busy carousel. Instead, she headed for the passenger pick-up area where her ride would be waiting.

Even though it wasn't necessary, her driver held up a sign that said "Greystone". Manny had been driving Tessa around as long as she could remember. He was one of her best friends in the world. Actually, he was one of her only friends. She loved the man as much as she loved her own father and would usually stay at his home when she was in town. Soon after she transitioned, Tessa went to visit Manny and his husband, Lawrence. Both men were longtime employees of her family, and they knew the truth of the Gargoyles. When Tessa told the men who her mate was, she had cried. And laughed. And cried some more. They dubbed Gregor "Greystone" as a codename. Since Tessa wouldn't tell her family she was mated to a full-blood, it was their secret.

Manny was smiling, his beautiful face almost cracking. "My girl, how I've missed you." The older man pulled Tessa in for a hug and a kiss on the cheek. "No luggage? I'm hurt. I was hoping you would be staying with us a while."

Tessa snaked her arm through her friend's as they walked. "Sorry, Man, but this is a quick brief with the fam and then I'm headed to New Orleans. I have a lot to tell you, so let's get to the car." They strolled arm-in-arm looking like father and daughter instead of driver and passenger. Tessa hated coming to New York for these short meetings. While she loved her mother, Tessa preferred the times when she was staying with Manny and Larry. She had long ago asked that Manny not drive the limo when picking her up. She wanted to be able to sit next to him and chat, not be separated to the back of the lonely monstrosity that shouted, "Look at me, I'm somebody."

Tessa couldn't help but smile when Manny opened the passenger door to his personal vehicle. He may appear refined, but he was as much of a speed freak as she was. While she preferred the Chevrolet, Manny was a Dodge man. The Challenger was sleek and bad-ass, and she knew there was a hemi under the hood. Even with technology finally getting back to where it had once been, there was nothing like these classic muscle cars.

Tessa pulled her seatbelt across her body, clicking it in place, all while enjoying the rumble of the engine. Now that the weather was getting colder, she would be pulling her own car out of the garage and parking her bike. Manny got as far as heading north on the 678 before he couldn't wait any longer. "Okay, Missy, spill it. You look different than the last time you were here. Does this have anything to do with Greystone?"

Even though it had everything to do with her mate, she still had to grin. "Manny, you know me too well. Actually, it does." She sighed then continued. "He knows. I screwed up, and now he knows. Not only does he know I'm his mate, but he knows about half-bloods." Tessa started at the beginning and told him about Isabelle taking the job at the Pen, about finding Tamian, and about flying off the roof.

"Why is your brother in jail?" Manny knew Tamian well and was shocked to hear of him being behind bars.

"The do-gooder put himself there on purpose, but I can't really fault him for it. He's trying to find Gordon's location just like we are. Hopefully, he'll be able to accomplish this without anyone else dying." Tessa filled

Manny in on the ruse at the World Council Delegation that had gone horribly wrong. "Right now, he's in solitary. I'm not sure how he expects to gain any information from the general population when he's stuck in a hole."

"So you jumped off the roof. I always miss the good stuff." Manny was chuckling.

"Yeah, well, it was good until Gregor phased and came after me. He was *pissed*. He knew at the bar that I was his mate, he just didn't know who I was exactly. Now he knows, and I have a feeling he's going to be a pain in my ass. Manny, the Gargoyle King has found his mate, and she's a human. I need to tell him that Goyles have been mating with humans for a long time now. He needs to know."

Manny grabbed Tessa's hand. "You'll do the right thing, sweet girl. You always do." He released her hand as they pulled up to the entrance to her parents' estate. Manny waited until he got the all-clear from the security patrol that had followed them for the last hour. He placed his forefinger on the scanner, and the gate opened. He and Tessa often joked about "keeping their digits" intact. If either one ever lost a finger, whoever took it would have access to the compound.

Elizabeth was waiting at the front door when the car pulled into the circle. Tessa leaned over and kissed Manny on the cheek. "Thanks, Man. I'll come back soon when I can stay awhile."

"You do that. At least call me. I want to hear more about you and Greystone." His eyes were wet with unshed tears as Tessa got out of the car.

"Andrea!" Elizabeth was now down the steps and welcoming her daughter into her arms. With the aging process having stopped, Elizabeth didn't look any older than Tessa did. They held each other in a tight hug then Tessa pulled back. "I know you called me here, but we have problems. Full-blooded ones."

114

"And what might those be?" Tessa's head jerked at the sound of her father's voice. *Well shit.* Why had her mother not warned her they wouldn't be alone? She left the warmth of her mother's embrace and went to Xavier. "Dad! I can't believe you're here!" She hugged the man she rarely saw anymore and looked around his shoulder at her mother who was shrugging.

"Tessa, my girl. How are you?" her father asked.

Xavier was smart and very adept at reading body rhythms. She had to get hers under control. She smiled her best smile and turned to her mom. "With the exception of being extremely tired, I'm great. I've been up with Isabelle. She finally transitioned."

"Let's get in out of the cold." Elizabeth made her way into the massive home Tessa had partially grown up in. The housekeeper, Cassandra, was standing just inside the door. As soon as Tessa crossed the threshold, she was in the older woman's arms. It had been a while since Tessa visited, so it didn't surprise her she was being smushed by everyone.

"Cassandra, how are you?" She loved the older woman like a grandmother. Having been whisked away when she was a baby, Tessa never knew her biological grandmother. She felt the tears falling down the older woman's cheeks. "Hey, now, what's up with the waterworks?" Tessa wiped away the tears with her thumbs and searched her eyes? "What's wrong?"

"I've just missed you is all," she whispered.

Tessa patted her on the shoulder and responded, "Well, I'm here now. After I speak with the 'rents I will come see you in the kitchen, okay?" Cassandra nodded then excused herself.

"What was that about?" Tessa asked when the housekeeper was out of earshot. Her mom gave a slight shake of her head. Whatever it was, Elizabeth obviously didn't want to discuss it in front of Xavier.

115

"Let's go have a seat." Xavier ushered the women to the lounge at the side of the house. The room was a sunken area with four sofas surrounding a fire pit in the middle of the room. Both Tessa and Elizabeth loved a fire. Once they were seated, Xavier asked, "Now, what is this about the Gargoyles?"

Tessa didn't miss that her father eluded her question. He had questions of his own and she had to answer them. She didn't dare look at her mother. That would give away that she was omitting some of the truth from what she was telling. "It appears the King has found his mate. A human."

"Yes, Rafael said as much when he all but threatened me at the Elder Council. Why do you feel this is a problem?" Xavier may be leaning back, seeming relaxed, but he was not shielding his own vitals. He knew about Rafael?

"Because he and his Clan are searching for answers. Answers that Isabelle and I both have. Answers that Rafael and his mate need. Nikolas Stone found one of Jonas' journals at the library. It was the first one where he talks of meeting Caroline. Nikolas came calling, asking if Isabelle had the other journals. His timing couldn't have been worse. She had just found out what she is, about Gargoyles, and the news Jonas is alive. Hell, she even came face to face with Caroline. Imagine Belle's shock at not only watching a brother she didn't know she had transition, but seeing her mother for the first time in probably twenty years. A mother who looks as young as she does. Dad, Isabelle has taken a job at the Penitentiary working for Gregor Stone. He was there when she began her transition. He knows about us. Therefore, Rafael knows about us. It's just a matter of time before they start demanding answers."

Elizabeth, who had been quiet until then, turned to her mate. "My darling, you have to tell her."

"Tell me what?" Tessa wasn't used to being kept in the dark.

Xavier stood and began pacing the room. Tessa had never seen her father appear anything less than calm and collected. The version of the man before her was anything but calm. "Rafael's uncle, Alistair, is the one who convinced Jonas' Clan to ostracize him. Alistair was at the meeting when Rafael announced to the room that he had found his mate and he suspected Jonas was really a shifter. I'm afraid Rafael has opened a can of worms that could lead to another Clan war."

"Gargoyles were put on earth to protect humans. Why did Alistair want Jonas banished?" Tessa stood and walked over to the window, taking in the vastness of their property.

"Because Alistair is a prejudiced old fool. He felt the line should be kept pure. In his opinion, mixing with humans is an affront to the species." Xavier leaned his backside against the bar, crossing his arms over his chest. "I shut down the meeting as quickly as I could. Alistair not only loathes humans, he also holds a sore spot for his sister as well as his nephew. He despised his brother-in-law because he was of Italian descent, not Greek. He didn't care that Athena had found her mate. When Edmondo was slain, Rafael should have taken his place on the Council. He refuses to do so. Therefore Athena still has the family vote, and it pisses her brother off."

"So this is why Jonas is so hell bent on keeping the mate bond from everyone. It makes sense now." She turned to her mother and asked, "Is this the problem you wanted to tell me about?"

Elizabeth joined her at the window and took Tessa's hands in her own. "No, but the other can wait for now. This is more important, Sweetheart. Your safety and well-being are more important to me than anything else we need to discuss."

"I'm not worried about me, Mom. You know I can take care of myself. Dad, I understand why Jonas wants to

117

keep the human bonding info secret, but after what you just told me, shouldn't the King be told the truth? Wouldn't it be better if he had all ammunition at his disposal?"

"Better for whom? If Rafael knows the truth about bonding with humans, he will mate with his woman and have children. His brothers and cousins will do the same thing. Not only will the Goyles be at risk, but their families as well."

Tessa didn't want to hear this. She had enough to worry about with her cousins transitioning and having children. Now she had to watch out for the full-bloods, too. "I'm afraid we might be too late. I think they are already mated. Fully."

"How do you know this?" Her father knew she and Elizabeth were very close and told each other almost everything.

Elizabeth squeezed her daughter's hands. "Tell him the rest. Tell your father who your mate is."

Twenty

Gregor's phone pinged with a text notification. "Your woman is on her way to New Orleans. If you care."

He replied to Julian: "I would appreciate a background check."

His phone pinged again. "I knew you'd say that. Already on it. Either she doesn't exist, or someone as good as I am has covered her tracks."

"Search for everything on Andrea Flanagan."

"WTF? Are you serious?"

"Just keep it quiet for now."

"Ten-four."

Gregor wasn't ready to accuse his mate of being the Montague baby, not that accuse was the right word to use. She couldn't help if she was part of the destruction of the world thirty-three years earlier, but he knew in his gut it was true. How he knew was beyond him. Dante was the one with the voodoo-like feelings. It could have something to do with the mate bond. Gregor had never studied or asked anyone about the bond, because he thought his chances of finding his were slim to none.

First New York and now Louisiana. He couldn't stand it. Gregor had to have more information on Tessa, and Tamian was going to give it to him. He headed to the lower level, stopping to talk with Deacon when he passed him in the corridor.

"Deacon, anything happening?" Like ninety-nine percent of the guards, Deacon was a shifter.

Deacon held out his hand for a fist bump. "Good morning, Brother. All's quiet except for the albino. He must have been having a nightmare. I was going to take St. Claire's breakfast to him when I heard Alexander yelling. I looked in and he was fully phased. He was pale; well, paler than usual. He yelled out, "Rebekah, I'm so sorry." I don't know who she is or what he did to her, but the dude can talk, obviously. When he saw me at the door, he asked for a cigarette. I slid him a patch, but you and I both know that will only help him for about two point five seconds. I did tell him that if he would give up Flanagan, you would get him a carton of smokes."

"If he gives up Flanagan, I'll buy him a whole fucking truckload. Thanks, man."

Gregor stopped at Vincent's door and peered in. The albino was once again on the floor doing push-ups. Even though he didn't work out as much as Frey did, Gregor couldn't imagine being a shifter and cooped up in such a small confine. He opened Tamian's cell door as quietly as possible. He motioned for Tamian to follow, and they headed toward his office.

Gregor poured them both a cup of coffee then motioned for Tamian to take a seat. "I hear your cell buddy had an outburst this morning."

"Yeah, it's not the first time he's had nightmares. He mumbles in his sleep, and most of it isn't coherent. This Rebekah's name has been spoken more than once. So has Flanagan's. Now that we know he can actually talk, I think it's time you bear down on him. I'm no psychologist, but I truly believe if you offer him cigarettes and sunshine, he'll give you something. The man is obsessed with both."

Gregor barked out a laugh. "Sunshine? He looks like he hasn't seen a ray of sun in his life."

"Maybe that's why he craves it so much. When something you love is taken away, it's all you can think about." Tamian's pained expression told Gregor the man knew this from experience.

"I agree. I want to transfer you out of solitary into gen pop. You up for that?" The original plan had been to put Tamian in general population to see if any of the inmates talked about Flanagan. When they captured Vincent, the plan changed. Now that he had determined the man knew something, his job there was finished, and he could do what he was originally brought in to do.

"Absolutely. It will be interesting to listen in on all the crazies." He laughed before taking a sip of coffee. "How's Isabelle? I have never actually witnessed someone's first transition, but I hear it can be quite painful."

Gregor was confused. If Tamian was a half-blood, surely he had gone through his own transition. "Are you telling me you haven't phased yet?" He knew Tamian wasn't comfortable talking about himself, he just didn't know why. "Look, your sister and I are mates. Eventually, we *are* going to be together. That means you and I are going to be brothers. I get you have your secrets, and I also get you're probably trying to protect Tessa. I just don't know why or from whom. I care about her. Yeah, those emotions stem from the mate bond, but that will only get stronger. If you know anything at all about the bond, you know she and I belong together."

He could tell Tamian was conflicted by his facial expression. "Like I said before, mine and Tessa's story is a little different."

"I'm pretty sure I have figured that part out. I know who you are, who she is. You said you wanted her to be the one to tell me your story, but she's gone. I can't wait for her to return and possibly tell me what I need to know." Gregor was getting agitated. Why did the fates think he was capable of dealing with a hothead like Tessa or her closed lip brother?

"What do you mean you know who we are?"

"I may look like a big oaf, as your sister calls me. I actually have a brain inside this stubby body. When you think about the facts, it doesn't take a genius to figure out Tessa is the Montague baby and you are her clone." Gregor stopped because Tamian had literally jumped to his feet. "Calm down, man. I'm not shouting the news from the rooftops. I just put two and two together and came up with

121

the answer. I figure if you are the clone Jonas created, then you are probably something even more special than the other clones in the world. I have a feeling you were given a little extra something during the process. If I'm right, you are probably one unique shifter."

Gregor knew he had hit home. Tamian sat back down and slumped in his chair, leaning his head against the back. "If you figured this out, who else has? Shit, I need to talk to Andi. We need to leave, get out of New Atlanta."

"Whoa, easy. You don't need to leave. In fact, you are probably safer here in New Atlanta than you would be anywhere. Tessa's my mate, so you know I'll protect her. Rafael is King, and he will protect you both. You have a big family now, whether you want it or not. You and Tessa will become part of our Clan."

"Do you know where Andi went? I really need to talk to her before we discuss this any further."

"I heard she was headed to New Orleans." Gregor didn't want to tell him he was having Tessa investigated.

"Ah, hell. Andi tends to get in trouble when she goes to Louisiana. I need to get out of here. She thinks she can take care of herself, but sometimes she gets in over her head."

"What exactly is she doing there?" Gregor was the one getting agitated now. He didn't want to hear his mate was in danger.

"Not what, who. I'm sure you don't want to hear this, but she has a *friend* she hooks up with when she goes to check on our cousin. That's what Andi does for the family: she's a watcher. She keeps an eye on all of our cousins who are spread out over the world. Andi has a tendency to attract some pretty unsavory characters wherever she goes, but this one, he takes first prize."

"And just who is this particular unsavory character?" Gregor stood from his chair and ran his hand through his short hair. He was going to New Orleans and bring Tessa home, or at the very least, keep her safe and out of the clutches of another man.

"His name is Jacques Dupart. He won't be hard to find. He owns a seedy bar on Ursulines called Jacques' Place. If he isn't with Andi, he'll be at the bar." Tamian was giving this information freely.

"Why are you being so forthcoming about all this? Up until now, you've been pretty secretive."

"Because I don't like the guy. Even without Andi being mated to you, I don't want to see her with someone like Dupart. I'm not asking you to go after her. I think you know by now how stubborn she is. She has her mind made up that even though you're her mate, she's not going to give in to the pull. But if you were so inclined to make a trip to the bayou, it wouldn't hurt my feelings in the least. I agreed to stay in here and get information, and that's what I'm going to do. But like I told Andi, someone has to watch the watcher."

"Where does Tessa stay when she's there?" Gregor pulled out his cell phone and was dialing Rafe.

"She has her own place in the Garden District. Hand me a pen, and I'll write down the address." Gregor slid a pen and paper across his desk. While Tamian was writing, he spoke to his brother, "I need the jet. Now. New Orleans. Of course it has to do with a woman. Yes, a particular redhead." He hung up and called Deacon. "Can you come in here?"

Gregor took the address as Tamian said, "I would rather you not tell Andi where you got the information. I have kept an eye on her her whole life without her knowing it, and we have a great relationship. I don't want her to start hating me now. She thinks she's ten feet tall and bulletproof, but we both know that isn't the case. "

"I will do my best to keep you out of it, but I won't make you a promise I can't keep. I really appreciate all you're doing, St. Claire." Gregor stretched across his desk to shake hands. Deacon knocked and walked in. "You rang?"

"I did. We are moving forward with our original plans; St. Claire is going to gen pop. Put him on the D block in one of the empty cells. Also, I am taking a short trip to Louisiana, and I want you to take over while I'm gone." Gregor had been giving Deacon more and more responsibility around the prison so that one day he could assume the role of warden.

"You got it, Boss. St. Claire, let's go get your things and cuff you up. We can't have you strolling in to your new home without restraints."

Tamian followed Deacon but stopped at the door. "I know you care for Andi, bond or not. I truly hope she comes around sooner rather than later. You'll be good for her." With that, he followed Deacon down to solitary to get his few belongings.

Gregor hoped Tamian was right. He wanted to be good for Tessa. Good to her. If her job was to travel the world and watch over her family, he would be more than happy to leave New Atlanta and watch over her.

On the drive home to grab a travel bag, he called Isabelle.

"Hello?" Isabelle answered the phone almost immediately.

"Isabelle, this is Gregor. How are you feeling?"

"Hello, Warden. I'm doing really well. I was actually thinking of returning to work tomorrow instead of waiting."

"That's why I'm calling. I have to go out of town, and I don't want you coming to the Pen without me there. It's not that I don't trust you; I would just rather be there with you while you are getting re-acclimated. I do remember what it's like to transition. I hope to be back in a couple of days. You can get back to it then."

"What if someone needs medical attention?" He liked that about Isabelle, ever the doctor.

"My cousin is on call. If there are any emergencies, he'll take care of them. I tell you what, since you have just changed and Tessa is out of town, why don't you take down his number, just in case." He waited for Isabelle to get a pen and paper, before giving her Dante's information. "You take care, and I'll see you soon." *Dammit.* He realized just as he hung up that he had given her Dante's phone number but not his name. Hopefully she wouldn't need to call him.

Gregor had mixed emotions about this trip. On one hand, he would be close to his mate. On the other, if he had to watch her with another man, it would probably crush him. *Or*, his beast may be the one doing the crushing.

Twenty-One

The flight attendant in first class handed Tessa another plastic cup. It might be a little early in the day to start drinking, but after the morning she'd had, she deserved some alcohol. Her mother finally convinced her to tell her father about Gregor. If he was shocked by the news, he didn't show it. Xavier was over seven hundred years old and had seen a lot in his lifetime. She doubted there was much that could surprise him.

Before her conversation with her father, Tessa had been of the mindset that Rafael should know about human bonding so he and his newfound Queen could begin making little Gargoyle princes and princesses. Now, she wasn't so sure. If what her father said about Alistair was true, did she really want to be the cause of more death? She already felt guilty about her cousin losing his life posing as Magnus. Tessa had always been so headstrong, so sure of her beliefs. Now…

The pilot came over the radio and announced they would be landing in approximately fifteen minutes. She downed her drink and gave the empty cup to the attendant. Tessa was wary about this visit. Normally she loved coming to New Orleans. This was one of her favorite homes. With the exception of New Atlanta, she spent more time here than any other. She was very fond of her cousin, Lillian. Lilly was a talented artist who had a display set up at Jackson Square. Tessa's home was filled with various paintings she'd bought from her cousin.

Tessa loved the free spirits that lived in the city. Whether it was the voodoo or witchcraft, or just the vibe that came from the riverside area, she truly felt right at home. The only downside was Jacques. Tessa had tried to break things off with the man the last time she was here. Their relationship, if you could call it that, had run its course. If she was honest, she liked the sex, but couldn't stand the man. When she first met Jacques in his bar, she had been young and intrigued by his brazenness. She thought of him as a kindred spirit. However, the more she got to know him, the less she liked about him.

Being a shifter meant enhanced hearing. On her last trip, she had overheard a phone conversation in which he was making a drug deal. Not just a small, I need some weed to get me through the week, deal. This was a major transaction in which he was the distributor of a lot of heroin. She had made the mistake of telling him she moved antiquities. Did he expect her to help him with his shipment? The excitement that had once shone brightly was now dimmed to the point of pitch black. The man wasn't used to hearing the word no, so when Tessa told him she didn't want to see him anymore, he hadn't taken her seriously. She knew he had eyes all over the city, so getting in and out without him knowing would be tricky. If she had to face him, she would deal with it.

After departing the plane, Tessa hailed a taxi and headed to her house. The ride was quick, and she paid the driver handsomely for getting her home safely. She hated taxis, but they were a necessary evil in this town. She climbed the steps to her porch then opened the mailbox and pulled out a few advertisements. All utility bills were paid online, a year in advance. The name on the deed was one of her many aliases: Tabitha Stone. If Gregor ever found out she used his last name as often as she did, he would probably get a bigger head than he already had. He also had a lot to do with her not wanting Jacques.

As soon as she realized he was her mate, she began fantasizing about being his wife. She might act like she hated his guts, but she was totally infatuated with the Gargoyle. Who wouldn't be? Gregor Stone was a stocky, gorgeous specimen. She had spied on him over the last three years whenever she could. The one fantasy she used most often when she was in bed at night with her vibrator was when he was in the boxing ring. She had followed him to his cousin's dojo and watched through a side window as her shirtless mate sparred with his much larger cousin. Gregor was probably the shortest of his Clan, but he was the most beautifully built. As Gregor had jabbed and kicked, Tessa had moaned and swooned.

Not only did he have the body of a god, he also had the most mesmerizing eyes she had ever seen. She never allowed herself to look at them long, because she knew she would get lost in their blue depths. Now that she knew the full story of why her uncle had been banned from his Clan, she was even more confused than ever. Her heart wanted her to throw caution to the wind and go after Gregor. Her head told her to hold off and do the smart thing. She would just have to wait and see which won out.

Tessa usually called her next door neighbor to let her know she was coming to town. Gladys was an older woman who lived with a cute little dog. Most animals didn't take to shifters, but Toby didn't seem to mind Tessa. Gladys had never married, but she still entertained gentlemen often. She had told Tessa that she got bored easily, and if she never married, she wouldn't have to worry about divorce. Tessa flipped the thermostat up a few degrees to knock the chill off. She threw the junk mail into the recycle bin and headed for the refrigerator. She didn't keep it stocked with food, but she always had beer.

She twisted the top off a bottle and took a long pull. After she relaxed for a bit, she would see if Gladys was home. If she was, Tessa would visit with her for the remainder of the day and go see Lilly tomorrow. She pulled off her boots and turned on the stereo. Normally, she opted for hard or classic rock. Today she was in a pensive mood, so she opted for some classical. She sat on one end of her leather sofa, pulling her feet under her. Placing the bottle on the end table, she leaned her head back. Closing her eyes, she let her mind wander to the Gargoyles, one in particular.

The doorbell ringing woke Tessa. The classical music had lulled her into a nap. She slowly walked to the front of her house and peered through the sheer curtains that covered the long windows on either side of the door. The silhouette was that of a short person. Gladys. She opened the door for her neighbor.

"Hello, Dolly. I came to get your mail and heard the music." Tessa stepped back to allow her friend in then shut the door and locked it. Gladys' nickname for Tessa always brought a smile to her face. There was nothing doll-like about Tessa, and they both knew it.

She hugged the older woman before leading her into the living room. Tessa's home was one of the smaller houses in the district. Considering she spent so little time in the city, it didn't make sense to purchase a huge house. She had considered it an investment. Eventually, all the cousins would transition and she would not have to travel as often. She loved this city and hoped to spend more time there in the future, just not on official family business. Would Gregor like New Orleans?

"Can I get you something to drink? I think I have a bottle of wine somewhere." Tessa rarely drank the stuff, but she kept it for Gladys.

"I'm fine, my girl. I want to know how you are. You don't look happy. Tell Gladys your troubles." The older woman sat down next to Tessa on the sofa and patted her leg.

"I never could get anything by you, could I? I have some major decisions to make. I couldn't do that with the distractions back home, so I decided to come here for a little down time." Technically, she wasn't lying. She did have major decisions to make, and Gregor was a distraction. A big one.

Gladys knew Tessa had more than one home. Being an archaeologist meant that she traveled the world, and having have homes in multiple places made sense. When she was younger, the cover had been fun, adventurous even. She had gone on a few digs with real archaeologists to see what it was like and had thoroughly enjoyed herself. Now, she was ready to settle down a little. She enjoyed watching over her cousins, but most had transitioned. When she no longer had to worry about them, she would need to find something else to fill her time. Blue eyes came to mind. She would like to fill her time with Gregor. She'd like to fill herself with Gregor. *Fuck.*

"Tabitha, did you hear what I said?"

Tessa sighed. "I'm sorry, Gladys. My mind was elsewhere. I'm afraid I'm not going to be very good company today."

Gladys patted her leg. "You have man troubles, I can tell. I sure hope it has nothing to do with that Jacques person."

"How do you know about him?" Tessa never brought Jacques back to her home. She had no doubt he had followed her and knew where she lived, but she tried to keep him separate from her personal space. The first few times she visited the city, she had stayed in a hotel. When she realized how much she loved New Orleans, she searched for a small house and had found the one next door to Gladys.

"He's been coming around, asking about you. He's a shady character, that one. How did you get messed up with him, anyway?"

Tessa had a cover story for just about every situation. "He was looking for a certain rare object and hired me to find it. When did he come by here?"

"When didn't he? He knocks on your door and then sits in his car, waiting. Eventually he gives up. I've called the police a couple of times, but when he sees the patrol car, he drives off. He came to my door once, asking if I had seen you. I told him in no uncertain terms that your whereabouts was none of his business."

"Oh, Gladys. Thank you for looking out for me, but you are right. Jacques Dupart is not a man to be messed with. I was hoping this trip would be drama free, but it seems I'm going to have to have a chat with him. But you, you do not open your door to him again, okay?"

"Okay, but you be careful. If he isn't a nice man, you shouldn't be around him either." Gladys stood, crossing her arms over her chest. "Promise me you'll be careful, Tabitha."

"I promise. And I apologize for not being good company. I'll make it up to you tomorrow."

"I can cook dinner, if you'd like." Gladys was not the best cook in the world, but she tried hard and always made a decent spaghetti.

"I would like that very much. Thank you, Gladys."

"No need to thank me yet. Get some rest, and I will see you tomorrow."

Tessa shut the door behind her neighbor and leaned against it. "Fucking Jacques. What are you up to?" She hadn't seen him in almost six months, and the last few times they had been together had been less than stellar. He couldn't understand why their sex life had gone from down and dirty to non-existent. She couldn't tell him it was because he disgusted her. She needed to come up with a plan to get rid of him once and for all. She hated the idea of selling her house, but the man had lived here his whole life. He definitely wasn't going anywhere.

Her stomach growling reminded her she hadn't eaten in a while. Cassandra had insisted on feeding her before she left for the airport. When she asked the older lady why she was sad, Cassandra told her they were happy tears. Finding one's mate was a big deal, and she hoped Tessa blessed them with little shifters before Cassandra was too old to enjoy them.

Tessa laughed and played it off. The thought of having Gregor's children made her nauseous after the conversation she'd had with her father.

Knowing there was nothing to eat in the house, Tessa decided to walk to the local Irish pub and grab a sandwich. She was taking a chance on one of Jacques' men seeing her, but she needed the fresh air. Instead of going out the front door, she went out the back, and snaked through some of the neighbors' alleys. If Jacques was around, she wanted to avoid him as long as possible.

Twenty-Two

Gregor's flight had taken forever. Not really, it just seemed that way. He spent the short forty minutes studying everything Julian could dig up on Jacques Dupart. On the surface, the man seemed like an honest business owner. His bar, Jacques' Place, was lucrative, even if it was a seedy dive. The tourists more than likely avoided it since it appeared to be a rough joint. The locals probably called it home. The man in the picture was not the type of man he figured Tessa would go after. But then again, he knew very little about his mate, including what type of man she found attractive. The guy in the picture was the complete opposite of Gregor: long blond hair, dark eyes. He was dressed in a suit and tie. His bio put him at six-two, two hundred twenty pounds. That didn't bother Gregor. Being a shifter, he wasn't intimidated by anyone.

Gregor punched in the address for Tessa's home and set out in his rental car. The ride from the airport was lengthened due to rush hour traffic. He didn't know the area, so he had to rely on the GPS to navigate the busy streets. Half an hour later than he should have arrived, he pulled onto her street. Slowly, he took in the beautiful houses that lined the road. Finding Tessa's home was easy since the number was nailed to a post on the porch. The pretty little house was nestled between two larger ones. Gregor sat at the curb, car idling, while he thought about something else Julian had dug up: the house was registered to Tabitha Stone.

Gregor's heart was swelling with encouragement that his mate really didn't hate him. Why else would she be using his name as her alias? Tabitha. That was better than Trixie, but it still wasn't her. Neither was Andrea. No, she was definitely Tessa. An older woman walking a small, fuzzy dog was headed down the sidewalk toward him. She

133

stopped and tapped on the passenger side window. He rolled it down and asked, "Can I help you?" The woman was eyeing him suspiciously.

"I was just about to ask you the same thing, young man. Are you lost?"

"No, ma'am. I was just calling to see if my cousin was home before I knocked on her door." He held up his cell phone.

"Your cousin, huh? I need to see some identification."

Was she serious? This woman had to be close to seventy. Yet here she was, ready to defend her neighborhood. He grinned, "Of course. I'm going to reach in my back pocket and pull out my wallet. Please don't shoot me."

"Don't be a smartass. I'm not going to shoot you." The small dog was yapping. "Hush, Toby."

Gregor showed his warden's identification badge to the lady, hoping to instill a little bit of trust. "See, Gregor Stone, Warden."

"Tabitha never said she had such a handsome cousin. You just missed her. If I had to venture a guess, I'd say she walked down to McFadden's. It's the Irish bar on St. Charles."

Gregor flashed his best smile at the lady. "Thank you…" He didn't know her name.

"Gladys. I live right there." She pointed at the large house to the left of Tessa's.

"Thank you, Gladys. It makes me feel a lot better knowing Tabitha lives next door to someone who watches out for her."

"She needs someone looking out for her. I hope you're here to get rid of that bum, Dupart."

"Yes ma'am, that's exactly why I'm here." Gregor hated that Gladys knew who Jacques was. That meant the man had been around. He didn't have a plan where Tessa's

134

lover was concerned. Gladys gave him one last look, then she and Toby turned back the way they'd come. He searched on his phone for the address to the bar. If Tessa had walked, it shouldn't be too far. Gregor decided to leave his car parked where it was and take a stroll himself.

McFadden's Irish Pub was a familiar place for Tessa. She ate there every time she was in the city. It, like The Tavern in New Atlanta, was home. The owners and bartenders knew her by name, well her alias anyway. They treated her like she was part of the family, no matter how much time passed between visits. She pushed through the front door and immediately heard, "Tabby!" Fiona, one of the owners, was coming around the bar to pull her in for a hug. She hugged the woman back and grinned. "Fi, how the hell are ya?"

Fiona was a beautiful, Irish woman with an equally gorgeous husband. Wherever Fiona was, Roy wasn't far behind. "We are very well, thank you." Her smile was so big Tessa was nearly blinded by it. When Fiona's hand moved to her stomach, Tessa knew there was a very good reason for her friend to be so happy. They had been trying a long time for a baby.

"This is seriously good news. I am so happy for you both." Roy was leaning against the post that separated the bar area from the kitchen. His face was adorned with his own smile.

"Now, come on. Sit down. You have been scarce these last few months. We need to catch up." Fiona led Tessa to a table close to the bar. This way they could have a little bit of privacy for girl talk, and Roy could keep an eye on his wife. Roy brought Tessa her usual draft beer and a cup of tea for his woman. He kissed her cheek gently then went back to the bar.

"Wow, Fi! A baby! This is so exciting." Tessa kept the conversation away from her as long as she could. She talked about cribs and strollers and diapers, anything to keep the topic on their first child. She knew having an alias was imperative in her life, but if there was one person she hated lying to, it was Fiona. She was the one true girl friend Tessa had.

Roy interrupted long enough to bring Tessa's sandwich and refill her pint glass. Eventually the topic of babies had run its course and Fiona asked the inevitable, "Have you seen Jacques? He has been tearing the streets apart searching for you. Tabitha, what's going on?"

Before she could answer, she heard Roy say, "Oh, fuck."

Speaking of the devil had brought him straight to her. *Shit.* Jacques walked right up to the table where she and Fiona were sitting. It was no coincidence he was there. Someone had tipped him off. "Tabitha." The one word caused a chill to run up her spine. Why was he so reluctant to let her go?

"Jacques, what are you doing here?" Tessa picked up her glass and finished the beer, holding the glass up for Roy to see it was empty.

"I happened to be in the neighborhood and saw you sitting here. Can I not stop in to say hello? I have missed you." He didn't bother waiting for an invitation. He pulled a stool over from a nearby table and sat next to Tessa.

"That's nice, but my friend and I were in the middle of a conversation." That wiped the smile off his face. She knew he was full of shit. The table was away from any of the windows. He either followed her, or someone had seen her and called him. Tessa wasn't scared of the man. Even though she was a woman, she was a shifter. The only male she would lose a fight to would be another shifter.

Roy placed her beer in front of her, and she gave him a small smile. "Thank you. Would you please bring me a to-go box for my sandwich? I seem to have lost my appetite." She knew she was pushing it with Jacques, but she hated the fact that he was stalking her.

"You don't have to be rude. I just want to talk to you." Jacques picked up a french fry off of Tessa's plate and bit the end of it.

"I'm not the one who sat down uninvited and started eating someone else's food. Fiona, please forgive my *friend* here. He usually has more manners." Tessa stood and retrieved the Styrofoam container from Roy. "I will let you get back to work. We will finish our discussion later." Tessa was pointedly looking at Fiona, attempting to telepath her sincere regret at bringing potential trouble to their establishment. It must have worked because Fiona stood and walked over to her husband. Tessa pulled out a couple of twenties and laid them on the table.

Not bothering to speak to Jacques, she grabbed the to-go box and stood in front of her friends. "I apologize. It was lovely to see you both, and I am so happy for you. I will do my best to come back before I head out of town." She kissed Fiona on the cheek and turned toward the door.

She didn't get far when she felt a huge hand grab her upper arm. "Where the fuck do you think you're going?"

The pub was only a few blocks from Tessa's house. Gregor intended to stay outside and wait for her to come out. He had no idea how he would explain his presence other than he had, in fact, followed her for no good reason. He could tell her Tamian asked him to follow her, even though her brother had specifically asked to be kept out of it. For now, he would just wait and see how she reacted.

Gregor felt Tessa's emotions coming from inside the bar, and these were not good ones. His mate was pissed. There were tables visible through the front window of the pub, but he didn't see her. "Get your fucking hand off me." He might not be able to see her, but he sure as hell heard her. "I just want to talk, Tabitha. Why are you acting like such a bitch?" He could only guess who was speaking to her that way. He wasn't going to wait and find out. He calmed himself and walked inside.

The scene before him was enough to cause him to fully phase. However, seeing Tessa putting Jacques Dupart in his place had his beast calming down. A little. "I said, take your fucking hand off me before you lose it." Tessa's emotions were supercharging now. It was a wonder she wasn't phasing. Gregor needed to defuse the situation before they were both showing fangs. He stepped closer and cleared his throat.

"Hello, Sweetheart. So sorry I'm late, but I was caught in traffic." He didn't know who was more stunned, Tessa or Jacques. He strolled right up to her and kissed her on the cheek. "I don't believe we've met. Gregor Stone." He stuck his hand out to the other man who was still staring at him.

"Stone?" Dupart asked incredulously.

"Yes, Gregor Stone. And you are?"

Jacques didn't answer his question or shake his hand. Instead, he accused Tessa, "Stone? You're married?"

Gregor put his arm around Tessa's shoulders and pulled her to his chest. Her face was priceless. "Yes, Tabitha. Tell the man. You're taken."

Tessa finally closed her mouth and leaned in, putting her arm around his waist. "That's right. Though, we were separated for a while."

"Un-fucking-believable. You are really something, you know that?" Jacques kicked over the nearest stool and stormed out of the bar.

Gregor's smile turned to a deep frown. "Yes, Tabitha. You are something."

She pulled out of his embrace. "What the *fuck* are you doing here?" She seethed through her teeth.

"Watching that ass. I told you to keep it safe, and it appears you were doing anything but. And you should watch your language. You curse too much."

The couple who had been standing off to the side watching the excitement took the opportunity to approach Tessa. "Are you all right?" The pretty woman was eyeing Gregor as warily as she had been Dupart.

"Yes, I'm fine. I am so sorry that jackass caused a scene. Fiona, again, congratulations on your wonderful news. I am going to take my sandwich and my…Gregor and head home."

Twenty-Three

Tessa grabbed Gregor's arm and practically dragged him from the pub. Once outside, he could tell she was gearing up to light into him, but he stopped her. "Tessa, we have company." He leaned in close so only she could hear him. "Your friend is across the street, watching. If you want to get rid of him, kiss me." Gregor knew he was taking advantage of the situation, but he didn't care. He would use any excuse to get close to this woman.

Tessa glanced out of the corner of her eye and noticed Dupart across the street, leaning against a light pole with his arms crossed over his chest. With her free hand, she slid her fingers into Gregor's short hair, pulling him down, closer to her face. She didn't hesitate to open her mouth for him, seeking his tongue. He fisted her hair in one hand and pulled her to him with the other. Her body was coming alive, the arousal scent floating up to invade his nostrils. His cock was hardening, wedged between their bodies. "Get a room," was yelled by a kid in a car going down St. Charles Street. "I think that's a very good idea," Gregor breathed into her mouth.

"Yes, let's take this somewhere a little more private." Tessa grabbed his hand and threaded their fingers together. He walked with her back to her house, enjoying the quiet before the storm. He knew she wasn't going to just let this go. Her emotions were a mixture of lust and anger. He was going to get an earful for following her out of town.

When they arrived at her house, Tessa still didn't say anything. As soon as the door was closed, instead of yelling at him, she dropped the food container to the floor then pushed him against the wall, hard. If Gregor hadn't been there to witness what happened next, he never would have believed it. His mate dropped to her knees and blew him. He could feel the adrenaline coursing through her body like white water rapids. She practically ripped his pants open to get to his hard cock. Tessa didn't take care with his erection; she grabbed hold as soon as it was free of his jeans and slammed it home to the back of her throat. "Oh fuck," he moaned.

The sight of his dick sliding in and out of her wet, warm mouth, her red hair bobbing up and down, and the sound of her moans had him close to shooting his wad down her throat. "Oh gods. That's it. Suck it hard." Gregor had a feeling this was a once in a lifetime occurrence for him, so he slowed his breathing and calmed his body. He wanted this to last as long as possible. Tessa pulled his jeans down farther on his legs, never losing the pace. He imagined her lying on her back, head hanging off the side of the bed with the outline of his dick in her throat as he slid in and out. If he ever got another chance to do this... That thought fled his brain when he felt her mouth leave his cock.

Gregor immediately missed the warmth. Tessa was looking up at him. Surely she wasn't such a sadist that she was going to stop. When she grabbed him with her hand, he realized she was giving her mouth a break. One hand stroked his cock, twisting the engorged head. Her free hand wiped the saliva off her chin then grabbed his balls. Fuck! That felt so good. She tugged on his swollen sac with just enough pressure to be painful yet still enjoyable. Her mouth once again replaced her hand, and she set the rhythm to match the movement of his hips. "Gods, Baby, seeing your pretty, wet mouth wrapped around my dick is so fucking hot. Oh, fuck yeah." As much as he was enjoying this, she was probably getting tired so he allowed his body to ramp back up.

When Gregor fisted Tessa's hair, a low groan escaped from her throat. He pulled hard enough to be painful, and she moaned even louder. His girl liked it rough, too. He took over the pace, thrusting in and out, fucking her mouth. "You suck so fucking good, Baby.

Swallow my cock. Take it all the way down." Tessa grabbed hold of his thighs, encouraging him on. When he couldn't hold off any longer, Gregor gripped her hair tighter, holding her face to his crotch as his come coated the back of her throat. Once she had sucked him dry, she rose from her knees to stand in front of him. Instead of wiping her chin, she crashed her mouth to his. The taste of his spunk on her tongue had his dick filling out for round two. In all his years, he had never tasted himself on a woman's lips.

The ringing of Tessa's phone had her pulling away. "That changes nothing. You need to go. Now." Leaving him standing with his semi-hard cock and his jeans around his thighs, Tessa picked up her to-go box and walked away.

Tessa knew she had just screwed up. Big time. Kissing the man was one thing, but having his cock in her mouth was going to be the death of her. There was no way she could deny him anything, but she had to. Fuck! Why did he have to be so enticing? Oh, right, the mate bond. Even if that weren't the case, Gregor Stone was irresistible. The man was built like a heavyweight boxer. And his eyes. Those godsdamn eyes. She made the mistake of looking at them when she was giving her mouth a break from sucking his glorious dick.

Tessa liked sex. She had been with several men over the years, but not enough to be considered a slut, yet enough that she knew when a man was going to be good in bed. Her mate was going to ruin her for all other men. When she finally gave in, and she was certain she would if they had sex, it would all be over. Gregor was muttering under his breath by the front door. She tried not to laugh. It was rude to leave him in such a state, but she needed him out of the house so she could take care of her own aching need. She had no intention of letting him get her naked.

"Tessa." Gregor growled her name. Growled.

"Gregor." She didn't growl back. No, he would probably like that. He was more than likely still turned on by the blowjob.

"You can't just suck my dick then walk away." His jeans were back in place with his button up shirt untucked. This was a look she was getting used to. The night at The Tavern when he rocked her world, he had been dressed less casually, really put together. She preferred this just fucked look on him.

"I can, and I did. I won't apologize for the blowjob. I blame that on the fucking fates. The mate bond and the adrenaline rush of you going all cave man at the pub... that got my juices flowing."

"I like when your juices are flowing. You're still turned on. I can smell your arousal from here. Let me take care of that for you." Gregor's nostrils were flaring. His Gargoyle senses had kicked in.

"I can take care of that myself. I don't need you or any other man. What I do need is for you to tell me what the fuck you're doing here. How did you even know where to find me?" Tessa opened the fridge and pulled out two beers. She could really be a dick and not offer him one, but she just didn't have it in her.

Gregor took the offered bottle and downed half of it. "That's not important."

"It's very important. If you're spying on me, that's one thing. If someone is offering up information freely, that's another."

"Maybe I just want to keep my mate safe." Gregor drank the rest then tossed the empty bottle in the recycle bin.

"I'm not your mate. Not until the fangs break the skin, and that's never going to happen." She had to change the subject. "How's Tamian?"

"Other than being worried about you, he's fine. He has made really good progress with his undercover work. I moved him into general population before I left to come here."

"Why would he be worried about me? Unless you told him where I was going."

"I might have mentioned it. He wanted to be the one to come after you. Since he's doing undercover inmate duty, he asked me to keep you safe; so here I am."

Tessa grabbed another beer out of the refrigerator and handed it to him. If he kept up this pace, she was going to need to go to the store.

"Your brother obviously keeps tabs on you, because he knew this Dupart was trouble. He was right. You wanna tell me about him? How did you get hooked up with a smuggler?"

"Smuggler? No, Jacques owns a bar." Tessa wasn't about to tell her mate that he was exactly right.

"I hate to break it to you, Red, but he is indeed a criminal. Jacques Dupart has been smuggling and brokering deals for a long time. He started off small, but his empire has grown over the last few years. That must be what he wanted you for. He thought you were an archaeologist traveling the world. Did he ever ask you to pick up packages on your trips?"

Tessa felt like she had been slapped. "You think the only reason he wanted me was to use me as a mule? You know what? Go to hell. Get the fuck out of my house, out of New Orleans, and out of my life." She drank the rest of her beer and opened the cabinet for a bottle of tequila.

"I didn't mean that he wouldn't find you desirable." Gregor couldn't back pedal fast enough. Too late. This only made the decision to stay away from him easier.

144

"I said get out. I wasn't joking. Nothing you can say now will make me want to truly be your mate. GET THE FUCK OUT!" Tessa hated losing control, but she was losing hers, quickly. She was so close to phasing, and she never wanted to give him that. Never wanted him to see her cry.

When he moved closer, she lost it. "GET OUT!" She threw the half-full bottle of tequila at his head. If he hadn't been a shifter with quick reflexes, she would have hit him. Instead, the bottle hit the far wall and smashed into hundreds of pieces, clear liquid splashing on the floor.

Gregor held his hands up in the defensive position, "Okay, gods, I'm sorry. I'll go. But I'll be watching you. I'll always be watching you." The look on his face was one of torment. Tessa didn't care. This was for the best. Gregor turned back one last time before he walked out of her home.

Tessa pulled another bottle of tequila out of the cabinet. This one was full. She unscrewed the cap and didn't bother getting a glass. She grabbed another beer and took both liquids to the living room where she cranked the heaviest metal music she had available. It didn't take long for half a bottle of liquor to numb the ache in her heart. Her last thought before she passed out was *fuck you, Stone*.

Twenty-Four

Kaya was surprised when she looked up from a report and Dane was sitting across from her. She hadn't heard him come in. "Damn, Abbott, this new you is a lot quieter than the old you. What's up?" She sat her pen down and gave him her undivided attention.

"I want to meet Rafael. I need answers, and I figure I better get them from the right person. I'm tired of not knowing what to do, who to talk to, who to trust. If he's the King, he should shoot straight with me. Right?" Dane was sitting still. Stone still. Just like Rafael was capable of doing.

"Yes, he will shoot straight. I can arrange a meeting. When that happens, you will find out more than you bargained for. I want you to promise me you will keep a level head. You are new to all things shifter. Rafael is over five hundred years old, and like you said, he's King. This means he will expect you to serve the family in the same capacity as all the other shifters. Can you do that?"

"I honestly don't know, but I'm willing to listen. What I do know is I need answers, and my family has been less than forthcoming. Sure, they told me bits and pieces, but I need the whole scenario. I'm a detective; I gather facts. For now, I'm treating my life as just another case, and until I know all the facts, I won't be able to make a decision."

"Fair enough. I will set the meeting for tonight, if that's not too soon."

"The sooner the better. Now, about the latest victim. Same victimology as the others. CSU found what appears to be skin under this one's fingernails, so hopefully, we have a break. We need one. I suggest doing a press conference alerting the public to take precautions."

"I have already set it up. I was just waiting for you to return and confirm we have a serial killer. Do you want to take lead on the camera? You're favorite reporter will be out there." Kaya wasn't a fan of Katherine Fox. While she was probably good at her job, she was a nuisance. Now that Kaya thought about it, she possibly fit the profile of the murder victims.

Dane's brows burrowed deeper between his eyes. "You always do the press conferences. What is going on with you? Why are you pushing things in my lap?"

"I'm not pushing anything. I simply offered you an opportunity. Damn, Abbott, forget it. I'll let you know when and where you will meet with Rafael."

He didn't proceed to get up. "I'm sorry. You're just different. I'm not used to a Chief that doesn't have everything and everyone by the balls. I've never known you to relinquish any control. I would be more than happy to do the press conference." Dane then stood. "Are you going to be at the meeting tonight?"

"Yes, I'll be there."

Dane nodded. "I'll go prepare a statement."

"You have twenty minutes. And you might want to tell your little friend to watch her redheaded ass."

"Nah, she doesn't look anything like Tessa Blackmore." Dane didn't bother elaborating. How in the hell had he put that together? Jasper.

Kaya leaned back in her chair. It seemed both she and Dane had changed over the last couple of weeks. He was right. Before she met Rafael, she never would have offered for anyone to do any aspect of her job. Now that it was possible for her and Rafael to have children, she was thinking more and more about retirement. She picked up the phone and called her mate, asking for a meeting between him and Dane.

Gregor was grateful for the trees in Tessa's yard. He reached out with his senses, and when he determined there was no one around, he opened his wings, launching himself into a tree. He stayed perched on a limb until Tessa's heartbeat calmed. The slow count meant she was probably asleep. He enjoyed her taste in music, even though he was sure she was using it as a means of escape. He often listened to hard rock when he wanted to let off some steam.

Tessa had failed to set the alarm on her doors before she passed out. He was going to stay where he was until she woke up and he knew she was safe. It was too early for her to be asleep for the night, but consuming copious amounts of liquor, if that's what she'd done, would have her snoozing for a while.

Now that he knew about Dupart and the role Tessa was likely supposed to play in his little empire, Gregor needed to keep an eye on her. He hadn't meant to hurt her feelings. He only wanted her to see what type of man she had been keeping company with. Most women would have cried, but not his woman. He was thankful to be a shifter than when that bottle had been hurled at his head. Even though it wouldn't truly hurt, smelling like eighty proof would've sucked. He leaned against the tree trunk and settled in.

Gregor didn't want to take a chance on being seen. He was high enough in the tree that humans wouldn't detect him. Still, he would wait until the sun was down before he eased out of his hiding spot. Gregor planned on tailing Tessa until she was ready to come home. Home. This was home for her, or at least one of them. What if he had really screwed up with her, and she decided to stay? He would have to convince her otherwise. Or move to New Orleans.

Sitting still for hours gave Gregor time to formulate a plan, at least when it came to dealing with Jacques. He called Julian to get the phone number for Dominic Dubois, the leader of the Louisiana Clan. He was going to enlist his help in shutting down Dupart. It might take a while, but if the man was in jail, he couldn't bother Tessa.

His cousin answered the phone quickly. "Julian."

"Hey, Jules. Did I catch you at a bad time?" He was talking quietly, even though he knew humans wouldn't detect the sound of his voice.

"No, I am waiting on the press conference to come on. There has been another redhead death. Are you whispering?"

"Sort of. I'm right outside Tessa's house. I was hoping to convince her to come home, but now I might try to persuade her to stay here until these murders are solved." Gregor was convinced these killings had everything to do with Tessa.

"Hang on, the news anchor is on the screen." Julian was turning the sound up on the television. A woman's voice was coming through the phone. "This is Katherine Fox reporting live from the New Atlanta Police Precinct..."

"Fuck me," Julian whispered.

"Is she that pretty?" Gregor was laughing until he heard his cousin growling.

"Oh fuck, I don't feel so well. NIKOLAS!" Gregor had to yank the phone away from his ear when Julian yelled out.

"Godsdamn Jules, what the fuck?" There was no answer on the other end, only muffled talking. "Jules...JULES...JULIAN!" Gregor whispered as loudly as he could without actually yelling.

"Hello? Gregor?" Nikolas was on the line. "Let me see, do you have warts? A growth of any sort?"

"What? Nik, what the fuck are you going on about? And what's wrong with Julian?"

"Oh, I think he just figured out who his mate is. That reporter, Katherine Fox. She came on the screen, and he

149

keeled over. I was just searching for the side effects. Hang on, Dane Abbott's coming to the microphone."

Nikolas was silent so that Gregor could listen in.

"Thank you for coming on such short notice. As you are aware, there have been several young women murdered in the last couple of weeks. Earlier today, another victim fitting the same description, washed up on the bank of the Chattahoochee. We have called this press conference to urge the women of New Atlanta, especially those with red hair and green eyes, to take extra precautions. If you have loved ones or friends with these physical characteristics, please contact them. All of the women were last seen in well-populated areas. We believe they were taken during daylight hours then disposed of at night. Our UnSub, or Unknown Subject, is most likely a good-looking male in his early thirties, possibly pretending to need assistance. If you have any information that would help us stop this killer, please call the crime force hotline at the number shown on your screen. Thank you."

Once the detective had finished speaking, Nikolas was back. "Did you need something?"

"Yes. I need Dominic's phone number. I have a little project for him."

"Sure thing. I'll text it to you. Would this have anything to do with your woman's lover?" Nikolas snickered as he typed away on the computer.

Gregor growled into the phone and hung up. He was going to kick some geeky ass when he got home. Before he could do that, he had to take care of one Jacques Dupart. Gregor had met Dominic several years ago when Rafael called a meeting of all Clan leaders. Before the Unholy were created, the Gargoyles watched over the humans, just not as closely as they had to now. There were always monsters out in the world, but most weren't so bad that the human police force couldn't take them down. As soon as the first Unholy were unleashed into the world, Rafael wanted to prepare the Goyles. Special prisons were built in all major cities.

The Unholy army originated in New Atlanta, but Gordon Flanagan soon spread his lunacy across the country. He had been trying to flush out his wife and daughter for the last thirty-three years. Gregor had to wonder what Tessa thought about all the killing being done in her name, her mother's name. He didn't blame her for hiding from the madman, but it had to bother her that Flanagan would stop at nothing to reclaim what had been taken from him. Rafael was already making plans to up the search for Flanagan. Gregor was going to hurry that along by pressing Vincent. Now that the albino was talking, Gregor was going to make sure the words he spoke had meaning.

The music coming from Tessa's house was now being played at a normal volume. His woman was awake. Her phone was ringing, and he listened as she answered then spoke to someone named Sophia. That's the same name she had mentioned to Isabelle. Tessa mostly listened, cursed a little, listened again, and then hung up. She was mumbling to herself about Egypt, Gregor, Gargoyles, and men in general. Gregor turned his face toward the sky and whispered to the fates, "I know you put her with me for a reason. Just give me the patience to deal with her until she comes to her senses."

With Tessa safe for the time being, Gregor quietly descended from the tree and walked to his rental car. He would call Dominic and set up a meeting. For now, he was going to take a walk down by the river. He would come back later and keep watch over his mate for the night.

Twenty-Five

Dane nicked his lip. Again. He had to get his fangs under control before he met Rafael. How had his life become this fantasy novel gone bad? Kaya put her blinker on, indicating they were turning into a driveway. There was no one behind him, so he didn't bother. He stopped behind her, waiting. Instead of punching in a code to the security box, she spoke into the box and the gate opened. Must be voice recognition. High tech. When Kaya told him the meeting with Rafael would be at his home, he never imagined it would be the massive structure coming into his view.

Kaya parked in front of a large garage, and Dane parked beside her. He calmed himself. The pep-talk she had given him came back to his mind. She had told him all his questions would be answered, and he would be welcomed into the Clan. He angled out of his car and walked over to a waiting Kaya. "You ready?" She asked him.

"As I'll ever be." Actually, he was very ready. Tessa and Caroline had given him some information, but not enough. Tessa had told him to be quiet around the Gargoyles, but if they were as Kaya described them, he wanted in. He had already met two of them, and they treated him as an equal, not a cast-off. Half-blood or not, he wanted to play in the big leagues, not the minors. The front door opened, and an older man smiled at them. When Kaya passed by, she kissed him on the cheek. "Good evening, Jonathan. I'd like you to meet Dane Abbott. Dane, Jonathan. He and his sister Priscilla take care of the manor."

Dane shook the older man's hand and told him it was a pleasure. Kaya continued on through the spacious place as if she lived there. She knew exactly where she was going, so he followed. He had expected to meet in an office setting, but instead, she led him to the kitchen. An older woman, Priscilla he presumed, was pulling cookies out of the oven. "Kaya! There you are, dear. I baked cookies. You must be Dane. What beautiful eyes you have." Dane couldn't help but grin as she rambled on.

"Priscilla, don't scare our guest off." A deep baritone voice came from behind Dane. He turned to see a tall, dark-haired man smiling at Priscilla. Kaya immediately went to him, and it was as if the rest of the world disappeared for them. When Kaya said she knew Rafael, she failed to mention just how well. When they broke from their kiss, the man turned to Dane. "Rafael Stone," he said as he held out his large hand. There was no power grip, no throwing the testosterone around to mark his territory. It wasn't necessary. This was Rafael Stone, King of the Gargoyles. His presence alone did the talking.

"Mr. Stone, Sir, uh... My King." Dane didn't know what to call him.

"Rafael is fine for now." He was smiling, so Dane hadn't screwed up... yet. "Priscilla, thank you for the cookies. If you'll excuse us, we're going to stay in here for a bit." The older lady patted Rafael's cheek as she walked by.

As Kaya pulled a spatula out of a drawer and scooped the cookies onto a plate, she asked, "Dane, would you like something to drink?"

"Water would be great, thanks." He really wanted a shot of whiskey. Or two.

Rafael motioned to the stools at the island. "Dane, please have a seat." Rafael, who was wearing faded blue jeans and an untucked button up shirt, sat on one of the stools at the island. His feet were bare. This was certainly not what Dane had been expecting. Kaya placed a glass of water in front of Dane and milk in front of Rafael. She poured herself a glass of wine and joined them. Rafael picked up a cookie and offered one to Dane. "Priscilla's cookies are to die for." He shoved the whole thing in his mouth, moaning as he chewed. Kaya was laughing at him.

153

Rafael drank half his milk, wiped his mouth on his sleeve and then spoke to Dane. "I appreciate you driving out here to meet with me. I was going to do this at the office, but I realized it would be better for you to see the real me. This is the Rafael Stone that most people don't know, never see. This is where I am most comfortable. And this is the *me* that I want you to get to know. Not just as your King, but your friend as well.

"We are aware you have recently gone through your transition. First, I want you to know, this is all new to us, the Gargoyles. Until a couple of weeks ago, we didn't know half-bloods existed. What I would like is for you to tell me your story. Start at the beginning, if you would please."

He glanced at Kaya, and she nodded. "I'm not sure what to say, really. One minute I was fine, the next I felt like I had the flu. I went to the doctor, but she couldn't figure out what was wrong with me. Then this happened."

"Okay, can you elaborate a little for me? We need to know everything you know, especially about your parents." Rafael grabbed another cookie, this time eating it in more than one bite.

"I'm not sure how much I'm supposed to say, but I've been thinking about that. I was left to my own defenses my whole life, not knowing the truth of who and what I am. Don't get me wrong, Caroline explained a lot of it to me. I haven't seen her or Isabelle since I transitioned. Tessa did stop by, but she was hurrying out of town. I know they're my family, but to me, family doesn't throw you to the wolves with no survival guide. This is a lot of shit to take in, and I just thought I would have someone helping me through it. I don't want you to think I'm some pussy whiner. I'm not. I just…"

Rafael interrupted him, "Dane, Son, it's okay. I don't think less of you because you are adjusting to being a shifter. If anything, I admire your strength. Gargoyles are born into families where being a shifter is first nature, not

154

second. Children watch their parents phase from the time they come into this world and are taught that they, too, will be shifters."

Dane couldn't believe Rafael was proud of him or that he had called him *son*. He guessed being over five hundred years old earned him the right to call anyone whatever he wanted to. "Thank you. It is a lot to get used to. Jasper has tried to help, but I wanted to talk to my family first and find out if it was okay to speak freely about all this. Since they aren't around, I'm making that decision for myself. If Gargoyles aren't supposed to know about half-bloods, maybe the Gargoyles shouldn't be mixing things up with humans." Rafael flinched just the slightest at that.

"Here's what I know: Isabelle Sarantos is my sister, Caroline Wexler is my mother, and Jonas Montague is my father, biologically speaking. I was put up for adoption when I was a baby as were some of my other siblings. The older ones were sent to live in various countries around the world. Isabelle was the exception. She's the youngest, and Caroline didn't want to give her up, but something happened that caused Caroline to leave when Isabelle was young. I didn't catch the part as to why Isabelle thought Montague was dead. Caroline didn't tell me that she's my mother; I overheard her and Tessa talking about it. Isabelle was also kept in the dark about being a shifter. When I went to her for medical help, she couldn't figure out what was wrong with me and called Tessa in. What Isabelle didn't know was that Tessa was already watching me. When I started my transition, Tessa had to tell her the truth. Some of this they told me, some I overheard when they thought I was asleep.

"I don't blame Isabelle for not coming to me; she has her own demons to face. I do blame Caroline. How can a mother..."

Kaya reached across the island to place her hand on Dane's arm. A low growl came from Rafael's throat, and she quickly pulled her hand back. Talk about intense.

"Can I ask a question?" Dane had told himself he was going to find out everything. When Rafael nodded he asked, "Are you two living together?"

Rafael didn't hesitate. "Yes. Kaya is my mate, therefore she is my Queen. Your Queen."

"Come again?" Dane knew things would be strange but *Queen*? That would explain the jealous warning when Kaya touched him.

Kaya spoke up, "I know this is a lot to take in, but quite a bit happened while you were away. For whatever reason, the fates have decided that the Gargoyles can mate with humans, as you now know. It could be because the females of their kind are nearly extinct. For the bloodline to continue, the Gargoyles are now able to mate with humans and have children, just like Jonas and Caroline."

Rafael elaborated, "We didn't know this was possible until I met Kaya. The first time I spoke to her on the telephone, I felt the mate pull. I tasked one of my cousins with the job of finding out everything he could on the subject of mating with humans. That search led him to Isabelle, and in turn Tessa. I need you to tell us all you know on the subject."

"That's just it; I don't know anything about it. Any conversation I had with Isabelle was before I knew she was my sister, and that was pertaining to my diagnosis. When I was with Tessa and Caroline, I was trying to control my phasing. They really didn't tell me anything useful. Caroline did mention how the Unholy came to be." Dane told them about one of his older brothers, Gabriel, being used as a pawn by Gordon Flanagan. He had been found by some of Flanagan's men when he was going through his initial transition. The scientists took his blood and studied his DNA, somehow using both with the army they were

156

creating. When Gabriel was no longer needed, he was thrown into the river and presumed dead. "This is the reason some of the younger siblings and I were put up for adoption, for our safety. I'm sorry; if I had more information I would gladly give it to you. Even though Isabelle is Montague's daughter, Tessa seems to be the one with firsthand knowledge of the man."

"Yes, Nikolas said as much after he spoke with her." Rafael stood and rinsed his glass out in the sink before putting it in the dishwasher.

"Nikolas?" Dane had heard of Nikolas Stone and had seen his picture in the local newspaper.

"Nikolas is my cousin. You will meet him on Sunday if you come for what I've dubbed as family day. Priscilla makes a buffet breakfast. You can come and stay all day or just drop by when you feel like it. I have several brothers and cousins that live here in New Atlanta, and even the Clan members that aren't related that closely are welcome." Rafael told Dane a little about each of the Clan that lived in New Atlanta. "I consider all of the Clan family whether we are related by blood or not. You are now part of our family."

Dane nodded. "I would like that. Do they all live here with you? I mean this place is so big..." He was interrupted by a voice coming from the back door.

"Honey, I'm home!" Jasper came into the kitchen with that ever present grin stuck to his face. "Oh, hey partner. I didn't know you were going to be here." Jasper helped himself to a cookie before opening the refrigerator and grabbing a bottle. "Beer anyone?"

Twenty-Six

Tessa heated her sandwich in the microwave. While it was nuking, she called her mother. "Hey, Mom. Sophia just called. She received a cryptic message telling her that Sam and Monica have been abducted, and if she wants to see them alive, she would have to travel to Egypt. She was given an address, and the note said she would get more information upon her arrival."

"This was what I wanted to talk to you about when you visited. I was afraid something like this had happened. When I couldn't get in touch with Sam, your father started checking around. He can't prove it, but he believes that Alistair is causing another stir with regards to Jonas. Andrea, please tell Sophia not to go after them. This is more than likely a trap."

"Right. Like she isn't going to go after her parents. Do you honestly think if someone told me you and Dad had been taken that I'd sit on my ass and do nothing? Sophia loves both her parents, but if something happened to Sam while she did nothing to find him, it'd kill her. Besides, she's already gone; she called me from the airport. I am going to check on Lillian first thing in the morning, and then I'm going to go after Sophia."

"Andrea, no, you can't! It's too dangerous," her mom declared, with her father yelling in the background, "Here, let me talk to her." Tessa hung up the phone before she could get orders from her dad to stay put. Since she lived in the States, technically Rafael was her King. Xavier was King in Italy, but he liked to throw his crown around with her since he was her father. There was no way she would let Sophia go off to a foreign country alone.

Shifter blood kept Tessa from getting too drunk or having massive hangovers. The sandwich and glass of water helped clear the alcohol from her system and the fuzziness from her mind. She had a lot of planning to do. Knowing Gregor was lurking about didn't help. She needed to be as far away from him as possible, and going to Egypt was just the ticket out of town. With Sam missing and Ezekiel still away, Tessa decided to tell Lilly the truth about being a shifter. With no one to help her through the transition, she needed to know what to expect. Tessa would go to her stand in the Quarter first thing in the morning.

Tessa grabbed more water from the kitchen as she dialed Dane's number. She felt bad that she had left both him and Isabelle to their own devices so soon after transitioning, but there was only one of her. By the time Sophia was able to help, all the cousins would probably have changed. It was the cousins' kids that Sophia was going to watch. She was the only child of the half-bloods old enough to go through a transition, and so far she hadn't. That didn't mean she wouldn't. When Dane's phone went to voice mail, Tessa called Belle.

"Hello?"

"Hey Belle, I was calling to see how you're doing and when you are planning on returning to work."

"I'm doing really well. I have the phasing under control, but I'm getting restless staying at home. I had planned on going back to work tomorrow, but Gregor called and said he had to go out of town. I'm to wait until he gets back. Since I don't know when that will be, I am going to my own clinic and get some work done. I want to look through Jonas' notes to see if there's anything I can do to help the inmates that Henshaw tampered with."

"That sounds like a great plan. Listen, I wanted to let you know that Sophia isn't around." Tessa filled Belle in on the note, Sophia leaving for Egypt, and Tessa's plan to go after them all. "I'll be home tomorrow night, but only long enough to pack for the trip. Have you talked to Dane?"

"No, I tried calling, but it went directly to voicemail. I left him a message to call me."

159

"Same here. If you do talk to him, try to get a feel for where he is with the Gargoyles. We need to stay as tight-lipped as possible around them. I found out some more information about why your father was banished. Rafael's uncle was the one who instigated that. It seems he's humanphobic or whatever the word is."

"I think the word you're looking for is anthrophobic. And who is Rafael?"

Tessa was relieved Belle was talking and hadn't hung up on her. "Rafael is one of Gregor's brothers, but more importantly, King of the Gargoyles in the Americas. Technically, he is our King, but until the half-bloods are acknowledged by the Gargoyles, we will continue on as we have been. I have a feeling it won't be much longer until he wants us all under his rule. With Gregor knowing about us, I am certain he has already told the King."

"So, that Nikolas that came by, is he their brother?"

"No, he's a cousin. There are a slew of cousins in and around New Atlanta. I would have to ask Sophia for a list. She has been keeping up with that information since she was old enough to write. She probably knows more about the Gargoyles than most of them do. The other two brothers are Dante Di Pietro, who lives in New Atlanta, and Sinclair Stone, who lives out west."

"Why does this Dante go by a different name?"

"Beats me. Maybe one day you will get the chance to ask him yourself. I'm going to get off here and make my travel arrangements. It was really good talking to you, Belle."

"You too. See you when you get back." Belle disconnected on her end, and Tessa was glad her cousin was being inquisitive about her new world.

Gregor parked his rental in the paid lot across from the casino then walked east toward the river. The day was losing its light, and this was one of Gregor's favorite times of day. When the sun faded, giving way to the moon, the blood coursed through his veins. The cells that fabricated his being ignited, as if they knew night was growing closer. Gargoyles relished the dark, reveled in the lack of sun, giving them the opportunity to spread their wings and soar. The breeze off the Mississippi River tugged at his shirt tail and softy blew through his short hair. Gregor ran a beefy hand through his cropped cut.

This brought to mind a few hours earlier when Tessa ran her fingers through his hair just before she kissed him. Even if it was a kiss to fool Jacques Dupart into believing they were together, it had been one of the best kisses of his life. Tessa's mouth was crafted perfectly for his, and now that he had tasted her essence, no other woman would do. If he was truthful, he didn't want any other woman. The few he had on speed dial could be removed from his phone. Gregor was determined to make Tessa his, no matter how long it took.

Sitting on a bench, looking out over the water, Gregor pulled out his phone and deleted every woman who was listed for nothing more than fucking. After that was done, he called Dominic.

"Salut." The voice coming the line was definitely French.

"Hello yourself, Dominic. This is Gregor Stone."

"Ah, Gregor. What can I do for you?"

The sound of silverware being placed on a plate came through the airwaves. "If I caught you at a bad time, I can call back."

"No, I was just finishing my meal. What's up?"

"I am in New Orleans on personal business, and I wondered if I could meet with you about a little problem I have."

161

"Of course. Anything for the King's brother." Dominic wasn't being sarcastic. Rafael was a great King, and the leaders of the other Clans respected him and offered their services freely and eagerly.

"Excellent. How about eight a.m. at Jackson Square?"

"I will be there. I must say you have me intrigued." The grin in his voice was apparent over the phone.

"Yeah, well, as much as I would love to take care of this myself, I have a prison to tend to and just don't have the time. Thank you, Dom. I will see you in the morning." Both men said goodbye, and Gregor rose from the bench. He wanted to check out a certain bar before heading back to Tessa's for the night. He walked along the river a little farther then crossed the train tracks and headed west toward Ursulines Avenue.

Gregor had never spent any time in Louisiana. He'd never had a reason to, until now. He wanted to see what the allure was. Tourists filled the sidewalks along with street entertainers, drunks, and vagrants. Young people all dressed in the same drab clothes sat on the sidewalks, some playing instruments for spare change while others just sat and talked. One such young man was walking with a dog draped over his shoulders. People would ask about the dog, was he hurt or did he just like to be carried. Gregor was certain it was a ruse for the man to get attention as well as money.

Once he crossed over Bourbon Street, the crowds thinned out. The busiest road in the French Quarter seemed to be the barrier for tourists. It marked the edge of *let's take a look over here* and *I don't think we should venture over there*. Gregor did venture on, noting a few of the locals who lived past the famous street sitting on stoops, enjoying the night. Even though Halloween was a couple of days away, the air in the southern town was still warm and sticky.

Gregor's shifter ears picked up the noise coming from the bar on the next block. He didn't have a plan if he happened upon Tessa's ex-lover. He walked into the crowded room and scanned the patrons. As luck would have it, the man was nowhere to be seen. Gregor raised his voice over the noise and ordered a draft beer crafted at the local brewery. He gave the bartender a ten and told him to keep the change. Leaning against the crowded bar, he sipped his beer and looked around again. The customers could easily fit in at The Tavern. He finished his beer, and seeing no sign of Dupart or any nefarious deals being made, he headed back to his car.

The crowd had picked up even more as Gregor eased his way along the various streets that led to the river. Young boys wore flattened aluminum cans tied to the bottom of their shoes, tapping out a rhythm while another boy banged away with drums sticks on an overturned pickle bucket. A man dressed in a coconut shell bikini and a long blonde wig was strutting down the sidewalk as well as he could wearing five inch heels. Young women wearing nothing but body paint were walking in the middle of the street, stopping for pictures whenever asked. These sightings didn't disturb Gregor, but neither did they hold any appeal. Having lived over five hundred years, he had seen a lot of shit in his time. The only sight that held his interest at the moment was around five foot eight with long red hair.

Gregor found an empty church parking lot close to Tessa's house. He didn't see any signs posted stating overnight parking was prohibited. Getting his rental towed would be a pain in the ass. He locked the vehicle and took off walking. He wasn't the only one on the sidewalks. Even though it was late in the day, individuals were jogging, walking their dogs, strolling with their babies. He tried to avoid those with dogs since animals could sense he was something other than what he appeared to be. He couldn't

163

help glancing into a baby carriage as a young couple passed by. A tiny, round face with eyes as blue as his own stared back at him. The couple didn't hesitate to allow him to coo at their infant. It was a little disconcerting they weren't scared in the least. There was no fear coming from either of them. He ran a beefy finger along the fat jaw that was grinning at him then thanked the couple for allowing him that small pleasure.

Gregor wanted children. Always had. In the past, he tried not to think about kids, even though he built his home with the hope of one day filling it with children. Now that he knew Tessa was his mate, he couldn't help but thinking about little black haired boys and petite red haired girls running all over his cabin. If it were up to him, he would be building on additions to make room for more kids. He trusted when he finally got Tessa to see they were meant to be together, she would want a houseful, too. After all, she was the one who would be carrying and delivering the babies. Julian's background check into Tessa had come up lacking. He didn't know any more now than he had before. She or someone she knew was just as good as Julian with their computer skills. Tessa Blackmore was still a mystery. One he intended to crack.

As he closed in on her house, he scanned the streets for any sign of someone who shouldn't be there, someone who might be spying on Tessa for Jacques. He doubted the man was brave enough to stalk her himself knowing Gregor was there. At least he hoped not. Seeing no one lurking, he stealthily ascended the tree outside Tessa's window and settled in for the night.

Twenty-Seven

Tessa finished her coffee and helped Gladys clear the breakfast dishes. Gladys had drilled her about her handsome cousin, and Tessa had lied her ass off, making shit up on the fly. She had to laugh at her older neighbor gushing so hard on her mate. She knew how gorgeous he was, but to hear her old friend go on and on about him was quite amusing. They said their goodbyes, and Tessa hopped the streetcar on St. Charles and headed to the Quarter. She was excited about seeing Lilly. She just hoped they had enough privacy this early in the morning where they could speak freely.

The early morning crowd was sparse. Tessa loved this time of day in the city. She could enjoy her town without the throngs of drunk tourists marring her morning walk. Jackson Square came into view and Tessa felt her breath hitch. The fence along St. Peter Street where Lilly showcased her artwork was bare. The black iron bars were void of the colorful masterpieces that normally brightened the dull walkway. She knew she was early, but any other time she had visited, Lilly was already setting up her display.

One of the tarot readers, John, according to his sign, was unfolding his table and chair. Tessa decided to ask him about her cousin. "Excuse me, I'm looking for Lilly. Does she not set up along the fence anymore?"

"Good morning. Yes, she does, but she's been sick the last few days. She is supposed to be back today, but I guess she's running late. Would you like a reading while you wait?"

Tessa had never let anyone read her cards. It wasn't that she didn't believe in the occult, quite the opposite. She knew better than most there were those among the humans who were more than they appeared to be with just a glance.

She, herself, was much more than just a red haired biker. Sure, there were charlatans among those with true abilities, but the vibe coming from this man indicated he was the real deal. "No, thank you. I have a feeling I know exactly what my future holds for me, but I do appreciate the offer. I'm going to grab a coffee. Would you like one?"

"I would love one. Black, please." John smiled and continued setting up his area.

Tessa walked down around the square until she came to a lesser known beignet stand. Café du Monde was still thriving after almost two hundred years. Several other shops used the same recipe and served the same coffee, they just didn't have the historical name nailed to their door. By the time she had the coffees and returned, Lilly was setting up her artwork. She handed John his coffee, and as she did, he told her, "Listen to your heart. Your mind is reeling with doing the right thing, but always listen to your heart."

Tessa should have been shocked, but she wasn't. She just nodded and turned toward her cousin. "Lilly! I was afraid I had missed you. John said you have been sick. Are you all right now?"

Lilly's wavy blonde hair was tied back away from her face. Her long flowing skirt was as colorful as the artwork she painted. "Tabitha! Oh, it's so good to see you again." She set down the painting she was affixing to the fence and pulled Tessa in for a hug. Her usually sunny smile was absent from her beautiful face. Tessa knew it was more than sickness.

"Please tell me, are you okay? You look... different." Tessa stepped back but kept her free hand on Lilly's arm. Her eyes were pleading with her cousin to confide in her. Lilly didn't know they were related, she just thought of Tessa as a very good customer.

"I am still under the weather, that's all." Lilly was looking around as if she were searching for someone.

"What's going on? You seem very distracted"

"I... Tabitha, I..." She grabbed the picture she had been hanging and strung it along the fence. Tessa offered her the next picture to hang next to it. All of a sudden, Lilly stiffened. She jerked her head around as if she were expecting a monster to be behind her.

"What is it? What has you so spooked?" Tessa didn't know who or what to search for. The air held an unusual quality, now that she was concentrating. If she didn't know better, she would swear Gregor was close by. Shit. Had he followed her? Of fucking course he had. Scanning the area was futile. Her mate wasn't out in the open. "Is this about a man? Has someone hurt you?"

"No, it's nothing like that, I'm just... honestly, I don't know what I am. There are just some things that can't be explained, and if I told you, I doubt you would believe me anyway."

Holy shit, had Lilly transitioned? Was this why she was so freaked out? "I have a very open mind. As a matter of fact, I believe I know what has you so jittery. Something happened to you recently that you can't explain and you don't understand." Tessa lowered her voice. "You weren't sick, were you? You experienced something that you should have been prepared for. Dammit, I should have been here for you."

Lilly's brown eyes were wide now. She placed her hand over her mouth, and Tessa knew there were fangs behind her lips. "Lilly, I can explain everything. I should have told you a long time ago about what was going to happen, but the family thought it best to keep things quiet. I am so sorry you had to transition alone."

Tears were slowly leaking from her cousin's eyes. "So I'm not a freak?"

"No, gods, no. What you are is special. And my cousin. We have so much to talk about, but I don't want to do it out here in the open." Tessa wanted to tell Lilly all about the shifters, but she couldn't do it where prying ears could possibly overhear something.

"I can get John to watch my stuff. I really need your assurance that I'm not crazy." The tears had stopped, but wet eyes held a look of optimism.

"If there is somewhere private we can talk, it would be great."

"Help me hang the rest of the pictures, then we can go to my studio. It's not far from here." Tessa helped Lilly, and before long, they were crossing the street and entering a small art gallery.

Gregor was glad to be out of that damn tree. He would do anything to watch over Tessa even if it meant spending all night awake, wedged between two branches. It might have been close to impossible to follow her to the square if she hadn't told Gladys where she was going. With her taking the slow-ass trolley, he was able to get to his rental car and park in a paid lot before she arrived at her destination. He already had his coffee and was standing next to a column outside an old museum watching Tessa talk to a blonde. Dominic walked up behind him, "Which one of those two is causing your bad mood?"

Gregor took in the Louisiana Clan leader. There was only one way to describe Dominic Dubois: pirate. His long, black hair was tied at his nape with a leather thong. His white shirt with the thick, turned-up cuffs would have looked silly on a lesser man. His leather pants were tight, so tight Gregor wasn't sure how his junk was still functional. The tall, leather boots were authentic. The only thing missing was an eye patch. He grinned at the man, and they shook hands. "The redhead. She's my mate."

Dominic finally smiled. "It's a bloody good thing, because I plan to claim the blonde as my own."

Gregor eyed the women and sipped his coffee. "About that, you might want to wait."

"And why's that?" Dominic stood next to Gregor as the women spoke softly to each other.

"Because the fates have decided we can mate with humans. If you claim this one and your mate happens along later, what will you do then? Break her heart?" Gregor inclined his head toward Lilly.

"Ah, that's what I've been experiencing. I do not think I will have to break anyone's heart, my brother. I do believe she is my intended."

Gregor took his eyes off the women. "The blonde's your mate?"

"Aye, I do believe she is. A long time ago, it was foretold to me by a gypsy that my mate would be a fair-haired witch. Now that you have told me we can mate with humans, I have faith Lilly is she. I have had stirrings for the lass. What about you? How do you know the redhead is your mate?" Dom took a drink of his own coffee.

"It's a long story, but she admitted she is my mate. The short of it is, she is a half-blood; her father is a Gargoyle, and her mother is human. For some fucked up reason, she won't have anything to do with me because I'm full-blooded. I am still trying to get to the bottom of that one. When we're together, the mate bond makes things so fucking good, then she remembers who I am and kicks me to the godsdamn curb. It is getting annoying. A couple of nights ago she scared the shit out of me, and I phased with no choice. The beast took over, and there I was, wings and all."

Dominic laughed. "Yes, I can imagine that happening with my Lillian. I would rather die than to see one strand of her fair hair harmed. Tell me, do you feel the need to constantly be around her? To touch her in some way?"

"It's maddening, but yeah, I do." Lilly jerked her head in their direction, and Tessa looked around as well. "I do believe they have caught our scent." Gregor pointed his cup in the women's direction. "I wonder what has Lillian so upset."

"I do not know, but I intend to find out. She has not been at her spot by the fence in several days. I couldn't just barge into her home and demand to take care of her, now could I?"

"You could, but you might've gotten a surprise, like a naked man in her bed."

Dom growled at Gregor. "Whoa, man. I was just making a statement. Don't go for the sword."

"Why is it I have never heard of a half-blood or the fact Goyles are mating with humans?" Dominic crossed his arms over his chest.

"We just found out about it ourselves. A few weeks back, Rafael was being framed for a multiple homicide. The police chief, who was investigating the murders, happened to be his mate. He couldn't believe it might be possible, so he had Nikolas search the archives. When he came up empty, Nik went to the public library. Long story short, he found a journal written by a Gargoyle who has been posing as human. It appeared to be a work of fiction until Nik actually read it. It was a diary detailing the Goyle's mating with a human and being ostracized for it.

"We have since found the Gargoyle's daughter. She is the current physician at the prison and my mate's cousin. She was at work when she began her transition. My mate is called a watcher. She helps the half-bloods go through their initial change. Dom, I think I know where Lillian was these past few days. I'm pretty sure being around you set off her transition."

"Transition? What makes you think she's a shifter?" Dominic asked skeptically.

"Because the change is triggered when the half-bloods meet their mate. At least that's what I was told. I think my mate has been watching Lillian all this time, knowing she would eventually transition."

"So you think Lillian is one of these half-bloods?"

"If my gut is right, yes, and those two are related," Gregor indicated their women by inclining his head.

Dominic was silent. Gregor got it. The knowledge that mating was possible was a stab through the heart. If this Lillian happened to be a half-blood, that meant she was more than likely kin to Tessa. However, he didn't have time to hold Dom's hand while he digested the information. He needed to get down to business. "What do you know about Jacques Dupart?"

Dominic drank the last of his coffee, tossing the empty cup in a nearby trash receptacle. "He owns a bar on Ursulines that serves as a front for his little side business. And by little, I mean his drug slash arms empire."

"Why has nothing been done to stop him?" Gregor wasn't accusing Dom, not yet. Most of the Gargoyles kept out of human business unless it was absolutely necessary.

"You know the answer to that question, Brother. We do not step in unless we absolutely have to. What's this about?" Dominic's eyes were trained on Lillian who was now walking away from her art stand with Tessa in tow. Gregor didn't answer the question until the women were out of sight.

"Somehow my mate got involved with him. She travels the world posing as an archaeologist while she is really keeping an eye on the half-bloods. He put her in his bed to get her married to his world. She broke things off, but it seems he is having a hard time with the word *no*."

"And just what does that have to do with me? Like I said, you know we don't get involved unless someone is in danger. Do you think he's a threat to Tabitha?"

Gregor cocked an eyebrow. "How do you know her name?"

"I make it my business to know about anyone that comes into contact with Lillian on more than one occasion. Tabitha has purchased several paintings from her, but comes by often enough just to chat. Question, if she's your mate, why is she in bed with another man?"

The dregs of coffee were no longer sitting well with Gregor. He tossed the cup into the garbage. "She wants nothing to do with me, so mated or not, she has been living her life without me in it. I intend to rectify that aspect of our relationship and soon. For now, all I can do is vow to keep her safe. I cannot do that here since I run the prison, so I am asking you to step in. Do what you can to get Dupart off the street."

"The local police have been trying to pin him down for years. What makes you think I can do it when they can't?"

"Because they don't have Julian. I have already spoken to my cousin, and he is at your disposal. Any information you need, he can get it. Here's his cell phone number." Gregor handed Dom a business card. "I'm not asking as a service to the King, I'm asking as a favor for myself. I will owe you one. Hell, you get Dupart locked up, I'll owe you however many you ask for."

Dominic grinned, "You have a deal. The Unholy have been too quiet for too long. I would love to have something to fill my time other than stalking Lilly. Now that it's probable she's my mate, I don't have to keep my distance, do I?" Dom had the same hopeful look in his eyes that Gregor knew all too well from looking in the mirror.

"No, you don't," Gregor said as the mate bond alerted them both to their women. Across the street, the door to the art gallery opened, and Tessa and Lilly exited the building together, arm in arm. "Now's your chance."

Twenty-Eight

Dante was examining the latest redhead victim when his cell phone rang. He pulled his latex gloves off and answered. "Yo."

Deacon was on the other end. "Hey, Dante, we have an incident and since Dr. Sarantos is at home, Gregor told me to call you. One of the inmates had a seizure. We got him stabilized, but I thought you should know."

"Do you know if he has a history of epilepsy?" Dante was washing his hands preparing to leave.

"No. I was going to look through the doc's files, but her door is locked."

"Okay, I will call her before heading that way. Just keep the patient calm, and strap him down if you have to."

Dante hung up. When Gregor said he was going out of town, he had given Dante Isabelle's number for emergencies such as this. He pulled up her phone number then hit send. "Hello?" He should have been expecting the gut check. Dante already suspected she was his mate. Now that her voice was flowing through the line, he was certain. "Hello? Who's there?"

"Dr. Sarantos, I apologize for the delay. This is Dante Di Pietro, Gregor's brother. He gave me your number in case there was an incident at the Pen. I am sorry to say there is, indeed, need of my assistance with an inmate. The reason I am calling is to find out if you have any anticonvulsants on hand in the clinic. One of the inmates has had a seizure."

"Oh, do you need me to take care of it? I don't mind driving out there if you're busy." Sunshine. Her voice felt like sunshine on a cold day washing over his body.

"No, that isn't necessary. If you will confirm the availability of the drug, I will be on my way."

"Yes, there were several different doses in the cabinet. I assume you have a key?" Sunshine was cooling off a bit.

"I do have a key. Under normal circumstances, I would not step in when you are perfectly capable of doing the job you were hired to do. However, when my brother tasks me with keeping you away from the Pen during his absence, I have no choice but to comply. Personally, I have to agree with him. Without him there to keep you safe, I prefer you stay where you are. Now, I am needed, so I will say thank you and goodbye."

Dante hung up before she could impart any more discomfort to his slowly collapsing self-control. He gripped the bridge of his nose with a thumb and forefinger, willing himself to calm the fuck down. How in the gods' names could a voice cause his libido to shift into high gear? Rafael hadn't been lying.

He found Trevor and told him where he was going. The ride from the morgue didn't take too long this early in the morning. He pulled up to the back door and headed directly to the clinic. Deacon met him and informed him there had been no further seizures. Dante nodded. What's his name? I want to go through his medical file." When Deacon gave him the inmate's name, he said, "I'll be right back."

Dante pulled his keys out of his pants pocket and found the one that would unlock Isabelle's office. As soon as Dante stepped through the door, he felt it. He was going to lose his breakfast. Instead of backing out of the room, he steeled himself. Breathing in deeply, he filled his lungs and sinuses with the glorious scent that was all Isabelle. He continued taking his mate's essence into his body until he could withstand being in the room without passing out. He opened the file cabinet and quickly found the patient's folder. He scanned Dr. Henshaw's notes, noticing there were no previous illnesses. What he did find was that

175

Henshaw had given the patient several injections of...holy fuck. Henshaw was dosing the inmate with Unholy blood. This wasn't good. Wasn't good at all. Shit, he needed to talk to Rafael. He returned to the clinic, unlocked the medicine cabinet and found the strongest dose of anticonvulsant he could find. After pumping a syringe-full into the patient, he observed the inmate for half an hour. Dante told Deacon, "Keep him strapped down for now."

Dante went back to Isabelle's office. Inmate files were stacked neatly on her desk. He sat down in her chair and opened the first one. He wasn't shocked to find the same type of notes written in the chart. He laid it aside and opened the next one. Every file Dante opened had the same alarming information. What had Henshaw been up to? Was he trying to create his own Unholy by injecting their blood into healthy patients? That must have been why he was in the Basement when he let the Unholy get loose a couple of weeks ago. If Isabelle had read through these files, she knew what the man had been about. Had she mentioned it to Gregor? Dante didn't know who to talk to first, Isabelle or Rafael. Dammit.

He owed it to Rafael to inform him of what had been going on, but he owed it to his mate to find out her side of the story before he went to his brother. He once again called Isabelle.

"Dr. Di Pietro, is everything okay? Were you able to find the medications?" Isabelle calling him by his surname was somewhat disheartening. Did she not feel the connection? What if she felt it but didn't want him for a mate? Tessa didn't want anything to do with Gregor. Had she convinced Isabelle that all Gargoyles were bad?

"Yes, Isabelle. I found the medication, and he is resting now. That's not why I'm calling. I would like to come see you and chat about some of the inmates, if you don't mind."

"Come see me?" His shifter hearing picked up her heartbeat. It was speeding, but not in the way it would if she were aroused. No, she was scared.

"I assure you, I mean you no harm, Isabelle. I also want to check on you. I know you recently transitioned, and since Tessa isn't around, I thought..."

"Oh, well then, thank you. Yes, I would like the company. Where did you want to meet?"

"Once I check in on the inmate and feel certain he will have no further episodes, I will be headed your way. I can come by your home, if that's convenient." Dante was interested in seeing what type of home she owned. Gregor had already been there, and Dante felt a tinge of jealousy. Not at his brother. He knew Gregor had no design on Isabelle other than as a boss. No, Dante wanted to be the only man to enter Isabelle's home. Was it a modest home since she lived alone, or was it posh and ostentatious?

"I'm not home right now, but I can meet you there in about half an hour. Will that be sufficient travel time?"

"You're not home? Where are you? I mean, sorry. What I meant was I can come to you, if that is more convenient." *Dammit, calm yourself. Don't scare her any more than she already is.*

"Oh, well that would be nice. I am at my clinic. It's over on..."

"I know where it is. I will be there in thirty minutes."

Dante gave Deacon instructions regarding the inmate's care. He was going to talk to Isabelle then come back to relieve Deacon from watching the man.

Thirty minutes proved to be more than sufficient travel time. Dante was about to knock on the door to the clinic when it was pulled open. Had he not filled his being with her scent earlier, he might have fallen to his knees. His mate was a dark-haired beauty with bright, chocolate eyes. "You must be Dr. Di Pietro. I see the family resemblance."

She stepped back, allowing him passage into the waiting area.

"I am, but please, call me Dante. You make me feel old addressing me by my title."

"My apologies. But you are old, are you not? You're a Gargoyle." Isabelle was looking at him clinically, like she would a sample under a microscope.

Dante's face was impassive. "I am 563. I guess to you I *am* old. For a Gargoyle, I am but a babe."

Isabelle's brown eyes were taking in his entire six-foot-four frame. He put her at approximately five-seven. If she were lying down, he would better be able to ascertain her height. Most bodies he observed were in the supine position. It took him a few seconds to realize her eyes were wide and her heartbeat was once again erratic.

"I need to ask you a question, if that's all right," she stated shyly.

"Of course. What would you like to know?"

"Have you visited the Pen any time in the last week, other than today?" He could see the wheels turning behind her beautiful eyes. She was wondering if he was her mate.

"Yes, I have. Why do you ask?" He wanted to tell her the truth, but he was afraid. She was gorgeous and he was... well, he was just Dante.

"It's just that...Tessa said I...what I mean is...why do you use the last name Di Pietro when your brothers go by Stone?"

Dante's heart sunk. Was she scared he was her mate? If so, he would just have to accept the rejection should she determine him to be less than suitable. "I use our family surname to separate myself from the others. Too many Stones in one location makes it harder to keep up the charade that we are not related. Now, may I ask you something?"

"Yes, of course, but why don't we have a seat. May I offer you something to drink?" Dante had to wonder if she was this proper all the time. He had witnessed the whirlwind that was Tessa when he and Gregor went to The Tavern. He couldn't see Isabelle in a biker bar setting, but he was all right with that. At present, she was dressed in a pair of dress slacks and a short-sleeved sweater that accentuated her figure nicely.

"No, thank you."

Isabelle cocked her head to the side and asked, "No, you don't want to have a seat, or no, you don't want a drink?"

His usually expressionless face softened for her. Unconsciously, he ran his index finger down her cheek. "I would love to have a seat, but I do not require a drink." Isabelle shivered under his touch. Her pupil's dilated, and her breathing hitched. Fuck, the mate pull was affecting her.

They sat in adjacent chairs, neither one leaning back. Their knees were inches apart. "You had a question?" She asked him breathlessly.

"How do you feel about Gargoyles?" He, Dante Di Pietro, was a chicken shit.

"I, well, uh, I..." She nervously tucked a strand of hair behind her ear.

"Never mind. I probably don't want to know the answer anyway. Why don't we talk about the inmates?"

"No, I'd rather talk about you. Honestly, I'm just a little nervous. You have to understand, until a couple of weeks ago, I wasn't aware Gargoyles even exist. Imagine my surprise when I found out I am half Gargoyle. I was privy to the information for all of a few hours when I found out my father, whom I thought was dead, is really alive. I saw a brother I didn't know I had transition right before my eyes. I ran into my mother whom I haven't seen in approximately twenty years, *and* she looks my age. *Then*, I myself begin transitioning in front of your brother who is supposed to be the bad guy. I was told I shouldn't talk to Gregor, or you, because your kind ostracized one of their own when he fell in love. So when you ask how I feel about Gargoyles, my answer would have to be conflicted."

"Who told you not to talk to me? Your father?" Dante would ring Jonas Montague's fucking neck if he attempted to keep them apart.

"No, Tessa did. She has her reasons. I'm just not certain they are valid."

"What do you mean?" He didn't want to have to tell Gregor to put a muzzle on his mate, but he would if she interfered.

"Tessa was keeping the family secrets so the Gargoyles wouldn't find out about us: the half-bloods. Now the secret is out of the bag."

"So now that the secret is out, and you know Tessa is mated to a Gargoyle, what are your opinions on the matter? You do know Gregor is her mate, do you not?" Dante should just come out and ask her. Again, chicken shit.

Isabelle nodded, "I guess it's safe for them since she isn't merely a human. I mean, if they have children, the offspring will have three-quarters shifter blood, right? So the man who is so prejudiced against humans might back off and leave them alone."

"What are you talking about? What man?" Dante was positive this conversation just went from bad to worse.

"Some uncle of the King's. I didn't catch his name since Tessa was in a hurry to make her travel arrangements."

Holy shit. No way. No fucking way. Dante needed to call Gregor and have him interrogate his woman. "So if you were to find out your mate is a Gargoyle, would you be okay with that?"

Isabelle's hands twisted in her lap. Dante could hear her heartbeat speeding up. He didn't want to make her nervous, he just wanted to know if he had a snowball's chance in hell of finding happiness.

"Are you suggesting... you and I are...? I don't really have a choice, do I? Not that I have anything against you. I mean, I'm half Gargoyle after all. I just don't understand how everyone is on board with the fates deciding who we are supposed to spend our life with. Look at Gregor and Tessa. She has been fighting the bond for three years. And you, you deserve someone who isn't plain or..."

Dante couldn't believe she was speaking of herself that way. "Isabelle, you are one of the most beautiful women I have ever met in my very long life. I'm not just saying that because of the bond either."

Isabelle continued ringing her hands, so he took a chance and held them between his own. She flashed her eyes up to his. He continued, "I am unsure about the whole mate bond as well. Instead of jumping in with both feet, we can pretend it isn't there, or if you like, we can take it slow and see how it goes." Dante was giving her time to adjust. It would crush him if she didn't want to at least explore the possibility of being together.

Isabelle bit her bottom lip while thinking of how to respond. He really wished she wouldn't do that. It only drew attention to her mouth, and her mouth was beautiful. Full red lips were enticing enough without her white teeth making indentions in the lower one. She finally squeezed his hands and replied, "I think I would like taking it slow. Honestly, I've been in love before. At least I thought it was love. It could have been a young girl's infatuation with a confident, older man. When I married Alexi, I thought it was for life. It wasn't. I don't want to screw this up, but at the same time, I don't want to withhold the relationship destined to be your one and only. Does that make sense?"

Dante hated hearing about her love for another man. While he didn't want Isabelle to hurt in any way, he was glad the other man was dead, else he might have to take care of that himself. When Nikolas was searching for the daughter of Jonas Montague, he had found out the tragic story behind her husband's demise. "Yes, it makes sense. I know I'm not much to look at, and I'm sure your late husband was probably very handsome. Please don't lie to me just to spare my feelings, and definitely don't pursue our relationship out of a sense of duty. I've been alone over five hundred years. I can handle going the rest of my life without my mate if she doesn't find me worthy."

Isabelle surprised him when she leaned in and placed her lips to his. It was a simple, chaste kiss, but it was heaven none the less. "You are definitely worthy," she whispered against his mouth.

Trying not to think about the tingle on his lips, he told her, "I will give you some space until you are settled into your new job and your new body. I will call you and ask you for a date, and we will proceed as any other couple would. If you need to see me or just want to talk to me before that time, please give me a call."

Isabelle gave him a small smile and nodded. "Now, about those inmates."

Twenty-Nine

Gregor was feeling empty. He had called Tessa, offering to fly her back to New Atlanta. When she declined, he asked that she at least let him drive her to the airport. Again she turned him down. She told him to move on with his life and find someone else to fulfil his time as well as his bed. Then she hung up. Being a shifter herself, she knew it didn't work that way. Maybe she could find another man to take to bed, but he would not give up. It would kill him to watch her be with someone else, but he would never take another woman to his bed, not while there was still a chance with his mate.

He didn't bother going home for a uniform before he headed to the Pen. As soon as he arrived, he called Deacon to his office for a report. Nothing too traumatic had happened, and Dante's patient was back in his cell. Now that Gregor was back in town, he would call Isabelle and have her return to work as soon as she was ready. The one thing of interest that happened was Vincent Alexander had changed his note. Now, instead of it reading *cigarette,* it read *Isabelle.* There was no way Gregor would allow Alexander anywhere near Isabelle without several shifters being right there with her. If she could get any useful information out of him, he was willing to try it. At least once.

Deacon left the office to make his rounds, and Gregor slumped down in his chair with his head leaned back, eyes closed. His thoughts wouldn't quieten. The events of New Orleans played in his mind like a movie on repeat. His desk phone rang several times before he relented and answered. "Stone."

"Warden Stone, this is Elizabeth Flanagan. If you care at all for my daughter, you will stop her from going to Egypt." The line went dead, and the dial tone buzzed in his ear. Gregor looked at the receiver like it was a snake.

183

"Fuck. FUCK!" He slammed the receiver down in its cradle and ran his hand through his hair.

He called Deacon on his radio and told him he was in charge again; Gregor had an emergency. Then he called Isabelle. She didn't answer her home phone so he called her cell. "Hello?"

"Isabelle, it's Gregor. I need Tessa's address." He was already in his Hummer, headed out the gate.

"Is everything okay?" Isabelle was going to protect Tessa, he knew it.

"No, everything is not okay. I have to stop her from leaving the country. Where does she live?"

"Gregor, I don't know if I should..." She was stopped by another voice in the background. Was that Dante? "Oh, okay, I will text it to you. But Gregor, she really does need to go to Egypt. One of our cousins is in trouble."

"I will work that out with Tessa. Thank you, Isabelle."

If someone was in trouble, his mate was not the cavalry. They could find someone else to ride in and save the day. His cell phone pinged with a text message from Isabelle. Once he had the address, Gregor put the pedal down. He arrived at Tessa's home in record time. He angled out of the Hummer and strode to the front door. Calming himself, he used his senses to check the area. The shower was running, and Tessa was singing.

Even though the house sat back off the road, he didn't take a chance someone could see him picking the locks. He stole his way to the back door, and luckily, the alarm was not set. He would have to speak to Tessa about that. After a quick job on the lock, he let himself in. He looked around Tessa's house. It was much larger than he expected. The family must pay her well for her to have this home as well as the one in New Orleans. The furnishings were comfortable. Photographs lined the walls. Pictures of exotic locations as well as random people were scattered throughout. Not one of the pictures included her though. He sat down in a chair in the living room admiring the stone hearth. It reminded him of a smaller version of his own fireplace. He sat back and enjoyed the tunes Tessa was singing with a radio. His mate had a decent voice. The water turned off. Gregor willed himself to stay calm.

Tessa walked out of the bathroom, wrapped in a towel. She paused, sensing someone in her house. As she rounded the corner to the living room she shrieked, "What the FUCK are you doing here?" Gregor was sitting in her recliner, ankle crossed over his knee. "Being an officer of the law, you should know the meaning of breaking and entering!"

"The alarm wasn't on," Gregor said nonchalantly staring at the unlit fireplace.

"Bullshit. I locked the doors and set the security. What are you doing here?" She seriously didn't want to know the answer.

"I came to ask you about bonding. You seem to be the expert on the subject."

"You have five seconds to clear out, Stone." Tessa hitched the towel higher around her breasts.

"Or what? You gonna kick me out?"

"No, I'm gonna call the police. See how the Chief feels about her mate's brother breaking the law."

"Go ahead and call her. While you have her on the phone, tell her what you know about humans mating with Gargoyles."

"I'm going to put on some clothes, if you don't mind."

"Be my guest." Gregor went back to staring at the fireplace.

185

"Be my guest," Tessa mumbled as she disappeared into her bedroom. She dropped the towel as she pulled open her dresser drawers, looking for something, anything to cover her body. *Son of a fucking bitch. She'd teach him.*

"911, what's your emergency?"

"This is Tessa Blackmore. There's an intruder in my house."

"What's your address Miss Blackmore?" Before Tessa could respond, a roar came from behind her.

"What the fuck do you think you're doing?" Gregor was coming at her, fully phased. His massive wings filled up her room.

"Proving a point." Tessa forgot she was naked. Gregor's eyes scanned her body. His nostrils were flaring and his chest heaving. *Oh shit. He's feeling the mate pull.*

"I'm sorry, there's no intruder. It's just my husband." Tessa hung up and threw the phone on the bed.

"Why aren't you screaming?" Gregor had his head cocked, frowning.

"It's not like I've never seen a Gargoyle, and besides, I don't scream."

He laughed, "I bet I can make you scream."

Tessa rolled her eyes. "You need to get out of here and let me put some clothes on." He wasn't backing up. No, he was inching forward. "Stone, listen to me. Phase back. You don't want to do this, not now."

He wasn't changing. She knew she smelled too good to him. She opened the night stand drawer and pulled out her gun. "Stop, Stone. Don't make me shoot you."

"You won't shoot me, Red." He took a couple more steps in her direction.

Fuck this. She cocked the hammer and aimed at his meaty thigh. "Not one more step."

Gregor didn't bat an eyelash. He lunged for Tessa and the gun went off.

"Fucking hell, you shot me!" Gregor was staring at the scratch on his leg. "You fucking shot me!"

"I told you to stop. Maybe next time you'll listen." She put the gun back in the night stand and turned toward the closet. At least she could put on her robe. She didn't make it two steps before she felt herself being hurled through the air, landing on her back on the bed. Gregor was on her, his powerful body keeping hers in place, strong hands holding her arms above her head. His claws and wings were gone but his fangs, those were front and center. Her eyes focused on his but she could see the fangs threatening in her peripheral vision.

"You shot me, Red. What should I do about that?" Gregor's hard cock was pressing against her bare pussy. His shredded cotton shirt was rubbing against her nipples as he moved over her. His breath was in her ear as he scraped a fang along her chin, down her neck, landing on her shoulder.

"I think you should get off." Tessa squirmed under him, not sure if she was trying to push his big body off hers or get a little friction going.

"Oh, I'll get off all right, but not before you do." He released her hands as he kissed her shoulder then slid down her body taking a stiff nipple into his mouth. He flicked the bud with his tongue then sucked on it causing fire to shoot through Tessa's body. He nicked her skin with his fangs. The pain was sharp, but at the same time so very sensual. He licked the drop of blood he'd drawn before he continued down her stomach, stopping to take in the tattoo above her hip bone. If he lingered long enough, he just might figure it out. He obviously had other things on his mind, because he moved farther down until his face was between her now spread thighs. She really should have him in a leg lock, not opening farther for him. Damn mating pull. Her body was fighting with her brain. It knew the male on top of her belonged there, even if her head was telling her hell no.

187

The first swipe of his tongue on her clit had her fangs coming out. "Stop."

The second flick in her wet folds had her claws bursting forth. "You need to stop." Her pleas were weak, even to her own ears. Her hips pushing up into his face told him her words were lies.

The nip of skin on the inside of her thigh had her ready to throw him on his back and fuck him into oblivion. There was no way she could say no to this man. Gregor licked her folds again then inserted a thick finger, plunging in then retreating, hitting her g-spot on the way out. He added a second one then finger fucked her while he tortured her clit with his tongue. Tessa's claws found purchase in her bedding while her body writhed under Gregor's face, wanting more.

"More, oh gods, I need more." Her climax was so close. He fucked her faster, harder. His tongue gave way to his mouth as he sucked her clit hard. With his free hand, he grabbed a fistful of her long red hair and pulled. That was the catalyst she needed to finally come apart. The sparks shooting from her core matched those she saw behind closed eyes. Gregor was right. She screamed.

If she had not been somewhere else mentally, she would have heard the car pull up in the drive. As it were, she was oblivious to the person moving through her house until she heard, "Freeze. Don't move."

She felt Gregor stiffen as the cop drew back the hammer on his gun. Tessa quickly phased back, hoping the officer hadn't seen her claws.

"Son of a bitch. You wanna get the fuck out of here so she can put some clothes on?" Gregor was talking to the cop, but his eyes were on her as he slid his body up hers to shield her nakedness from the other man.

The cop laughed, "Yeah, I'll give you two a minute." Why the hell was he laughing?

She expected Gregor to move off the bed. Instead he pushed her hair away from her face and kissed her softly. *Well fuck.*

Merrick ignored the ringing phone. The woman lying under him was too delectable to stop fucking. Red hair was splayed across white pillows; the contrast was almost blinding. Her wrists were bound with rope, and her arms were stretched over her head, putting her breasts on full display. Her creamy smooth skin was taunting him. There was not one blemish on her anywhere. No birthmark, no freckle, no tattoo, nothing. He needed to rectify that.

So far, he had been fairly gentle. Her moans filled the air as he thrust in and out of her wet pussy. When he pulled his cock out, her green eyes widened. He decided for his next trick she would need to be completely immobile. He grabbed more rope and bound her ankles tightly to the bed. When she started to complain, he rolled up an old t-shirt and gagged her mouth. Even though they were far away from civilization, he wasn't taking any chances.

Merrick caressed the pale skin but offered no words of comfort or accolades of beauty. No, this was the part he enjoyed the most. When a woman who had so easily offered her body to a stranger figured out she had fucked up. When the fear shone brightly in those green eyes, and she pissed herself knowing she was going to die. That was the biggest turn on Merrick had ever known.

He climbed back onto the bed and situated himself between her legs, licking her bare mound, sucking on her clit. Her body was betraying her. The pleasure overrode the pain and the fright, up until that moment she realized what was happening. Then, it was too late. He sucked on the tender flesh at the juncture of her thigh and cunt. He pulled the blood to the surface, the skin turning red then purple. As she wiggled and squirmed as best she could while being tied up, he marked a colorful path up her white skin until he got to her neck. He didn't bother lubing the condom. He thrust his cock into her still wet pussy. As with the other victims, he wrapped his large hand around her small neck and squeezed. As his orgasm neared, he gripped harder. Her life leaving her body was simultaneous with his seed leaving his. As the woman gasped her last breath, Merrick expelled his last stream of cum.

Needing to remove the smell of sex from his body, Merrick took a quick shower. As he turned the water off, he heard his phone ringing again. He wrapped a towel around his hips and looked at the caller I.D. *Fuck.*

"Mr. Flanagan, what can I do for you?" Gordon Flanagan rarely called unless he was pissed.

"You can tell me why you haven't flushed her out."

"Sir, I have another body ready to dump. If she doesn't come forward after this one, I will up my game. I was thinking I need to branch out to surrounding states."

"My patience is wearing thin." The phone disconnected. Merrick knew going outside Flanagan's game plan was risky, but his daughter wasn't taking the bait. For all he knew, she wasn't even in New Atlanta. An idea had formed while he was in the shower. He opened his duffle and pulled out a hunting knife. Before cutting the ropes loose from the bed, Merrick decided to leave a different type of calling card.

Thirty

"What the fuck are you doing here, Jenkins?" Gregor knew Jasper played for the other team, but gay or not, he didn't want anyone seeing Tessa naked.

"That's Detective Jenkins to you, and I'm answering a 911 break-in call."

"Since when do detectives answer those types of calls?" Gregor walked into the kitchen, removing his shredded shirt. He stopped just inside the doorway with his back to the hall. He was pissed at himself for not hearing Jasper come into the house. Gregor couldn't say anything to Tessa about not setting the alarm. He hadn't even locked the fucking door.

"Since I was in the vicinity. It's a good thing I did, too, considering the fangs were out. Seriously, I wouldn't want sharp teeth so close to my junk."

"You couldn't see my fangs."

"No, but I could see hers." He was pointing at Tessa who had just walked into the room, now fully clothed.

Gregor opened his mouth, but Tessa cut him off. "Out. Both of you out, now."

"I'm not going anywhere until I get some answers. Jenkins, I'll see you at the manor." Jasper grinned then gave him a two-fingered salute.

Before he could reach the door, his cell phone rang. "Jenkins. Fuck, where? I'm on my way." His shit-eating grin was gone. He pointed at Tessa, "You need to watch yourself."

Gregor waited until Jasper was pulling out of the driveway before speaking. He was pretty sure another redhead had just been found. He needed to lighten the mood, not darken it. "You taste so fucking good." He ran his tongue over his lips, savoring the last bit of her juices.

Tessa rolled her eyes at him and leaned against the kitchen island. "What do I have to do to get you to leave? I can't bully you out; you're a bigger bully. I can't shoot you; it doesn't penetrate. I can't tell you I hate you; you're too pig-headed to believe any woman wouldn't fall down at your feet worshiping at the Stone altar."

Gods, did she really hate him? The pain he felt earlier in his heart just increased a hundred-fold. "You can give me some answers. You tell me what I want to know, and then I'll go."

"Stone, I don't have time for your games or your questions."

"Then make time. It seems you are the all-knowing when it comes to bonding. How is that? How did you, Tessa-Trixie-Tabitha-Andrea-Flanagan-Blackmore become the mating Dalai Lama?"

"Wow, I'm impressed. How long did you spend practicing that one? You know what? Ask me your questions. The sooner I answer, the sooner I can be alone." She jumped up on the island, crossing her ankles. "What's your first question?"

"Do you really hate me?" Gregor shouldn't let her know she was getting to him. He shouldn't care as much as he did, but she was crushing his heart.

"No, I don't hate you. I just don't like you very much. Next question." She leaned back on her hands, her breasts jutting out in front of her.

"Are you going out of town again?"

"Yes, next."

"Where are you going this time?"

"I don't see how it's any of your business, but to speed this shit along, I'm going to Egypt. One of the other watchers has gone missing. His daughter has set out to find him, and she has no experience in that sort of thing. I'm the only one who can go after her and keep her safe."

192

"Who's supposed to keep *you* safe?" Gregor knew she wouldn't allow it, but he was going to either go with her, or at the least, follow her.

"I've been doing this a long time now. I don't need anyone watching my back." Her beautiful green eyes were dull. She truly believed she was alone in all this.

"Who is your father?"

She flinched. "Not up for discussion. I thought you wanted to know about mating."

"Okay, if Jonas was ostracized for mating with a human, why didn't he change his name? I mean, yeah, he modernized it, but he's been hiding out for hundreds of years. Why not change to an alias like you have?"

"My aliases are to keep Flanagan from finding me. Society believes Jonas to be dead. If the Gargoyles want to find him, they will, no matter what he calls himself."

"How many humans have mated with Goyles?"

"Honestly? I don't know the exact number. In our family the only ones I am certain of are Jonas and my father. If Rafael has mated with the chief, that would be three. As far as the half-bloods, I'm guessing around twelve." Tessa shifted so she was no longer leaning on her arms. Gregor was glad. While he might be an ass man, any part of his mate turned him on.

"How many children does Jonas have?"

"Seventeen. Well, sixteen now." Tessa hopped down and went to the refrigerator, pulling out two beers. She unscrewed the top off both and handed him one. This was getting to be a habit.

"Why sixteen? Do half-bloods die the same way Gargoyles do?"

"Because one was killed before he transitioned." Hmm, that was a conversation for another time.

"How many siblings do you have?"

"Just Tamian. My mother wanted more children, but my father wouldn't hear of it. She is going to remain young forever, and he will not risk her having another child."

"What do you mean remain young forever?"

"Just like the Gargoyles stop aging, when a human mates with a full-blood and has a child, the aging process stops. My mom looks as young as I do. As a matter of fact, we could almost pass for twins."

"Interesting. Are there any other side effects of the mating process?"

"None that we're aware of." Tessa leaned a hip against the counter and drank her beer, waiting on the next question.

"What happens when the half-bloods have children? Do those children shift as well?"

"We don't know yet; we are still waiting to find out. Now, I've answered your questions. I would like for you to go."

"One more question." Gregor knew the answer before he asked, but what the hell.

"What?" Her annoyed look was back.

"Will you have dinner with me?"

It took her almost a full minute to answer. "On one condition."

"Anything." He would promise her the moon if she would just spend some time getting to know him.

"I will have dinner with you if you promise to forget about us. I will give you tonight. After that, I'm out of your life. For good."

"Anything but that."

"Then the answer is no. Look, Stone, I'm sorry. Really, I am. If I were anyone other than who I am, we wouldn't be having this conversation. But I cannot be your mate."

"Okay. One night. But you have to give me all night. Not just dinner. I want you at my table then in my bed... all night. Afterwards, if you still feel the same, I will let you go."

"Really?" Tessa didn't look convinced.

"Really. One night is better than nothing. At least I will have the memories to keep me company." Gods, he knew he sounded like a sappy woman. He was going all in, counting on the bond to kick in and Tessa changing her mind.

Sighing, she relented. "Okay, one night. Then you have to let me go and not interfere."

"Deal."

Jasper and Dane arrived within minutes of each other. The dumping site was in a wooded area on the south side of the city. CSU was on the scene, taping off the area. Jasper had been in his new job a few days and was already tired of seeing the yellow barriers. He couldn't swallow the knowledge that a human life could mean absolutely nothing to someone.

Dante was at the scene, standing over the victim. He motioned them both over to where he was. Pointing at the body, he said "This is new." Instead of the victim being fully clothed, this one was naked from the waste up. Purple marks that resembled hickies dotted her torso, and words had been carved into her chest: **Andrea, where are you?**

"Who the hell is Andrea?" Jasper asked no one in particular.

"My guess would be Flanagan's daughter. If I remember correctly, that was her name. Dante, did the DNA evidence on the last victim give us any leads?" Dane asked, staring at the body.

"It did. Trevor called as I was driving over here. The DNA belongs to one Richard Merrick. He was dishonorably discharged from the Army several years ago. I have Julian searching for his whereabouts. I'm going to call him back and add the name Andrea to his list of searches for anything to do with Flanagan, just to be sure. If we are right, he is trying to flush his daughter out using lookalikes. There is also something off about the DNA of the victims, and I have Trevor looking into it. If he can't figure it out, I'll throw that to Julian as well." Dante walked off to where the victim was being placed in a body bag. Without another word to either of them, he left the scene.

"I will never get used to him," Dane said to the tail lights.

"Sure you will; he just doesn't have a reason to smile. All he sees is death, and most of the time it's useless killings like this one. I was just thinking I've been on this job less than a week, and I'm already feeling empty."

Dane nodded, "Let's take a walk."

When they were out of earshot of the others, Jasper sighed, "It's hard to wrap my head around the fact you've been seeing shit like this as long as you have. How do you do it?"

Dane sighed. "I guess the same way Dante has, you eventually get numb."

Jasper thought for a minute. "I've worked mostly as a firefighter the last half-century, so the trauma I've seen has been of a different sort. Very few fire deaths were arson. Most were accidents, not the brutal murder this was."

They continued walking, canvassing the area looking for clues as they talked. "I can't wait to meet Sixx. I hope he can turn my financial situation around the way he has for the rest of you. If you all have so much money, why do you still have day jobs?"

For Jasper that was an easy one. "If you help me move, you will get to meet him. As for working, have you ever taken a vacation and by the end of it you were so stir crazy you were jonesing to get back to your job?"

"Yeah, relaxing can be a chore." Dane laughed now that he thought about it.

"Imagine relaxing for over four hundred years. That puts a whole new spin on stir crazy." Jasper had come to the manor during Dane's meeting with Rafael. After grabbing a beer, he was invited to join the conversation. "What made you decide to open up?"

Dane stopped and squatted down, looking at a footprint in the dirt. "Kaya. She told me I could continue on the lonely path I was on, or I could have a family, a Clan. I had time to think about what I wanted. My biological family kept this shit from me my whole life. Sure, they may have thought their reasons were legitimate, but I'd rather have known what I was up against from the start. If they are so scared of whoever it is they're hiding from, I'd rather have all the knowledge of our kind at my disposal, as well as the backing of my Brothers. I may not be a full-blooded Gargoyle, but Rafael said that didn't matter to him. Jasper, I have felt alone my whole life. If I'm going to live forever, I don't want to be alone anymore. I think Kaya always thought she'd be alone forever, too. It's odd, thinking about her being a Queen. I've known her a long time, and if anyone can lead a group of Alpha men, it would be her."

Jasper understood what Dane was saying. Even though he was nearly five hundred years old, he never felt part of the Clan out west. He had hidden the fact he was gay, and it had been a lonely existence. He finally found a lover in Craig, but he had wanted to hide their relationship. Craig was convinced they couldn't come out as lovers and not lose their jobs as firemen. When Sin told Jasper it was time he moved, he freaked. He felt alone in his world where he knew people. He couldn't imagine moving again, starting over. It turned out to be best thing that ever happened to him. Now, he wasn't flaming, but he sure wasn't hiding his sexuality, and Rafael's Clan couldn't care less.

197

Get to know Dane time was up when he pointed at the evidence on the ground. "Let's get CSU over here."

Thirty-One

Tessa was an idiot. Pure and simple. Why in the name of all that was holy did she agree to this? At least she was driving herself and wouldn't have to rely on Gregor's generosity when she decided it was time to go. And go she would. If tonight went the way she was sure it would, Gregor would pour on the Stone charm and seduce her, appealing to her inner shifter to mate with him. She had to be strong, not only for her sake but his as well. She had already let the family down by spilling as much information as she had about the human bonding. So be it. Rafael was King, and as such, he had to make the hard decisions, whether they be about territories, family disputes, or what diapers to put on his little Prince.

She didn't need a GPS to tell her where her mate lived. When she first transitioned, she became obsessed with him. She followed Gregor often, sometimes to bars, sometimes to his home. Never did she get up the nerve to get close to him. Maybe it hadn't been nerves, more like self-preservation. As time went on and she realized she would never be with him in the way they were meant to be, she stopped following. Watching him go out of town to meet other women had been too much. That was when she decided to hook up with Jacques. What a disaster that turned out to be.

Gregor's property was secured tighter than a military fort. The gate was thick iron and the security box was state of the art, voice recognition. Since she had never been there, Gregor had left it open for her arrival. As soon as she drove through, it automatically closed behind her. The rumble of her Camaro was loud against the silence of the woods. She was surrounded by trees on both sides of the long, paved drive leading to Gregor's home. She expected a log cabin to be nestled among the Georgia pines. What she didn't expect was the massive log and stone structure that came into view as she drove out of a curve.

She put her car in park and just sat there. *Holy Mother of Zeus.* Tessa was in the midst of her dream home. Of course her mate would live in the woods in the type of house she had dreamed of ever since she was a little girl. She liked her house in New Orleans, but she had bought it as an investment. This… this house was what dreams were made of. Baking cookies with your little girl dreams. Sitting on the deck watching your mate throwing football with your little boy dreams. Relaxing in the hot tub after the kids had gone to bed dreams. Making love in front of the fire dreams.

The front door opened, and Gregor stepped out onto the porch. He was dressed casually in faded jeans and a long sleeve Henley. The sleeves were pushed up showing his massive forearms. His feet were bare. Gods, that was so sexy. He didn't move toward her, just stood with his hands in his pockets, waiting. Tessa grabbed her backpack from the passenger seat and angled out of her sports car. She didn't bother locking the door.

"Do you want to put her in the garage?" Gregor inclined his head toward the car.

Dammit, he was already being nice. "Nah, she'll be fine out here for one night." Tessa needed to remind herself this was one night only. Though her curiosity was peaked at what he had in the garage besides his Hummer and Harley. She slowly walked up the steps and stopped, leaving an arm's length between them.

Gregor took her backpack. "I hope you like Italian." He opened the door, holding it for her. She stepped into the spacious, open room. The floor plan was perfect. The large family room opened up to the kitchen and dining area. There were windows everywhere including a large sliding glass door leading out to a deck on the back of the house. Even though Gargoyles weren't affected by the cold, Gregor had a fire going. A large bearskin covered the hardwood floor in front of the hearth. She could already see herself naked underneath Gregor on that rug.

"Would you like something to drink? I have beer, wine, and most kinds of liquor you could want." Gregor was directly behind her, the heat coming off his large body warming her better than the fireplace could. His breath tickled her ear. She turned to tell him she'd love a beer, but as soon as she parted her lips, his were covering hers. He fisted her hair gently, tugging her head back slightly to make their mouths fit perfectly. He didn't push for tongue but her body instinctually gave it to him anyway. He kept the contact soft yet sensual. He broke the kiss then placed his lips on her forehead.

"Beer. Please." She should break her promise and leave. Now. Gods, she was fucked. After one kiss. Tessa admired Gregor's ass as he placed her backpack by the staircase then continued to the kitchen. The interior of the house was filled with manly furnishings. Two large leather sofas were secured between thick wood end tables. The hand-hewn dining table would seat twelve easily. The appliances were top-of-the-line stainless. She noticed the absence of a large screen TV, a staple in any man's home. He must have a media room somewhere in this monstrosity. A beer appeared in her line of sight, and she took the bottle and drank. "You have a lovely home. For some reason I always imagined you'd have a small cabin, not this huge lodge."

"And I always imagined I'd be filling it with a mate and a posse of kids." The hurt on Gregor's face was impossible to miss. He drank down his own beer. "Are you hungry? I have lasagna that's ready to eat. All I need to do is toast the bread."

"I could eat. Did you cook this yourself?" Tessa wasn't a bad cook, she just didn't take the time to learn how to make extravagant dishes since she lived alone.

"I did. When you've lived as long as I have, you find hobbies you enjoy so you don't lose your mind. I enjoy cooking. Since I don't have a housekeeper like most of the others do, it's either cook or eat frozen dinners. I prefer to cook."

Gregor moved gracefully around the kitchen, pulling a cookie sheet out of a cabinet. He sliced what looked like a fresh loaf of French bread, buttering it then sprinkling it with freshly grated Parmesan cheese. "Did you make the bread, too?"

"No. That is one art I haven't mastered. Priscilla, Rafael's housekeeper, baked it for us." He slid the pan in the oven and shut the door. Leaning his backside against the counter, he crossed his legs at the ankle.

Tessa couldn't keep her eyes off his bare feet. Normally she found feet ugly, but his were perfect. His toes slanted at just the right angle. "Do you like to cook?" His question was asked with a quirk of his lips. Did he know she was turned on by his feet? Of course he did. Gargoyle mates had built in libido detectors.

"I do like to, I just don't take the time to do it. I'm hardly ever in one spot long, and when I am, I don't bother cooking for just me. What other hobbies do you enjoy?" Tessa wanted to know everything about her mate, even if they couldn't be together.

"Masonry, carpentry, anything that has to do with my hands." He waved his hand in the air at his home.

"You built this place?" she asked incredulously. She shouldn't be surprised; his family created buildings, after all.

"Don't sound so surprised. Yes, with Dante's help, we built it from the foundation up."

Gregor took the bread from the oven, transferring it to a linen-lined basket and setting it on the table. He pulled a couple of plates out of an overhead cabinet and dished out a healthy portion of lasagna for her, an even larger one for himself, and placed those on rust-colored placemats. He retrieved two salads from the refrigerator, grabbing several different types of dressing. A vase of wildflowers sat in the middle of the table cloaked on either side by candles that had recently been burning. He must have seen her looking. "What can I say? I like a nice table." He lit the candles and placed the lighter back in his pocket.

Once everything was ready, he pulled her chair out for her. "I'm going to have a glass of wine. Would you like one or another beer?"

"I'll have wine, please." Tessa wasn't a wine girl, but when in Rome...

The meal was enjoyed with very little talk. The food was some of the most delicious Tessa had ever put in her mouth. She couldn't help the moans that escaped her throat with the first few bites. Gregor arched an eyebrow, and she shrugged. "Sorry, but this is delicious."

When their stomachs were full, Gregor asked if she wanted dessert. Tessa declined. "Gods, no. I need to unbutton my jeans now." Gregor growled. "Later, Stone. We have all night. Now, how about showing me the rest of this monstrosity you call your home."

Gregor showed Tessa everything except his bedroom. He must be saving it for later. Or maybe he had changed his mind and didn't intend to let her see it. She really couldn't blame him. If she had no intention of being a permanent fixture in his life, why share the most intimate part of his home with her? He led her to the back deck where they sat down and enjoyed the sunlight fading, making way for the moon. She could feel his gaze on her face, and she couldn't help but smile.

"This is perfect. Your home, the woods, the peace and quiet." She turned her face to his and again, she couldn't miss the sadness in his eyes. She laced their fingers together. She could pretend for one night that this was, indeed, perfect. After a few minutes of enjoying the serenity, she asked, "So tell me, what's hiding in your garage?"

"Ah, I wondered how long it would take for you to ask. Let's go take a look." Gregor released their fingers but waited on her to walk by his side. She missed the connection. He opened the side door that led into the massive two-story building. The view in front of her had her drooling. She should have known her mate was a car fanatic, too. And these weren't just any cars. Sitting before her were several classic hotrods, but the one she wanted to bow down and worship was a mint condition Camaro Super Sport limited edition. Her claws were itching to bust through the skin as her adrenaline pumped through her body.

"Tops out at two-forty. I had a Corvette Z06 engine dropped in it. Six hundred and fifty horsepower." Gregor was leaning against the hood of a mint Ford Mustang like it was any old vehicle.

"Do you ever drive these?" Tessa asked sweeping her arm indicating the hotrods. Her Camaro was a newer model she had modified to be faster yet more fuel efficient. What she wouldn't give to drive one of these bad boys.

"Nah, they were more of an investment. If I want speed I hop on the bike." Again, the sadness crept through his voice. He was killing her. This hardass, strong, built like a brick shithouse of a man, was ripping her to shreds with nothing more than the tone of his voice.

"I need another beer." Tessa couldn't bear to look at the vehicles any longer. All of this could be hers if she would just say yes. It didn't matter that they didn't know each other well or they hadn't spent any quality time together. If she gave the nod, Gregor would give her the world. On a fuel-injected, chrome-plated platter. She didn't wait on him to move. Tessa found her way back to the kitchen and helped herself to another bottle. She had half of it guzzled when Gregor's phone rang. Cursing, he answered it.

"This better be life or death, preferably death. She did? He is? Thank you." Gregor pocketed his phone. "I have a message for you from your mother."

Tessa was glad she didn't have a mouthful of beer. "My mother? What in the fuck are you doing talking to my mother?" All the sweet thoughts Tessa had been thinking just flew out the back door that was still slid open.

"Actually *she* was talking to *me*. She said to tell you Ezekiel is on his way to Egypt, so now you don't have to go." Gregor's smug look pissed her off. Did he think he could interfere just because her mother asked him to?

"Gods, you are so fuckin' frustrating!"

Thirty-Two

"What have I told you about that mouth of yours?" Even though there was nothing lady like about her vocabulary, Gregor preferred her brand of brazenness.

"As I recall you like my mouth." She was glaring at him. It was a look he had finally gotten used to and just ignored.

"Yes, when my dick is in it." If she was going to pretend she wanted nothing to do with him, he wasn't going to play nice. He didn't wait on a response. He turned and sauntered away from her only to hear the hammer being cocked. She wouldn't. There was a sharp pain in his ass. She did. She shot him in the motherfucking ass. Where the hell did she even get a gun?

"You fucking brat, you shot me! AGAIN!" He roared as he lunged for her. Gregor grabbed Tessa and threw her over his shoulder. He climbed the stairs two at a time until he opened the door to the only room he hadn't shown her. His bedroom. He sat down on the side of the bed, pulled her off his shoulder, and placed her across his lap. He grabbed the gun and tossed it out of her reach, then he smacked her ass.

"You bastard! What do you think you're doing?"

"Just where did you have a gun?" He smacked her again, causing her to wiggle in his lap.

"In the waistband of my jeans, where I *always* have a gun," she seethed.

He popped her ass again.

"What was that for?" she screamed at him.

Gregor gave her four hard smacks on her ass. "For...Being...A...Brat!" The first couple of smacks had her squirming, trying to get free. The third and fourth caused a different kind of squirm. She liked it rough. He raised his hand and popped her again, in a different place. She moaned then wiggled again. He grabbed one boot at a time, pulling them off her feet and tossing them aside. Using his shifter strength, he ripped her jeans down the back, exposing her thong.

Black lace. *Fuck me.* He grabbed a fistful of red hair, holding her in place and landed another slap to her left cheek. He rubbed out the pain before he struck the right cheek. Tessa was murmuring and squirming, and the scent of arousal was getting stronger with each slap on her ass. He rubbed out the handprint. Instead of another smack, he dipped his hand between her legs. The wetness on the thin material was proof she was as turned on as he was. He tore the lace off her body. He used her wetness to coat his fingers, then he slid them up to her pucker. His baser needs leaned to the rougher, darker side. Would she be up for a little backdoor play?

When Tessa arched her back, thrusting her ass to meet his fingers, he had his answer. His girl liked it dirty. He didn't hesitate. He ran his finger through her juices again then circled her hole, applying a little pressure at first. "Gregor," Tessa moaned again and pressed against his finger. He momentarily froze. That was the first time he could remember her calling him by his first name. When she wiggled again, he slid his finger in, rubbing the inside in a circular motion. "Oh gods, that feels sooo good." If it felt half as good for her as it did when he had it done to him, he knew she was going to come soon.

It was taking all his control not to come in his pants. "Pull my dick out. Suck me, Tessa. Fucking suck my cock." It was awkward with her lying across his lap, so he moved farther back on the bed so he could lie down, pulling her with him. His finger never left its hole, sliding deeper with each stroke. Tessa managed to get his jeans undone far enough to free his erection. She didn't play around. She sucked hard, taking him all the way to the back of her throat. He had received a lot of blowjobs in his many years, but no one gave head like his mate. He tried not to think of why she was so good at it. Instead, he pumped his finger in and out of her ass as she matched the tempo with her mouth. "Mmm." She was moaning around his dick, and he wasn't going to last.

"Oh fuck, Baby. Gods yes, suck it. That's it." Gregor pulled his finger out and dragged her pants off her legs. He then grabbed her hips, slinging her legs over his body so she was straddling his face. He kept his fangs in his gums so he wouldn't hurt her. He sucked and licked her clit, wanting her to come. Her strangled moans around his dick had him coming undone. He slapped her ass, and she orgasmed hard; her juices flowing as fast as he could lap them up. He was ready to come, but he wanted to be inside of her pussy when he did.

Gregor rolled out from under her body and raised up on his knees behind her. The sight of her pink ass in front of him was more than he could handle. Grabbing the base of his cock, he delayed his orgasm. He lined the engorged head up with her pussy and without preamble, drove it home. He didn't give her time to adjust; he thrust in hard. He slid his cock out slowly then pumped it back in. Tessa's claws were out, embedded in his comforter. He didn't care. His fangs popped out, cutting into his lower lip. Gods how he wanted to bite her. Claim her. *Fuck!*

"Greegoorrrrr," Tessa was panting as he pulled out then grunting when he slammed his dick back into her heat. "Gods, yes! Fuck meeee." Her ass was bumping his groin with every thrust. The sound of flesh meeting flesh was fueling his orgasm. He grabbed her hair, pulling her head backwards so she had to arch her back, pushing that beautiful ass higher. He slapped her right cheek, leaving a handprint, and she gasped.

"You... Are... Fucking... Mine." He punctuated every word with a hard thrust and came with a roar. Gregor ground his dick into her pussy, emptying his seed into her

208

body. He collapsed on top of her, his cock still pulsing. Even though he was spent, he wasn't ready to pull out and lose the connection. He raised his upper body so he wouldn't crush her, and admired the sight beneath him. Her sweaty hair was sticking to her skin. Her eyes were closed. He pushed the red strands off her beautiful face, drinking in the sheen of perspiration glistening her skin.

Gregor finally pulled out then continued to pet his mate, not caring that she was silent. At least she wasn't yelling at him. Or shooting at him. Her lips were turned up slightly. What he wouldn't give to see them in a full on smile. Letting her rest, he opened the drawer of the nightstand and pulled out a bottle of after-care lotion. He poured the cold cream into his hands, rubbing them together before he tended to her pink cheeks. As he gently massaged the lotion into her skin, Tessa purred.

Tessa had heard of subspace but had never experienced it herself. This might be just an imitation of the real thing, but she was floating. Her soul was hovering just above their bodies, her heart tagging along with it. She tried to get her mouth to stop smiling, but it was no use. Never had a man used her body so well, so completely, then took the time to care for her afterwards. After he lotioned her ass, the bed shifted, and Gregor rose. She wanted him back. The water was running in the bathroom, then it turned off. The bed dipped as he sat next to her, wiping between her legs with a warm washcloth.

Tessa felt herself being wrapped in the comforter she was certain was shredded. Gregor lifted her into his arms and carried her down the stairs to the family room. Gently, he placed her on the rug in front of the fire. He added a couple of logs before lying down beside her. The silence was punctuated by the crackling wood. A naked Gregor was on his side, head cradled in his hand. His other hand was trailing shapes across her skin until he stopped at her tattoo. Tessa should care that he was investigating the ink closely, but right now she couldn't muster the energy.

Gregor's fingertip caressed the swirling lines. When he had studied it enough, he dotted her skin with soft kisses. Tessa tried to focus on him, her mate. She needed to snap out of the high she was riding before she did something really stupid like confess her true feelings. This fog she was swimming through was going to really fuck things up, but it just felt too good. His gorgeous blue eyes came into view, his brow was creased with worry lines. "Hey, are you okay?"

Tessa just nodded. She opened her mouth to speak but was cut off by his breath. Gods the man knew how to kiss. Whether it was soft and sensual or hard and sexual, she wanted him to never stop breathing his soul into hers. She managed to reach up and cup the side of his head with one hand. Feeling his flaccid dick coming to life, she slid her hand down his neck, down his chest, across his ridged abs, until she found what she was looking for. His cock hardened in her hand, pulsing under her fingers. She wanted him in her mouth but couldn't make her body obey for more than a hand job.

As Tessa continued to stroke Gregor, she kept her eyes locked on his face. He rose up and situated himself between her legs, holding his body aloft with his hands. He kept his eyes locked on her hand that was stroking him. When he finally looked up, Tessa saw lust staring back at her. His normally crystal blue orbs were dark with desire. He rocked his cock into her hand, never taking his eyes off hers. She needed him. Tessa had to have him in her, on her, surrounding her with the strength of the Gargoyle he was. "Need you," she managed to whisper.

Just like that, her wish was his command. Using only his cock, he persuaded her body to open for him. With no foreplay, no teasing, just one swift movement, he was once again seated in her core. This time she would get to watch his face when he came.

This Gregor was completely different than the one in the bedroom. This man was slow and tender. The look in his eyes was a mixture of lust and wonderment. If she had to guess, she would say he was learning every inch of her from the inside out. He was going to memorize this moment in time so he could relive it once she was gone. At least that's what she was doing. She never realized someone could make love so slowly. Oh gods, he was making love to her. She felt the tears wet the back of her eyes. *Fucking Alistair. Why did his fucking uncle have to be such a prick?*

"Tessa." Gregor stopped moving. The tip of his cock was still inside her entrance, but Gregor remained motionless. "What's wrong, Baby? Talk to me."

When he called her Baby, the flood gates opened. The tears rolled down her cheeks, and she told him the truth. "We can't do this. As much as I want this with you, we can't have it. It's not safe. We have to stay away from each other."

"Why isn't it safe? Who are you scared of?" Gregor was down on one forearm. He used his free hand to gently swipe the tears from her cheeks. His face was so close. Too close. Oh shit, she'd already said too much. Tessa's brain was slowly beginning to function properly.

"Nobody, never mind. Please, make love to me." When he still didn't move, Tessa pulled her feet closer to her hips so she could thrust up, burying his cock inside of her. "Please, I need you."

The doubt was still there on his face, but he did as she asked. Gregor Stone made slow, sweet love to her on a bear skin rug in front of a crackling fire.

Thirty-Three

Tessa woke to the aroma of coffee and bacon wafting up the stairs, and the sound of Gregor singing a sexy Anthony Hamilton number. He loved to sing and wasn't shy about singing in front of her. Last night had been the single best experience of her life. After her mini-meltdown, Gregor backed off with the questions of why they couldn't be together. Instead he asked her about her life, her travels, her cousins. Gregor wanted to know everything about her, and she found it easy to talk to him about it all. What would it hurt? There was nothing he could find out that would ruin it for them. His uncle had already seen to that.

She in turn asked questions about his life, begging him to leave out his sexual conquests. Neither wanted to hear about the other's love life. Tessa found it interesting he and his brothers had paired up along the way. He and Dante were close, just like Rafael was close with Sinclair. He talked about the Clan and his parents. Anything she asked, he answered.

When he asked about all her aliases, she explained that she changed her name everywhere she went to keep Flanagan from getting any closer. Gordon was the one to name her Andrea, and she loathed anything to do with him. She went on to talk about her time with Jonas and how he had called her his little Nikola Tesla, saying she was going to grow up to be brilliant, too. She couldn't say Tesla, instead it came out Tessa. Jonas had called her that ever since. What Gregor didn't ask her was why she sometimes used his last name. For that she was grateful.

Gregor had shown her several sides, all different, but all good in their own way. He was tender when she needed it, but he was also wild when she wanted it. Gregor could probably open up a whole new sexual world to her if she would let him. Were things different, she would turn her body over to him and let him have his way. Last night had been a small sampling of what he would do. When he told her that her ass was his, he hadn't lied. When she agreed to spend the night, he drove straight to the adult store and purchased a new anal plug for her. He stretched her out with the plug while he fucked her. Later, when her body was ready, he replaced the plug with his cock. He rubbed her clit while fucking her ass. It was the most intense orgasm she had ever had.

She grabbed her backpack and headed to the shower. She would prefer to keep his scent on her skin for the rest of her life, but Tessa had to wash the last couple of rounds of sex off her body. After the anal play, they had taken a shower together. They intended to bathe only, but Tessa had insisted on soaping his body so she could feel every inch of his skin under her fingers. When she started sliding her hand up and down his dick, Gregor lifted Tessa up, wrapped his arms under her thighs, and impaled her on his cock. Eventually they bathed and wrapped themselves in a couple of thick robes. They found some leftovers to refuel their bodies before having sex on the kitchen table. The sofa was used for a blowjob and the stairs for eating her pussy. The hot tub had been talked about but they just never made it out there. At some point she had given out and fallen asleep draped over Gregor's body.

Now, reality was setting into her psyche. The ache she felt in her chest was of her own doing. All she had to do was walk down those steps and tell Gregor to bite her, make the bond official. She had come close when she had spaced out. No, she was doing the right thing for him. She had to keep him safe from his uncle and from her freak of a stalker. She needed to move away, put some distance between them. That would make the hurt less for both of them. Eventually.

She turned the shower off and grabbed a towel, wrapping her wet hair in it. She dried off and pulled on clean clothes she had brought with her. Instead of her standard jeans, she opted for more comfortable yoga pants. She slid a t-shirt over her head and put socks on her feet. She might be part shifter, but her feet still got cold. She found her comb and quickly detangled her long hair. She twisted it up, securing it with a clip, holding it away from her face.

Tessa padded down the stairs, stopping at the bottom to take in all that was Gregor. The man was standing in flannel sleep pants and nothing else. The muscles in his back bunched and snaked under his skin. He was singing a different song now, some Marilyn Manson tune.

Tessa crossed the kitchen, closing the distance between them. She didn't hesitate to walk into his open arms. Wrapping himself around her, he breathed in her clean scent. She enjoyed the feeling of being safe, cherished, wanted. Loved? Maybe not yet, it was probably too soon. If she stayed with Gregor, he no doubt would grow to love her.

"Coffee?" Gregor released her and opened the cabinet for an extra mug. He didn't wait for her to answer, just poured the liquid and pushed the milk toward her. He remembered how she took her coffee from their conversation during the night.

"Thank you. You didn't have to go to all this trouble for me." She poured milk in her coffee and stirred it around with a spoon.

"No trouble, I have to eat, so I just cooked a little extra." Gregor dumped scrambled eggs and bacon on two plates, popped some bread in the toaster, then sat down across from her. His mood was somber. She could change it with one word. She didn't. When neither one ate much, just pushed their food around, Tessa decided it was time to say goodbye. For good.

She stood to clear her plate but Gregor stopped her. "Don't worry about it. I will clean the kitchen later."

"Okay. Well, thank you for everything. I wish…"

Gregor cut her off. "Don't, Tessa. Just go." Gregor turned away from her and walked out the back door. She knew this would be hard, but she didn't think he would be so cold about it. She took one last look around at what she was letting go.

Gregor's heart was shredded. Completely ripped into tiny fucking pieces that would never mend. The last thing he wanted to do was go to the manor and be around his brothers, much less a happy Rafael and Kaya. Duty called, and he would bear it, because he had to. He was already late, but he didn't care. There was no way he could watch Tessa get in her car and drive off, so he had taken off through the woods at a dead run. When enough time had passed, he returned to his house and showered. The t-shirt Tessa had been wearing when she arrived was on the floor of the bathroom. It must have fallen out of her backpack when she was grabbing her things. Gregor lifted the soft cotton to his nose and inhaled. Tears pricked the back of his eyes, and he lost it. His fist found the wall-length mirror, shattering it into thousands of shards.

Not bothering to clean up the glass or his hand, he quickly dressed and grabbed his helmet then threw it back down. He knew the laws, but right then he didn't give a fuck. If he got pulled over between home and Rafe's, he'd just show his identification and tell the police to piss off. Passing the sports cars to get to the bike, he stopped in front of the Camaro. It was his pick of the cars in his collection. He should have known it would be Tessa's favorite as well.

Gregor rode his bike hard all the way to Rafael's. He parked in front of the garage and cut the motor. He didn't need shifter hearing to tell there was something going on.

The noise level in the manor would rival a sports arena. Gregor walked in the dining room just in time to see Dante phase. Wings knocked food platters off the sideboard. Rafael got in his face, "Stand down. NOW! That's a fucking order!"

Gregor cautiously stepped up next to his brother. As soon as he phased back, Gregor placed his hand on Dante's shoulder. "Brother, what is it? Talk to me." Dante was shaking with fury.

"These motherfuckers want to throw Isabelle to the wolf. I will not allow it."

Gregor had obviously missed something important. "Someone care to fill me in?"

Rafael was not happy. "If you bothered to be here on time, we wouldn't have to fill you in."

"Well excuse the fuck out of me for having a godsdamn personal problem. Fuck you, Rafe."

Dante was yelling at Deacon. Nikolas was sitting in the corner staring at the floor. Julian was arguing with Jasper. Some pretty boy he assumed was Dane Abbott was standing in the kitchen door looking like he would rather be anywhere else. The whole lot of them had lost their fucking minds. A shrill whistle rent the air. Kaya stepped into the room and glared.

"I don't know what the hell is going on in here. What I do know is the way you're all carrying on isn't going to solve anything." She continued on into the kitchen, grabbed a cup of coffee then went back to wherever she had come from.

Rafael tried to hide his grin and failed. "She's right. Why don't we take this outside so Priscilla doesn't have to clean up after anyone else? Just in case."

The men silently followed Rafael out to the patio. The tension was thick, but no one said a word. Rafael remained standing and addressed them as one. "Gregor needs to be brought up to speed. Julian, please go first."

216

"The breach in the computer system a few weeks back came from Jasper's computer. It has been determined Jasper isn't smart enough to have hacked into the system. No offense."

Jasper volleyed, "None taken."

Julian continued. "I have contacted Sinclair, so he can investigate Jasper's former boyfriend, Craig. Further, the email from Bartholomew Cromwell originated from somewhere in Greece. This mystery is proving to be a bit more difficult to crack."

Dante, having calmed down, asked Rafael, "Did you ever respond to the bid request?"

"Yes, the amount was so outrageous that even if it had been a legitimate request, they would have told me to sod off. That's not important right now. What is important is that Deacon has let us in on the tidbit about Alexander speaking and requesting to talk to Isabelle."

Dante started to argue, but Gregor put his hands on his chest. "Whoa, Brother. Do you need to tell us something?" Dante would have punched anyone else for touching him, but Gregor's hands and soft words had a calming effect.

"She is my mate. I needed to speak to her about something I found in the inmate files, so I went to visit her. We had a nice chat."

"A nice chat? Is she on board with being your mate?" Gregor's own heart was broken. That didn't mean he would hold a grudge against his brother if he found happiness.

"Not really. Since she had a less than perfect marriage that ended in tragedy, I can understand her reluctance at another relationship. I have offered to bow out, but I've also given her the option to call me, should she wish to see where things go. The chat I was referring to had more to do with the half-bloods than my mating with her."

217

All eyes turned to Dane who held up his hands defensively. "Hey, don't look at me. I've already told you everything I know."

Dante shook his head, frowning. "Isabelle was afraid to speak freely, because Tessa told her not to. Isabelle mentioned that the King's uncle was the one who ostracized her father. She didn't know his name, but she said he was the reason Tessa was so hell-bent on staying away from you."

"Tessa admitted as much last night. She wouldn't give me his name either, but it only makes sense that it's Alistair. He never shied away from expressing his contempt for our mother when she married outside of the Greek bloodlines. He is a purist. If marrying an Italian had him disowning his sister, imagine how he would feel about one of us hooking up with a human." Gregor wished Tessa had enough faith in him to keep her safe.

Julian spoke up, "Could he be the Greek who sent the email? Rafe, was he at the Elder Council?"

"He was there, but the email came in before I flew to Italy. Still, it could have come from him. He's never liked me, so maybe he was trying to flush me out of the office. He had to know I would be at the meeting, though. I need to call our mother. She and Xavier were acting funny, and X explained that not all the Elders were unopposed to humans. I knew he was hiding something. They both were, godsdamnit."

Gregor chimed in, "I did get some useful information from Tessa about the bonding. Gargoyles have mated with humans and successfully had eighteen children. Caroline had seventeen of those. Elizabeth only had Tessa because whoever the father is wouldn't take a chance on any more births."

Rafael frowned. "I thought she said the others were born successfully."

"She did. Her father is just so protective of her mother, one child was enough for him. And there's Tamian, so technically they have two children. When I asked, Tessa refused to name her father. She is definitely scared of whoever is behind the threats to the humans. She wouldn't speak of it, but it's the reason she gives for us not being together. Nikolas, you look like someone kicked your puppy. What's wrong?"

Nikolas closed his eyes and sighed. "I have been to the library several times to see Sophia and she hasn't been there. Yesterday when I went, someone gave me a note. All it said was she was sorry to leave now that I had found her."

"Did you say Sophia?" Gregor and Dante asked at the same time.

Nikolas straightened up, staring at both his cousins. "Yes."

"Hang on a second." Gregor pulled out his cell phone and prayed Tessa would answer his call.

"Gregor, if you're calling to..."

He cut her off. "Listen, you mentioned a Sophia. She wouldn't happen to be a librarian, would she?"

"Yeah, why? What's this about?" Tessa was in her car. He could hear the engine idling.

"Just curious. Gotta go." He thumbed the phone off and told Nikolas, "I know where your woman is. Egypt."

"Egypt? Why the fuck would she be in Egypt?" Nikolas was nearly shouting.

"Her father is missing. From what I gather, Tessa and two others in their family are called watchers. They look after the half-bloods who haven't transitioned yet. Sophia's father is one of the watchers and has allegedly been abducted. Tessa planned on going after them, but her mother called and wanted me to intervene."

"Hold up. The elusive Elizabeth Flanagan called you?" Dane was the one asking the question.

"Apparently she knows I am her daughter's mate, and she asked that I stop Tessa from going after Sophia's father. Tessa will probably still go after them even though someone named Ezekiel has gone."

"And how do you know that?" Dane again.

"Elizabeth called the Pen and left a message with me," Deacon confirmed.

Nikolas was bouncing on the balls of his feet. Rafael looked at him, "Do what you have to do." Nikolas didn't need further permission. He ran full speed to his car.

"Do we need to send someone with him?" Geoffrey asked.

Gregor wanted to be the one to go after Nikolas. Something tugged at his gut, something sinister regarding the trip. If Tessa was going anywhere near the sand, he wanted to be there for her.

"If he needs help, he'll ask. Now, back to Isabelle and the inmates. Dante, what did you find that you needed to speak to her about?" Rafael sat down. Tempers had leveled off for the time being.

"I got a call from Deacon when an inmate was having a seizure. I looked into his file for past episodes or allergies and noted that Henshaw had been dosing the patient with Unholy blood. There was a stack of files on Isabelle's desk. When I skimmed through them, I noticed he was giving all of those particular inmates Unholy blood as well. I wanted to speak to her about it. She had just started going through the files when she transitioned. Since she hasn't been back to work since, she only knew what little bit she had read. We have agreed to work together to test all the inmates who were being used as Henshaw's guinea pigs."

Frey whistled low, "I bet that's what the good doctor was doing in the Basement. He was extracting Unholy blood. But to what end? Was he trying to build his own army? Could he have been working for Flanagan?"

"We'll never know. Speaking of Flanagan, I hear St. Claire made good progress with the albino and he wants to speak to Isabelle for some reason. Dante before you get your wings out of joint, just hear us out." Rafael pinned him with a look daring him to phase again. "Not only do we have the murders at the warehouse, we now have the redhead killings. Dane, do you have any leads in the case?"

"Yes, Sir. The DNA found under victim five's fingernails matched one Richard Merrick, ex-army, dishonorably discharged. Dante asked Julian to search further into his whereabouts. The victim we found yesterday was not only strangled like the others, but she was also mutilated. He is getting desperate for whatever his endgame is. He sent us a message."

"What was the message?" Gregor asked Dane but had his eye on Dante who was looking at the ground.

"It said, 'Andrea, where are you?'"

Gregor ran to the back of the house and threw up. When his stomach was empty and he was no longer heaving, he returned to the others.

Rafael waited until he was back with the group. "Julian explained that Tessa is Andrea Flanagan. Dante, this just makes it that much more important to get information from Vincent any way we can. You know we will not allow him to harm your mate. We will restrain him, and we will have a full team in the room at all times."

Gregor placed a hand on his brother's shoulder. He knew exactly what Dante was feeling. There was no way he would want his mate in the same room with a psychotic shifter. At the same time, he would do everything he could to keep his brother's mate safe as well. Dante looked at Gregor and nodded. "Okay."

"Is there any more business we need to discuss before we head to the Pen?" Rafael asked each man, eyebrows raised. When he received no responses, he said, "Don't forget, tomorrow Jasper is moving to his own home.

Sixx had business to attend tonight, but he will be available tomorrow."

Rafael instructed them all to head to the prison. He told Jasper to hold up. "I got a call from Sinclair earlier. Craig's gone."

"Gone? What do you mean gone?"

"It appears he decided he didn't like the west coast any longer. He turned in his notice, packed his house up, and nobody has heard from him in weeks."

Jasper nodded. "I seriously doubt I hear from him, but if I do I'll let you know."

Rafael gave Jasper's shoulder a squeeze, "Good enough. Let's go protect Dante's mate."

Thirty-Four

Isabelle was surprised to receive a phone call from Dante so soon after he left until she heard why he was phoning. He offered to pick her up, but she declined, saying she could get to the Pen faster if she drove there herself. Within half an hour she was parking in her reserved spot. Dante was waiting for her by the back door. "Thank you for agreeing to speak with the inmate. I don't want to alarm you, but I do believe he has information on the whereabouts of Gordon Flanagan and possibly the Redhead Killer."

Dante softly held her elbow and escorted her into the building. The mate bond pulled at her. She was lightheaded and grasped onto Dante's arm for support. "Are you all right, Isabelle?" His beautiful face was a mask of concern.

"May I speak honestly?" She had to tell him what type of disruption his nearness caused.

"Of course. I prefer honesty at all costs. Please remember that."

"I will remember. It's just when you are near me, I can barely breathe. Thinking is almost impossible. I never knew the mate bond would be so strong, but it is. I know you said I would be protected when I am speaking with Vincent, but if you are in the same room as I am…"

Dante let go of her elbow. "Are you saying you don't want me near you?"

Isabelle steeled her nerves and took both of his hands in hers. "Not at all. It isn't a matter of want, Dante. It's a matter of being able to concentrate on the task at hand. Under normal circumstances, I would be nervous. These are not normal circumstances. I am asking that you stay close, just not so close as to disrupt my interview with the inmate."

"Agreed. I will be outside the door, out of your line of sight. That is the best I can give you. I apologize now if my nearness causes hardship for you, but you are my mate, and it is my duty first and foremost to protect you."

While it might not be a declaration of love, the truth of Dante's words caused her heart to stutter. She squeezed his hands before making her way to Gregor's office. The sight when she arrived was enough to make any woman nervous. There had to be at least eight large alpha badasses hovering in the outer waiting area. Gregor was giving instructions when she walked in. "Isabelle, there you are. How are you feeling?"

"Very well, thank you." Taking in each one of the men, she noticed that most of them resembled Dante and Gregor in some way. Gargoyles.

"Please, let me introduce everyone to you. Isabelle Sarantos, this is our King, Rafael, our cousins Julian, Geoffrey, Lorenzo, Jasper, Urijah, and Mason. You've already met Deacon." All of the men bowed their head and placed a fist over their heart. Odd.

"We have moved Vincent into the largest interrogation room there is and have secured him. All of us will be in the room with you, so you need not fear for your safety. So far, he has refused to speak in our presence. The few words he has said were mostly the ramblings of a mad man. He has had a couple of nightmares, possibly remembering someone from his past or feeling guilty over someone he murdered. We have no way of knowing if that has any bearing on his time spent with Flanagan. It is imperative we find out what he knows about Gordon. Do you have any questions?"

"No. I've never been involved in any type of interrogation, at least not where I'm the one asking the questions." It was hard not to remember the police drilling her relentlessly when Alexi died. Dante was at her back, giving a quick squeeze to her bicep.

"You can do this," he whispered in her ear.

"I'm ready." She straightened her spine. It was time for her to buck up and be more like her cousin. If she were here, she would barge into the interrogation room and take over. If Isabelle could channel her inner Tessa, all would go well.

The large room was located on one of the upper levels. All of the men stepped into the room, making a semi-circle. Dante paused just outside the door and touched her cheek. "You will be fine, and I'll be right here."

Isabelle nodded at her mate then entered the room. She had expected the same lost looking, broken man who had placed his hand on the window when she passed by. Instead, standing before her was a fully phased Gargoyle. *Tessa, think like Tessa.* "Hello, Vincent. Are those really necessary?" She pointed at his wings. Instead of answering, he bared his fangs at her. She allowed her own fangs to drop and her claws to spring forth from her hands. Baring her own fangs at the albino seemed to momentarily stun him. His wings vanished behind his back and his fangs and claws disappeared.

Isabelle retracted her own fangs but pointed at him with an extended claw. "Now, you behave." She retracted her claws and closed the distance to stand in front of Vincent. Not close enough where he could reach her, but she would not show fear by hiding behind the men. "You indicated by a note that you wished to see me. What would you like to talk about?"

Instead of focusing on Isabelle, Vincent was taking in all the shifters in the room. "Vincent, we know you can speak. The charade is up. If you wish for me to remain in the room with you, you will have to talk to me. Otherwise this little party is over, and you can return to solitary without a cigarette." Isabelle knew it was cruel, but she had stopped and bought a pack of smokes on her way to the Pen. She would reward him for good behavior, and she could think of no better reward than that which he craved most.

"Vincent, would you like a cigarette?" She pulled a pack out of her pocket, tapping it against her finger to loosen a few from the others. She pulled one smoke out and sniffed it, dropping the rest of the pack back into her pocket.

"Yes." His voice croaked from lack of use.

"Then I need you to answer a few questions for me. Can you do that?"

"Yes."

"Where is Gordon Flanagan?" Isabelle figured she might as well go for broke.

Instead of answering, Vincent jerked on his chains and grunted. The men behind her stepped up, but she held up her hand stopping them. Isabelle held up the cigarette and snapped it in two. Vincent immediately calmed.

"Let me make myself clear. I had a full pack of these when I walked into this room. Now I have nineteen. For every outburst, you lose another one. If you tell me what I want to know, I will give you every single cigarette I have left. Now, I will ask you again, where is Gordon Flanagan?"

"Merrick."

"No, Gordon Flanagan." Isabelle pulled out another cigarette and started to snap it.

"Merrick knows." Vincent eyeballed the cigarette like it was his only link to this world.

One of the men spoke up behind Isabelle. "Richard Merrick's DNA came back as the Redhead Killer. We need to find him, too."

"Vincent, where can we find this Merrick?" Isabelle sniffed the cigarette, taunting him.

"He always called me. I never saw him. Can I have the cigarette now, Izzy?"

"What did you call me?" In that moment, Isabelle had a flashback. She was a little girl bouncing on someone's knee.

Vincent retreated into himself, mumbling about sunshine and cigarettes. "Vincent, look at me." Isabelle took a step toward the inmate, and he lunged at her.

"He took her! He took her away from me!"

Dante ran into the room and grabbed Isabelle as the men converged on Vincent. Someone stuck a needle in his neck, depressing a plunger full of something into his body. Almost immediately he calmed. Dante pulled her away from the room. "Are you all right?" He ran his hands over her arms as if Vincent actually touched her.

"I'm fine, Dante. He didn't hurt me." No, he just shook her to the core calling her Izzy, taking her back to when she was a toddler. It must have been a coincidence. "I promise, I'm fine. What did they give him?"

"Hellebore root. It's one of the few things that has any effect on Gargoyles. Too much of it can cause total paralysis."

"How do you know how much to administer?" Isabelle asked over her shoulder as the other Gargoyles took Vincent back to his cell.

"Trial and error. It's been used for years to sedate the Unholy."

Isabelle would make note of it once she was back at work. As far as she was concerned, the sooner the better. She had made a connection with Vincent, even if only briefly. Had the men not been in the room, he might have opened up more.

"Can we not at least give him one cigarette? He did give us a name." Isabelle had promised one to him, and he didn't get it. She didn't like breaking a promise.

"He will be passed out for a while. You can up the dosage on his patch."

"Should I hang around and try talking to him again later?" She knew she could get through to him if she had more time.

"No, that is all." Isabelle turned to the voice speaking behind her. Rafael, the King. "We appreciate what you did in there. You handled the situation very well. We need to focus our efforts on Richard Merrick. Isabelle, it was a pleasure meeting you, and I look forward to spending more time in your presence." Rafael inclined his head to her then turned on his heel and left. All of the men spoke to her, congratulating her on a job well done. She honestly didn't feel like she had accomplished anything.

Gregor was the last one to return from wherever they had taken Vincent. "Isabelle, thank you. If you feel well enough, I hope you will return to work tomorrow. I think there has been enough excitement for today." He looked so sad. She hadn't noticed it earlier with her nerves firing inside her body. Now that the excitement was over, she was able to take in his features more clearly.

She reached out to touch him, but Dante stopped her. "Let him go. There's only one person who can ease his pain now. May I escort you to your car?"

Isabelle had the feeling she was being dismissed which was fine with her. It was Halloween after all, and she had candy to hand out later. "No, that's not necessary, but thank you for the offer." She walked away from her mate, knowing he was watching after her. Once she was in her car, she lost it. She shook uncontrollably and let the tears flow. Luckily none of the guards or Dante came out before she could calm herself. When the tears subsided, Isabelle started her car and headed home.

Vincent's brain was foggy. The woman in front of him was Isabelle. The little girl sitting on his lap was his Izzy. They couldn't be the same person. Could they? *No, that's not right, her name is Rebekah. Beautiful, sunshiny*

228

Rebekah. I have the ring in my pocket and I'm going to ask her to marry me tonight. Gabriel relished the sunshine on his face. It was a welcome reminder of the woman who brightened his very existence. Gabriel continued on his way home when his stomach clenched into a knot. He stepped between two buildings in case he was going to throw up. Leaning one hand against the brick wall of the factory, he took deep breaths, attempting to settle whatever bug had crawled into his system.

The heat crept up his neck, his hands began throbbing. His gums felt as if they were on fire. The pain searing through his back was unlike anything he had ever known. "Hey, buddy, you all right?" A voice asked from behind. He couldn't answer. Gabriel dropped to the ground, and his world went straight to hell.

"Holy Mother of God! Do you see this shit? Flanagan's going to give us a raise!" Voices infiltrated his ears. When he woke up, Gabriel was strapped to a table. Bright lights were shining in his eyes, causing the pain in his head to multiply tenfold. "What's your name?" His bottom eyelid was pulled down, and a flashlight was shining brighter than he could withstand. When he attempted to move his head, nothing happened.

"Good thing you clamped this freak down. He's a strong one." One of the men in white lab coats pulled his lip up, looking at his teeth. No, not teeth. His fangs. *Oh, gods, I've transitioned.*

"Hey, freak, what's your name? Is anyone going to miss you, or are they going to be glad to be rid of the circus act?" White coat number two measured his claws. "I asked you a question. What's your name?"

When the man held a needle close enough to touch Gabriel's eye, he whimpered, "Vincent."

"Vincent what? Do you have a last name, or should we make up one for you? Not that you will need one where you're going."

Gabriel knew he had to calm himself. He was strapped to a table and if his wings decided to come out, it would probably hurt like hell. "Alexander. Vincent Alexander."

Gabriel pulled the first name out of the air that came to mind. Vincent Alexander had been a bully of the worst kind. If anyone were to deserve this type of treatment, it was him.

"Well, Vincent, let's see what you're made of."

What happened after next was a blur. A painful, bloody blur. Gabriel had no idea how long he was abused, he just knew it was long enough to wish he were dead.

No, not dead. I swam. I swam out of the water. But Rebekah was gone. He took her away. Only Izzy was there, waiting for me. Vincent didn't want to think about the white coats anymore. He didn't want to sleep either, because that's where she was. His sunshine.

He dropped to the floor and, on unsteady arms, began doing push-ups.

Thirty-Five

Merrick's Mustang was packed full of clothes and weapons. There was little else in the small apartment that belonged to him. He was fairly certain he was safe hanging around New Atlanta, but he wasn't making any headway. Extending the killing field to the next state over would hopefully flush out Flanagan's daughter. His calling card to Andrea so far had done no good. The police had found the body, but another press conference hadn't been issued.

Just like Alexander's place, the rent on his apartment was paid up for a year. He didn't mind moving around, but he had grown fond of the busy area around New Atlanta. The city was teeming with bars which meant lots of women willing to have a one night stand. Having gone without sex while in the army had become tedious. Now he was making up for lost pussy. Merrick had decided to head north to Tennessee. The drive wouldn't take long and New Nashville was large enough for him to get lost there.

Traffic was heavier than usual with it being Halloween. Parents were driving their kids to the fancy neighborhoods to beg for candy. He pulled into a convenience store parking lot to fuel up. While the gas was pumping, he went into the store for a carton of cigarettes. After he paid, a colorful flyer on the door snagged his attention.

Fall Festival, County Fairgrounds

As he topped off the gas tank, Merrick thought back to his childhood and the festivals he had attended with his mom. They had been dirt poor, but she made sure they had enough money for at least a candy apple and a couple of rides. All of a sudden, nostalgia took over, and he decided he would check out this year's festival for old time's sake. He cranked the Mustang and headed toward the fairground.

231

Tessa had driven around all day and was no closer to finding the answers to the questions stabbing at her brain. If her subconscious asked her *why* one more time, she was going to go crazy. Stark-raving mad. Certifiable, put her in Milledgeville, nuts. She wasn't one-hundred percent sure the insane asylum still existed. Even better. She deserved to be locked up alone.

As soon as she left Gregor's, she made the mistake of calling her mother while she was driving around. What started off as a bitch session on her part soon turned into a crying fest. Tessa wasn't normally overly emotional, but now that Gregor was in the picture and she had tasted how good life would be living as his mate, her hormones had kicked into overdrive. Before they hung up, Elizabeth shocked her by telling her to follow her heart. Elizabeth thought by telling Xavier that Gregor was her mate, he would back off with the secrecy. She should have known better. Xavier was being overly cautious as he always was when it came to Tessa. Her mother reminded her she was a grown woman and should make her own choices, especially where affairs of the heart were concerned. Her father would just have to deal with her decision. Tessa thought back to the tarot reader. *Follow your heart.*

If only it were that easy. All her life, Jonas had drilled into her the importance of secrecy. When she stopped and thought about it, was he right in having her hide her existence? From Flanagan, yes. But to keep herself away from her mate when Jonas had forsaken his whole Clan to be with Caroline? Why was he any better than she?

Tessa pulled into the gas station to refuel. She walked into the store to see a smiling Peggy. She laid two twenties on the counter and told her fill-up on four. She hadn't driven the Camaro in so long she didn't know if forty bucks would fill up the tank or not, but it would be enough to get her where she needed to go. After chatting with the cashier for a beat, she went back outside. An advertisement for the Fall Festival caught her eye. She had never been to one of those festivals when she was little. She and her mom had been holed up in their huge house, hiding out from Flanagan.

She leaned a hip against the back quarter panel while the gas pumped. A family-themed Halloween function wasn't exactly how she wanted to spend her afternoon, but it might be better than going home alone and moping. The pump clicked off, and she returned the nozzle to its slot. After resetting the mileage counter, she headed her hotrod toward the festival.

The gravel parking lot was filled with SUV's and mini-vans. Tessa found a spot as far away from the other vehicles as possible. She backed into a spot close to the carnival ride trailers. She beeped the locks and set the alarm, cringing at the dust that was already settling on the hood. While she had spent a lot of money customizing her ride, she was very envious of the hot little number Gregor had stored in his garage. That had to have set him back a bit.

Tessa paid for an armband and ambled through the throngs of people already enjoying sugary treats on sticks and carrying stuffed animals under their arms. The food lines were ten deep. Carnival workers called out as she passed by, tempting her to try her luck at some silly game. Little kids were fishing for plastic ducks, older kids were throwing baseballs. The sounds and lights could cause a lesser woman to have a headache.

A very sad child ran into Tessa's legs. The tears must have clouded her vision because she looked up, startled. The little girl's mother grabbed her hand and apologized to Tessa. "I'm so sorry. She didn't win the duck." Tessa studied the booth behind the woman where the child had been playing.

"That duck over there?" Tessa asked the mother. When she nodded, Tessa told her to hang on. She walked up to the carnival worker and asked, "What do I have to do to win the duck?"

The teenager looked on the wall at the toy then told her, "Hit at least ten targets."

Tessa laid a five down and picked up the toy looking rifle. "Let's do this." The little girl had stepped up beside Tessa, her eyes wide. Tessa grinned at her. Raising the gun to her shoulder and aiming, shot after shot hit the target. Without counting, Tessa figured she had hit around thirty. She put the rifle back where she got it and asked the little girl, "What color do you want?"

"Purple, please." The little girl was smiling from ear to ear.

A fucking purple duck. Tessa told the worker, "The purple duck it is."

When the child held the stuffed toy securely in her arms, she wrapped herself around Tessa's legs. "Thank you, lady."

Tessa laughed out loud and ran her hand down the little girl's hair. "You're welcome, little lady." The mother also thanked her before she took the little girl's hand and walked off.

"That was really nice of you," the teenager working the booth said to her back.

Tessa looked at him and shrugged. "It was fun." She watched the mother and daughter wistfully then convinced her feet to move. Gregor had said he wanted kids. A houseful. She figured with the few Gargoyle offspring who had been born lately, all the males would want kids to carry on the species. The question was, did he want to be a father? Not just a sperm donor who relegated the parental responsibilities to the mother or a nanny, but a real dad who doted on his kids and taught them things like how to throw a football or how to ride a bike. All the things Tessa's own father hadn't had time for.

Tessa wasn't one to complain about her childhood. She had experienced things no other kid would even dream of. Sure, she played dress-up with her mother and had tea parties with dolls, but more importantly, Tessa had sat on a stool watching her uncle in the lab. He would teach her and quiz her about formulas and theories. Tamian had grown up the same way, learning from Jonas. Between the two of them, they could probably make their own clone.

Seeing a short line at one of the food shacks, Tessa decided she needed to try at least one treat that would probably cause instant cavities. The people moved up as the orders were taken, and the man in front of her turned right into her, spilling some powdered sugar covered waffle thing all over her. She attempted to wipe the white powder off her shirt. The man apologized profusely, trying to hand her a napkin. Tessa started to tell him she was fine and his assistance wasn't necessary until their eyes met. Some sort of recognition registered in her brain. The tall, well-built, very handsome stranger stopped talking. His mouth opened to say something then closed again. "Excuse me," he muttered as he abruptly brushed by her shoulder.

Tessa was no longer in the mood for food. What she longed for was something cold to drink. She doubted the family function would have a liquor bar. Whether it was female intuition or something more spiritual, the feeling in her gut told her the man she ran into was bad news. For her.

Not wasting any time, Tessa headed toward the nearest exit. She opened her senses, reaching, searching. Adults arguing, children laughing, separate it. Dissect it all. There, faintly. "I think I've found her, Sir. At the fairground. Yes, Sir, she looks just like the picture. Okay, I'll get her."

Tessa didn't wait around for tall, dark, and dangerous to catch up with her. She hurried through the

235

masses. As soon as she reached the exit she took off as fast as her booted feet would carry her. Before she left Gregor's house earlier, she had changed out of her yoga pants into jeans and boots. Her shifter hearing alerted her to the sound of feet gaining on her. She pulled her keys out of her front pocket and thumbed the key fob, hitting the remote start. She unlocked the car and practically dove into the driver's seat. She threw the gearshift into drive and shoved the gas pedal to the floorboard. The forward momentum closed the door just as she passed her pursuer.

Fortunately, he was still running behind her. Unfortunately, his vehicle happened to be within a few feet of him. Tessa dodged cars and festival goers as best she could without slinging too much gravel. The cloud of dust behind her blocked her view of the other vehicle. Dammit! Why couldn't she be closer to home? Closer to Gregor. When the dust settled, a black Mustang was visible in her review mirror. Unless the driver had modified his car, there was no way he would catch her. She took the car out of automatic and slid the shifter over to manual. The black car was keeping up with her but just barely. "Shit. SHIT! You're the son of a bitch who's been chasing me," she said to the image in her mirror.

Several miles down the road, an odd sound infiltrated Tessa's senses. She shifted her sight between the curvy road in front of her and the car in her mirror. She rolled down her window and the unmistakable sound of a helicopter floated through the air. "Fuck me." She could probably outrun the Mustang, but there was no way she could get away from a helicopter. She needed a bird of her own. She pressed a button on her steering wheel. When it beeped, she said, "Call Gregor."

It wasn't Gregor's night to patrol, but there was no way he could return home with Tessa's scent embedded in every room, every piece of furniture. He would have to burn the bear rug as well as his bedding. Fuck, he'd probably have to rip out the carpet and chop up the kitchen table, too. He and Tessa had made good use of every room in the house with the exception of the spare bedrooms. They would probably have gotten to those, too, but eventually she had worn down and fallen asleep.

Her red hair spilling over his chest was a vision that would forever be burned into his mind. Her sandalwood scent had permeated his nostrils. The way she moved her body, the smiles she gave him, the groans she released when they fucked, gods those things had taken purchase in his soul. Gregor had never made love to any woman in his five hundred years. Until last night. Until Tessa. He didn't even know he had it in him to be slow and gentle. Only once had his mate asked for slow. The other times his heart just told him he needed it. *They* needed it. Fuck his heart. It had lied. He opened his senses. The sun would be going down soon, and he would take to the air, find some Unholy bastards to shred.

The other Clan members had gone about their own lives. Some were getting ready to patrol, some were back at their jobs. Gregor just wanted to go. Anywhere away from where he was. Where Tessa was. He walked down the corridor to the men's room and took a piss. He was washing his hands when his phone rang. Fuck it. He didn't want to talk to anyone. He dried his hands then tossed the paper towels in the trash can. His phone stopped ringing but immediately rang again. Sighing, he pulled it out of its holder and answered it.

"Stone."

"Gregor! I need you." Tessa was breathing heavily.

Gregor's heart skipped about five beats. "What made you change your mind?"

"No, I fucking need you. I'm being chased, and there's a fucking helicopter after me, too. Godsdamnit! I don't know who the fucker is on my tail, but I'm pretty sure the asshole in the bird is Flanagan."

"Shit, where are you?" Gregor was running through the corridors. He tagged Deacon's shirt and dragged him along putting Tessa on speakerphone.

"I'm headed north on Forty-One. Dammit, I know these roads better than anyone, but with a chopper tagging my every move, I can't get away."

"Okay, Baby, stay on the line. I'm getting Frey on Deacon's phone." Deacon handed him his cell and he barked into the mouthpiece, "Frey, I need the bird. The big one. Now. Tessa's being chased and she thinks it's Flanagan. I'm headed her direction. She's driving north on Forty-One. We need to intercept her before something happens."

Gregor realized he had ridden his bike to work. "Deacon! Keys!" Deacon tossed him the keys to his truck and told him to go. He would call the rest of the Clan to help.

Gregor climbed into the tall four-wheel drive and told Tessa, "Baby, just hang on. I'm coming to get you."

Thirty-Six

Gregor was banking on Jasper and Dane giving him a police escort so any state troopers in the area wouldn't slow his mission. And he was definitely on a mission. How could Tessa have found so much fucking trouble in the few hours since he had seen her? Was this the danger she had been talking about? Deacon's four-wheel drive truck moaned under the strain of being pushed so hard. Sirens blared in the distance. The scene in the rearview mirror was two unmarked cars weaving around other vehicles that didn't have time to move out of the way.

When the vehicles pulled up alongside him, he was relieved to see Dane and Jasper in one car, Kaya and Rafael in the other. Rafael gave him a thumbs up, and he once more turned his attention to the voice on the phone. Gregor was glad Tessa had hands free calling. She continued to give him play by plays of what was happening and where she was. If it weren't for the helicopter, he was sure she could outdrive her opponent. For some reason, the helicopter wasn't pursuing her, it was just tracking her movements. Probably to keep whoever was in the Mustang from losing her. If it was Flanagan, he would want her alive.

Speaking of helicopters, the unmistakable whir of blades came into earshot, and Gregor knew Frey was closing in. Now for the hard part. To communicate with his cousin, Gregor was going to have to disconnect from his call with Tessa. As soon as he got a break in her cursing, he interrupted, "Tessa, I need to hang up for a minute. I have to tell Frey exactly where you and the other bird are, okay?"

"Fine, just hurry the fuck up. And Gregor, when you get here and you catch this motherfucker on my tail, I get first crack at him, you hear me?"

"I hear you, Red. I will call you right back." He disconnected and called Frey.

"Gregor, Julian has radar on the screen. I have the other bird's coordinates locked in. I'm about 15 minutes out."

"Roger that. Frey, I don't have to tell you to do whatever you have to do to keep Flanagan or whoever it is in the sky away from my mate."

"No, you don't. I see the Chief has chosen to take her role as Queen very seriously. We are getting out of her jurisdiction, and things could get ugly."

Gregor gripped the wheel tighter. He didn't care how ugly things got as long as Tessa came out of this unscathed. "You just do what you have to. I'm hanging up and calling Tessa back for an update."

The helicopter went on ahead and Gregor took the exit off the interstate that led to the smaller two-lane road. Dammit! He wished he were in the helicopter with Frey. Fuck it, he was going to get there quicker. He hit redial, and when Frey picked up, he told him to circle back around. Gregor found a pullover and shut the truck off. When the others pulled up beside him, he told them to go ahead and he would meet them there, wherever there was. He would call them if Tessa turned off this road.

When the Blackhawk was closing in, Gregor removed his shirt and phased, flying up to meet Frey so he didn't have to land. Lorenzo was in the co-pilot seat and pointed to his headphones. Instead of grabbing a set of cans and putting them over his ears, he shook his head and dialed Tessa. "Baby, are you still on Forty-One?"

"Yes, but the helicopter is trying to get me to pull over. He keeps dipping down in front of me. I don't know how much longer I can keep this up."

"Just hang on, Red. I'm in the bird with Frey and we should have the other helo in our sights very soon. Please, Baby, hang on."

Lorenzo pointed to the headset again and this time Gregor put his on. "I need to keep talking to Tessa, what is it?"

"Julian has confirmed the other bird is an Apache, and it's loaded with an arsenal."

"And he knows this how?" Gregor pulled one side of the cans off and put the cell phone to his ear so he could listen to Tessa.

"Beats the hell out of me. He's Julian. We need to be ready to phase and bail if necessary."

"Gregor, oh shit, Gregor I..." The sounds of glass breaking, metal crunching, and Tessa screaming were coming through the phone. Frey cursing came through the cans, and the sight that came into view stopped Gregor's heart. The other helicopter was hovering over one of the worst crashes Gregor had ever seen, and his woman was down there somewhere. Both cars had flipped and rolled down an embankment. The Camaro was on its top, jagged sheet metal jutting out at odd angles. The Mustang was wrapped around a tree. Once again, with no thought for humans in the area, Gregor dove out of the Blackhawk, phasing on the fly, to get to his woman.

As soon as his feet hit the pavement, Gregor retracted his wings and yelled, "Tessa! TESSA!" He ran down the embankment to the front of her car. Upon first glance he didn't see her anywhere. Sirens screamed behind him and artillery fire was going off in the sky. "TESSA!"

Both cars screeched to a stop beside the wreckage. Rafael took over, telling Dane and Jasper to secure whoever was in the other vehicle. Kaya called for an ambulance. Rafael climbed down to Tessa's Camaro and scanned the area behind the car. Red hair was spread on the ground, barely visible. "Over here!" Rafael called for Gregor.

The sight of Tessa's body pinned underneath the wreckage had Gregor roaring. He lifted the car off his

241

mate's lifeless body, flipping it onto its tires. "NO, NO, NOOOOOOOOOO!"

"Greg, don't move her," Rafael advised as they knelt down next to Tessa. It had been a long time since anyone called him that. He had insisted on everyone using his full name when he transitioned. Greg was the little boy he left behind. Now it was appropriate. He felt like a helpless child as he softly pushed Tessa's long red hair off of her face. Cuts crisscrossed her skin. Bruises were already forming. The femur of her left leg was visible. Her right arm was at an odd angle and the left was beneath her body. If she had been wearing her seatbelt she probably wouldn't be all cut up. Then again, she might have been crushed to death. He had no idea of the internal damage done by the car landing on her. Rafael cursed as a fireball lit up the sky. Even the possibility of his cousin being shot down couldn't drag Gregor's tear-filled eyes away from his mate.

Frey had flown combat missions in more than one war. He had never lost a chopper, and he wasn't about to lose this one. The Clan owned a commercial helicopter that was registered in the family's name. This bird, however, was not on anyone's list. Frey happened to have commandeered it several years ago and just forgot to return it.

Even though Lorenzo was a Gargoyle, he wasn't combat trained. Very few of the Stone Clan were. Still, it was good to have a co-pilot to be his eyes on the ground so he could keep his own eyes on the enemy. Whoever was flying the other helo had skills, but none that compared to Geoffrey's.

He maneuvered so he was alongside the other helicopter. When he was close, he could see someone leaning out the side door, eyes intent on the carnage below. Frey was staring at Gordon Flanagan. He needed to get them as far away from the wreckage as possible, and away from any neighborhoods below. When the other bird didn't move, Frey eased around, putting himself as close as he could without disrupting his family on the ground. He edged closer, getting their attention. Flanagan motioned to the pilot who moved away from the area. Kaya had already told Geoffrey to apprehend Flanagan by any means necessary. Even though she hadn't said the words, he interpreted them to mean dead or alive.

Both helicopters were military grade, loaded for bear. The Apache might be smaller and quicker, but Frey and his Blackhawk were almost one entity. Neither he nor Lorenzo were scared of being shot out of the air; they could phase and fly before they hit the ground. They just wanted to capture Flanagan with as little damage to the area below them as possible. Their plan was squashed when Flanagan's pilot maneuvered the bird into a quick one-eighty and opened fire. Frey dodged the rapid-fire rounds while returning his own volley.

A game of chicken ensued with both pilots proving to be unforgiving. "Do you want me to phase and take them out from inside?" Lorenzo was obviously ready to be on the ground. Frey glanced down and took in the number of rescue vehicles headed to the crash site. While humans usually never looked up, the constant spray of gunfire was surely garnering attention.

"If there were no civilians on the ground, I would say yes. It's going to be hard enough to get out of this situation without getting Kaya in trouble, much less ourselves. FUCK!" A small rocket barely missed the tail of the Blackhawk. If his shifter hearing hadn't alerted him to the Hydra being launched, they would probably be going down. "I'm tired of playing with this motherfucker. I say we go big or go home, and right now, I'm going big."

It might be overkill, but Frey locked on with a Hellfire missile. He pressed the red "fire" button, and within seconds, Gordon Flanagan's helicopter erupted into flames. Geoffrey didn't wait around to find out if the man lived or died. He needed to get out the vicinity and hoped like hell none of this came back on Kaya or the Clan.

He kept radio silence so that no transmission could be tracked. Lorenzo looked back at the smoke on the ground. "Do you see any survivors?" Frey asked as he flew east towards his home.

"No, all I see is smoke. Do you want me to call to the ground, find out how Tessa is?"

Frey's face became grimmer. If Tessa didn't pull through her injuries, Gregor was going to lose his shit. "Yeah, but call Rafe. Tell him unless it's imperative he has the bird for transport, we're going incognito."

Frey sent up a silent prayer to the gods that Tessa be okay. Lorenzo hung up and didn't speak. He appeared to be offering his own prayers. *Well fuck.*

Thirty-Seven

Kaya was talking to Curtis Standifer, the local Chief, attempting to smooth things over for being out of her jurisdiction. She explained she was there as family, not as an officer of the law. Rafael had called Dante and told him to get in touch with Joseph Mooneyham. Joe was a lone wolf sort of Gargoyle, staying out of Clan business. He was Chief of Staff at New Atlanta hospital, and one of the brightest doctors and surgeons in the States. Rafe explained the seriousness of Tessa's injuries, and how Joseph was the only one he trusted to work on her. He meant no offense to Dante and none was taken. They both knew Dante's limitations, and neither was willing to risk a mate's life because of pride.

The fire and rescue crews were using the Jaws of Life to extract the driver of the Mustang from his vehicle. Tessa was being secured to a board for transport. It broke Rafael's heart to see Gregor in so much pain. If the roles were reversed, he didn't know that he would be containing himself half as well as Gregor was. He hadn't moved from Tessa's side except to give the medics room to maneuver. A medical helicopter was on its way to transport her to the hospital.

Rafael was proud of Kaya. She had taken one look at Tessa and immediately went into Queen mode. She was not ordering her men around. She was consoling Gregor, and asking Dane and Jasper for assistance in dealing with the police and emergency crews. The only time she lost her shit was when Katherine Fox showed up, way before any news crew should have received the information. Kaya threatened Dane, telling him if he let Katherine anywhere near Tessa, she would rip his wings off with her bare hands.

The medical helicopter arrived and landed in the middle of the two-lane road Tessa had been driving on before she flipped. "We're ready, Sir." The medics were speaking to Gregor, but it was Rafael who spoke up.

"Take her to New Atlanta. Dr. Joseph Mooneyham is standing by with his team." They nodded, gently lifted the board holding Tessa, and carried her up the hill to the waiting transport. Gregor didn't move. He was immobile and still silent, having not said a word since he found Tessa's body. Rafael placed a hand on his shoulder, "Greg, are you going to ride with her?"

Gregor blinked back the tears and nodded. Rafael grabbed his neck and touched their foreheads together for strength. When Rafe released him, Gregor followed her broken body and climbed in the helicopter beside her. Rafael yelled after him, "We'll meet you there." The bird lifted off the ground, headed to the one man, the only man who could possibly put Tessa back together. If she had been fully human, she would not be breathing. But Tessa was tough, and Rafael had to believe the fates wouldn't put her and Gregor together only to tear them apart so quickly.

Rafael walked over to where Kaya was finishing her statement to the locals. "We need to go, Love." When the Chief opened his mouth to object, Rafael interrupted. "Kaya is the Chief of Police in New Atlanta. You know where to find her should you need further information. My brother needs his family with him. Now."

Rafael walked Kaya to her car, with Jasper and Dane going to theirs. Once underway, Rafael asked, "How bad is it?"

Kaya kept her eyes on the road. "If Geoffrey covered his own tracks, then not bad at all. I explained to Curtis what happened, how Tessa called Gregor who happened to be with us. He thought I should have called for back-up sooner than I did, but I explained we weren't absolutely sure of what was happening. I told him we don't know who the driver of the Mustang is or why he was chasing Tessa.

That's the truth. Do you think this Joseph is going to be able to save her?"

"If anyone can, it will be Joe." Rafael put his arm on the seat behind Kaya and placed his hand on her neck under her blonde hair. He had been itching to touch her for the last hour. The need to be close to her had not waned in the last few weeks. If anything, it had intensified. With Kaya going back to work, Rafael was still getting used to not seeing her twenty-four seven.

"Is he part of your Clan? I haven't heard you mention him before." Kaya was far enough away from the wreckage that she flipped on her lights and her siren.

"Joseph is hard to explain. He showed up about ten years ago. When new shifters enter an area, they are required to meet with the leader and declare their Clan. He refused to give me a Clan name but assured me he would gladly serve under my leadership. I didn't push it. We needed a good doctor on the inside. Rarely do we need medical attention, but on the off-chance we do, it needs to be one of our own."

Rafael could see the medical helicopter ahead in the distance. He called Julian to give him an update and have him call the others. A waiting room full of shifters might not be a good idea, but with Tessa as critical as she was, Gregor needed all the support he could get. "Julian, see if you can trace Elizabeth Flanagan's number from when she called the Pen. She needs to know her daughter's condition."

"I'm on it. Do you want me to call Nikolas back?"

"No, let him go. Sophia is his mate, and if she's in trouble, he needs to be there for her. We have a long wait ahead of us. Please get with Dante. I need you two to find out who was driving the Mustang. I also want to know if there were any survivors in the helicopter."

"Will do. And Rafe? Tell Gregor I'm there for him." The phone disconnected. If anything ever happened to Kaya, Rafe would not want to live. How could she have burrowed into his soul so quickly? He would just pray that Joseph could undo the damage to Tessa.

The medics constantly worked on Tessa to keep her stabilized. Her vitals were all over the place. Gregor stayed out of their way but did not move from her side. His hand was on her bare leg. He felt the tears wetting his eyes when he noticed the shirt that had been cut away from Tessa was actually his. She must have snagged it from his dirty clothes hamper before she left. She was laid out in front of him and everyone else in only her underwear. He wanted to cover the black lace panties, but the attendants were not focused on her crotch. He realized his own shirt was still wrapped around his waist, so he quickly shrugged it on.

Gregor studied the cuts marring Tessa's skin. He knew plastic surgery could heal those, but he didn't care. She would still be the most beautiful woman in the world if the gashes all over her body healed to pale pink lines. The important part was getting the internal damage fixed. The pilot alerted them that they would be landing soon.

Once the helicopter set down on the pad atop the hospital, nurses were waiting to take Tessa inside to surgery. The medics carefully lifted the board and Tessa onto the waiting gurney, and they all moved as one unit. Gregor followed until they came to a double door. Joseph Mooneyham was waiting for his patient. He nodded at Gregor. When he turned his eyes to his patient, he whispered, "No."

Gregor stepped up to the doctor he had met a couple of times. "What's wrong? Joseph, she's my m... she's my fiancée. You have to help her."

The other man nodded. "You have my word; I will do my best." Joseph directed the staff to the O.R. and Gregor shouted, "Wait!" He hurried to the gurney and leaned over Tessa, softly kissing her lips, whispering "I love you" against them. He knew it was too soon to declare his feelings, but he also didn't want it to be too late.

Gregor found himself alone. He glanced around feeling lost until one of the nurses came back out. "Mr. Stone, if you will follow me, I need to get some information." Gregor followed the nurse. He filled out the paperwork as if Tessa were indeed his fiancée. He listed himself as the individual responsible for payment. After that, he expected to be put in a small room where he would feel as caged as his inmates. Instead, he was taken to a large room that was filled with the faces he needed to see right now. Gregor prided himself on being strong, but at this moment, he felt anything but. The emotion roiling through his heart and mind was one he'd never experienced: despair.

Rafael was the first one to reach him, pulling him into a tight embrace. "Brother." One by one the others offered their own support, then they all settled in for what was sure to be a long night.

"Dante and Julian are working to find out who the driver of the car was and if there were any survivors in the chopper crash." Rafael was barely whispering, knowing the others' shifter ears would detect his words. They didn't need the humans to overhear any part of their conversation. Kaya was already privy to the knowledge, so she had gone seeking coffee for them all. "Deacon is manning the Pen, and Sixx is on his way."

Gregor just nodded then turned toward the door, waiting. Kaya came back with coffee, but he declined. His adrenaline was still at an all-time high, and he needed to calm himself. Caffeine would not help. The others settled into the less than comfortable waiting room chairs and let Gregor have his space. Time dragged on. Minutes then hours passed. The second hand on the clock was deafening as it ticked, so very slowly. If by some miracle Joseph was able to save Tessa, Gregor would spend every minute of every day making up for lost time. Even though she was the one to steal the last three years away from them, he would be the one giving them back to her. If she would let him. Maybe she only reached out to him because she knew he had the resources to help her out of the dangerous situation she had found herself in. He had to trust that she would not have called him if she didn't want him in her life.

Gregor could feel the pull of the moon. He wanted to go outside for some fresh air, but he would not be any farther away from Tessa than he was at this moment. Some of the others had gone outside for a break, never staying away long. Dante called with an update. The driver of the Mustang had been dead at the scene when they pulled him from the wreckage. His neck had been severed and the blood loss too substantial. He was identified as Richard Merrick. The Redhead Killer had been the one chasing Tessa.

This brought about another conversation. Frey was pretty sure the man in the other helo was Gordon Flanagan. At least he looked enough like him to make that assumption, but the man who died in the warehouse a few weeks back had looked just like a Flanagan too. Until the body was recovered and a positive DNA match made, they wouldn't know conclusively.

The night had turned into day when the waiting room door opened. Joseph walked through, looking like he had spent all night fighting Unholy. The man was worn out and weary.

Gregor couldn't stand the silence or the unknown any longer. "Joseph, please tell me. Is Tessa okay? Is she going to make it?"

Thirty-Eight

Before the doctor could answer Gregor, the waiting room door burst open, and Tamian ran in. He took one look at the doctor and said, "What the fuck?" Gregor didn't miss Joseph shaking his head at Tessa's brother. Did they know each other? It was possible. The Clan hadn't known Tamian was a shifter or that the half-bloods even existed a week before. They knew so little about Tessa and her side of the shifter family.

"I was just going to give an update on Miss Blackmore." He turned his attention to Gregor. "She is stable, although I induced a coma until the swelling around her brain shrinks. Her internal injuries weren't as serious as we thought once we got in there. She had bleeding we were able to stop. Both arms and her left leg had broken bones, all of which have been repaired. The left side of her body sustained the most injury. Both bones in her left forearm, and the radius in her right arm required plates and screws. Both arms are in temporary splints. Her left leg was quite devastated. Her femur required an intramedullary nail. She was very lucky the femoral artery was not punctured. The good news is once her arms heal, she will be able to use crutches to get around, and her leg will heal quickly. Her injuries could have been much worse."

"How long will she be in a coma? When can I see her?" Knowing his mate was alive had Gregor's adrenaline rising again. The beast inside knew his mate was close, and he wanted to be near her, touching her.

"We will need to monitor the swelling for a few days until it has gone down enough to ascertain whether there is any neurological damage. She is in recovery. We will be moving her into ICU within the hour. You can see her then.

251

Gregor, I need you to prepare yourself before you go in. She is hooked up to machines; wires and tubes are everywhere. She needs you calm and strong, yes?"

Gregor nodded. "Thank you, Joseph, I don't know…" He couldn't finish his sentence. The tears in his eyes and the emotion clogging his throat silenced him.

"You can thank me by taking good care of her. That woman in there is special. Someone will be down soon to take you to see her." Joseph walked off before Gregor could ask any questions. How the hell did he know Tessa was special?

The waiting room door opened again, and Isabelle came in, tears streaking her pretty face. She just stood there, looking as lost as Gregor felt. "Isabelle, come here." He opened his arms and she hesitantly walked into them. They didn't know each other well, but they had one common bond, and that was Tessa. Gregor explained her condition and that he was going to see her soon.

"I'm sorry I just got here. I didn't know. I got to work this morning and Deacon told me. When I finally checked my phone, I saw I had several missed calls from Dante. He is probably mad at me, but I turned the ringer off last night so I could rest."

"Shh, it's all right. You're here now. Besides, there was nothing you could have done during the night except worry like the rest of us. At least you got some sleep." Gregor released her from his embrace. He could tell she was overwhelmed with all the shifter testosterone in the room until Kaya came over, introduced herself, and took Isabelle away from him. Rafael's mate was making an excellent Queen.

Gregor told everyone to go home and get some rest. He knew Tamian and Isabelle would remain, but the others wouldn't need to go in and see Tessa. He assured them he was fine, and he would need them strong in the coming days. Isabelle and Tamian were talking quietly in one corner

252

of the room. He could listen in if he wanted, but instead gave them their privacy. If he weren't a greedy bastard, he would let them go in and see Tessa first, but he was.

Sooner than expected, a nurse came in and called for him. He wiped his hands down his jeans. He wasn't sweating, it was just a nervous gesture. "I'll be back soon so you can go see her," he told both Isabelle and Tamian. Again, they huddled together.

Gregor followed the nurse until they came to a sanitizing sink. "Please wash and dry your hands before you go into the patient's room." He did as instructed and once again followed the older lady down another hallway. The room she led him into had the nurse's station in the middle with the patient rooms surrounding the outer walls in a circular pattern. All the rooms had glass windows the nurses could see into. None of the curtains were closed, exposing everyone to passersby.

Gregor only had eyes for one patient. The nurse didn't have to tell him Tessa's room number. The mate bond took him to her. He stood outside her room, looking at her still body through the window. He willed his own body to calm. It would do no good for his claws or fangs to scare the humans. When he was ready, he entered her room and quietly stood over his mate, taking in the wires and tubing Joseph had warned him were present. Her beautiful red hair was matted together, some blood still present. Gregor wanted to pick her up and put her in the shower, wash it for her.

Now that the blood had been cleaned from her skin, Gregor was able to count the lacerations visible on her face and arms. He knew there were more hiding beneath the cotton hospital gown, but he wouldn't shock the nurses by unrobing her just yet. "Talk to her." A soft voice came from behind him. He turned to see the same older nurse standing in the doorway. "It helps if you talk to them. They can hear loved ones even though they're in a coma. She needs to know you're here for her, that you're waiting on her to return to you." The nurse smiled and left him alone with his woman.

Pulling up a chair, he sat as close to the bed as his knees would allow. Gregor picked up Tessa's once strong hand that was now sticking out of a splint. He gently held it, stroking her skin with his thumb. "Hey, Red. It's me, Gregor. I'm here, Baby. The doctor says you have a little bit of swelling on your brain, but he's optimistic you are going to be fine. You just need to get some rest. Tamian and Isabelle are here, too. They want to come in and see you. I really want to keep you all to myself, but you would probably rather see them than me anyway."

Gregor quieted and just admired her sleeping form. Fuck, was it just yesterday morning they had shared his bed together? It felt like a lifetime ago. He really didn't want to leave her, but her brother and cousin had as much of a right to visit with her since she wasn't yet his mate. "I'm going to go get Tamian now. But I will be back. I'm not leaving you, Red. I'll be here with you until you wake up. Then I will be here long after that, if you'll have me." He placed a soft kiss on her cut knuckles then one on her chapped lips. He needed to remember to go to the gift shop downstairs and get a lip balm for her.

He released her hand, and one of the monitors started beeping. The nurse came in and pushed a button, quieting the monitor. "What happened?" she asked Gregor. The nurse wasn't accusing him of harming Tessa, she was just concerned.

"I told her I would be back later and released her hand."

"Take hold of her hand." The nurse waited patiently while Gregor did as she told him. He sat back down in the chair and took Tessa's hand in his. The nurse smiled. "She knows you're here. You have a calming effect when you are touching. You let go and her heart started racing."

254

"I need to let her brother and cousin come see her. Will she be okay if I leave for a while?" Gregor wouldn't risk her health, not even for Tamian.

"She'll be fine. I will stay here with her until they come in." The nurse pushed a stray strand of hair off Tessa's forehead. He trusted her to keep Tessa calm until he returned.

"Thank you..." He glanced at her name badge. "Miriam. I will send Tamian and Isabelle in. I'll be back soon." Gregor lingered at the door, assuring himself Tessa would be okay long enough for the others to visit. His heart was once again beating erratically. His beast warred inside, not wanting to leave its mate.

Gregor found Tamian and Isabelle where he'd left them. He told them to follow him, and they could each go see her for a few minutes. Isabelle spoke to several nurses and doctors on the way to the ICU. She would most likely look at Tessa in a clinical way, being able to use her own experience as a doctor to stay calm when seeing her cousin. Tamian was another story. The waves of energy bouncing off the man were almost visible to the eye. He was going to have to calm himself before he went into the room.

"I want Isabelle to go first," Gregor told them.

Knowing the drill, Isabelle scrubbed her hands before heading to Tessa's room.

"Tamian, you've got to lock it down, man. I know what you're feeling. I may not have the psychic twin thing you two have, but she is my mate. She is aware of who's in the room with her, and she doesn't need you feeding her a shit ton of extra emotions."

Tamian nodded. "I'm trying. She's been my whole world up to this point. Growing up we were separated most of the time, but we still had the type of connection twins have. We are so deeply connected on a cellular level that I can almost feel her pain from here."

Gregor flinched. "She's in pain? Right now?"

"No, not physically. It's more an emotional hurt. Hopefully I will be able to get a feel for what's going on when I'm in the room with her."

Isabelle didn't linger long. She returned and had Tamian wash up then pointed to the correct room. She and Gregor were silent as Tamian made his way to his sister's room. Just as they turned to go back to the waiting room, alarms started blaring and Tamian yelled, "NO!"

Gregor didn't care about the one person at a time rule; he entered Tessa's room among hospital personnel trying to shoo both he and Tamian from the room. Neither one budged. When the nurses couldn't get Tessa's vitals under control, Miriam motioned for Gregor. "Get over here and hold her hand." He didn't hesitate. He gently lifted Tessa's hand closest to him and immediately her body began calming. The other workers looked at each other then at Gregor. Miriam smiled. "I believe she needs you more than she needs us right now." Gregor pulled up the chair that had been shoved away from the bed and sat down, not releasing Tessa's hand.

"I should go." Tamian turned to leave the room. He mumbled, "She obviously doesn't need me."

"St. Claire, stay. She does need you. I need you, too." Gregor lowered his voice so the nurses couldn't hear. "With any luck at all on my part, Tessa will agree to be my mate. That means you and I will be brothers. You might not feel it, but you are already part of our Clan. Now, please stay and be with your sister. If you need privacy, just do that mind speak stuff you do."

Tamian hesitated for a few seconds then returned to Tessa's side and gently lifted her other hand. Instead of speaking silently, he talked to her out loud so Gregor could hear him. He didn't talk about anything in particular, just let her hear his voice. Her body remained calm throughout the rest of her brother's visit. When the nurse finally came in to run one of them off, Tamian graciously accepted he would

256

be the one to leave. Before he left he shook Gregor's hand. "I couldn't have chosen a better Goyle for my sister. I know she's in good hands. I'll be in the waiting room if you need me."

Tamian's retreating form turned the corner. Gregor knew there were visiting hours, but he wasn't leaving. He had failed Tessa in not getting to her fast enough before the wreck. He would not fail her again.

Thirty-Nine

Three days passed as Gregor sat by Tessa's side, leaving only to shower down the hall and give quick updates to the Clan who visited. When Dante couldn't convince him to leave the hospital, he went to Gregor's home and grabbed a duffle bag filling it with clothes and toiletries. Joseph had obviously given instructions to allow more than one visitor since the nurses didn't try to run Dante off.

He visited every night, filling Gregor in on the happenings of the world outside and sometimes just offering silent support. The only body found from the helicopter wreckage who had come across Dante's slab was so badly burned, dental records would be needed to make an identification, and even that was a long shot. If the corpse was Gordon Flanagan, he would be surprised. As far as the redheaded victims, Trevor had confirmed the last two victims were also clones. He had spent hours analyzing the victims' DNA. The women had just enough genetic markers in common to be related.

Dante's head turned toward the door. Joseph walked into the room a few seconds later. Gregor never would get used to his brother's psychic nature.

"Gregor, Dante. It's time." The swelling had gone down around Tessa's brain and Joseph was going to bring her out of her coma. "If you will please head down to the waiting room, I will come get you when she starts waking up."

Gregor whispered in Tessa's ear he would see her soon and kissed her lips before walking out with Dante. He spoke to the day shift nurses as they passed the station. Spending several days in the hospital had given Gregor plenty of insight into the lives of the doctors and other personnel. Most of them gave tirelessly and cared deeply for all of the patients.

The waiting room had been a revolving door of family over the weekend, but now most everyone was carrying on with their normal routines. "Why aren't you at work?" Gregor asked Dante when they reached the waiting area.

"Trevor can handle the morgue, and I need a break from Isabelle."

"Is it that bad, being around her?"

"Yes, it is. My beast is becoming uncontrollable when she's near. It takes most of my energy to keep from phasing. The rest of my energy is spent not ripping her clothes off and taking her right there in her office. The sooner she and I figure out the extent of the damage Henshaw caused, the sooner I can hand the Pen back over to her fully. We agreed to take things slow and pretend the pull of the mating bond isn't present. But I have to tell you, Brother, I'm not sure I can keep the charade going. I am putting aside my feelings for her sake. It's the hardest thing I have ever done in my life." Dante was splitting his time between the morgue and the Pen, working twenty hour days just to be sure Isabelle got the inmates the care they needed.

Gregor could understand where Dante was coming from if he felt for Isabelle even half of what Gregor felt for Tessa. "I understand that. When Tessa told me we couldn't be together, it ripped me apart. She was protecting me. I'm the one who is supposed to protect her, and she was putting my feelings and well-being before her own. You're a good man, Dante. Isabelle will come around."

"I also hope the mate bond is enough for me..." He didn't finish his thought. He didn't have to. Gregor knew what was on his mind. Dante's sexual proclivities were different than most Alphas'.

Dante stretched his tall frame, extending his arms toward the ceiling. He rolled his neck, leaving his head hanging for a few seconds. Gregor knew this was his way of trying to relieve the tension. "Then there's her obsession with Alexander. She is convinced the albino can be saved. I have a bad feeling in my gut there's more there than meets the eye. I wasn't in the room when she interrogated him, but there was a strong current, a familiarity coming from the room. I can't put my finger on it, but I don't think she's going to let it go. I caught her sneaking him a cigarette."

"The prison is a no smoking area. At least not on the inside." Gregor was astounded at Isabelle's boldness. "I didn't take Isabelle for the break the rules type. Tessa must be rubbing off on her."

"Yes, well, she won't be doing it again anytime soon. I had a little talk with Deacon, and he has given all the guards strict orders she is not to be allowed near any of the inmates without an escort."

Gregor chuckled. The sound surprised him. He hadn't smiled, let alone laughed in the last four days. Not since a story Tessa told him when they were lying in bed caused him to laugh out loud. The smile on her face from the sound of him laughing was one he would never forget. She lit up like a child who had been given her first Popsicle. Now her beautiful face was covered with cuts. He would hire the best plastic surgeon in the world to have her scars erased just as soon as her internal injuries were healed.

Tamian walked in the door of the waiting room. "Any word yet?"

"How did you know Joseph was bringing her out?" Gregor cocked one brow. "Is it the bond you and Tessa have?"

Tamian grinned, "No, it's the charm I poured on one pretty little nurse. She called me."

Gregor shook his head. "I meant to ask you earlier, are you not mated? The other half-bloods transition when

260

they meet their mate. You've already transitioned, so you must be mated, right?"

Tamian had already dodged answering the question once before. Gregor hoped he would feel comfortable enough to confide in him.

"That's a long story. Maybe one day when this mess is all over, you and I can sit down and talk about it. For now, let's focus on getting my sister well." Tamian stuck his hands in the front pockets of his jeans and waited for Gregor to respond.

"Yeah, man. Whatever you want. I didn't mean to pry." Gregor absolutely did mean to pry. There was something distinctively different about Tamian. Maybe being a clone had something to do with it.

"Have you talked to your parents? I'm sure they would want to know Tessa's in the hospital."

"I talked to my mother as soon as Tessa was out of surgery. She wants to come see her, but she has to wait on our father to get back from a trip. He won't allow her to travel alone."

"Did you tell her there's a possibility Flanagan could be dead?" Gregor was still waiting on confirmation of that himself.

"That would be a blessing, but no. Until I have proof the bastard's body burned to a crisp, I don't want to get her hopes up. I'm looking forward to the day both Mom and Andi can breathe easier and not have to hide anymore."

Gregor didn't mention his uncle, Alistair. It seemed they both had crazed men in the branches of their familial trees. The three men sat quietly for a while, waiting on word from the doctor that Tessa had come out of her coma and they could go talk to her. The more time that went by with no news, the more worried Gregor got. He had started pacing the floor an hour earlier, and now both Dante and Tamian had joined him. Another hour passed, and the door opened. Once again, the doctor looked haggard.

261

"Joseph, is everything all right? Did Tessa come out of her coma?" Gregor swore if he got Tessa home and well, he was going to wrap her in a fucking cocoon and lock her away from the rest of the world.

"She is off all machines and breathing on her own, but there's a small problem." The doctor sighed.

"What kind of problem?" Tamian asked before Gregor could.

"She's not waking up. This happens sometimes. She is being moved to the lab for an MRI now. It will take about thirty minutes. I'll be back after it's complete." Joseph ran a hand through his hair as he walked off.

Dante pulled his phone out of his pocket. "Hello. Actually there's been a slight setback, but we're hoping an MRI will give us more information. Yes, I'll call you as soon as I know something." Dante disconnect and announced, "That was Isabelle calling to check on Tessa."

Tamian raised his eyebrows at Dante. "I didn't hear the phone ring. Or buzz."

Gregor clapped Tam on the shoulder, "That's something you're going to have to get used to. Just like you and Tessa have your mind speak thing going on, our brother here has his own ESP."

While they were waiting, several calls came in, all Clan checking on Tessa's status. Deacon assured Gregor he had the Pen under control. Julian reported that Nikolas had arrived in Egypt but was having no luck tracking down Sophia. Sinclair called from the west coast offering what little support he could. Rafael let him know Kaya was being drilled by the Governor. The local sheriff didn't believe Kaya when she told him she had no clue who was in the helicopter. Frey was back at the dojo, business as usual.

Gregor had yet to hear from Dominic. With Tessa staying out of New Orleans, Jacques Dupart was the least of his worries. He wondered if he should call Gladys. If he only knew how often Tessa checked in with her neighbor.

262

Did she have other homes where she would be missed if she didn't call someone? He had a lot to learn about Tessa, and he vowed to make it his mission to learn every single thing about her once she woke up.

An hour later, Joseph finally came back. "There was nothing on the MRI. We're just going to have to encourage Tessa to wake up on her own."

"I want to take her home." Gregor had to get out of this hospital before he went stir crazy, and leaving Tessa here was out of the question.

"I understand your frustration, but she needs to be monitored."

"I get that, but I have to get out of here. I think you can understand why. I will take her home with me and hire someone to monitor her condition. Just tell me what she needs other than an I.V."

While Joseph was thinking, Dante spoke up. "Isabelle and I can take care of the monitoring. There's no need for you to hire anyone."

Joseph frowned at Dante. "You and Isabelle?"

"Yes, you should know her. Isabelle Sarantos is the leading doctor in infectious disease and internal medicine in New Atlanta. She's very bright and most assuredly capable."

"Oh, I know her all right; I just didn't know you did." He turned to Gregor, "As far as Tessa goes, I will agree to you taking her home. I know with her being your mate, you would die before you risked her well-being."

Tamian spoke up, "Gregor, if you don't mind, I would like to be able to sit with her as well."

"Of course. As a matter of fact, why don't you stay at the cabin with us? I have plenty of bedrooms, and I would welcome the company."

Tamian looked surprised, but quickly smiled. "Thanks. I need to take care of a few things that have been overlooked while I was in the Pen. If you give me your address, I will meet you there later."

"*You* were in the Pen? For what?" Joseph obviously knew St. Claire didn't belong in prison.

"I was undercover." Tamian just shrugged. It was a gesture Gregor was getting used to.

"How long will it take you to get your home ready for a patient?" Joseph asked Gregor.

Dante answered for him, "I will transport Tessa in one of our buses. Trevor can ride in the back, if you do not object. I can set her up with everything she needs once we have her settled into bed." He pulled out his phone and called down to the morgue, telling Trevor what supplies to gather.

Gregor offered a small smile, "I don't mind, but Trevor may. You know he doesn't like me."

"He likes you fine, you're just scary looking," Dante deadpanned.

Gregor laughed out loud at that. If anyone was scary it was his baby brother.

"I will gather the necessary equipment for you to take home. Just make sure these get back to the hospital once she is well. This really goes against hospital policy. I guess being Chief of Staff, I can make executive decisions, can't I?"

"Yes, and this is the right decision. I have a feeling once I get her home, she will improve to the point of waking up. She's a free spirit, and this place is anything but free." Gregor was being selfish. He wanted to be able to sleep in his bed with Tessa. He wanted to be the one to give her a bath, wash her hair. He needed to take care of her, not sit in a chair and watch others do what he should be doing.

"Okay, Dante you get an ambulance ready, and Gregor you come with me. We will gather Tessa's things and get her ready to meet Dante on the lower level. Tamian, I guess I will see you around." Joseph shook hands with

Tessa's brother. Gregor had the feeling there was more going on with those two, but he would have to wait until later to find out what.

"Gregor, text me your address, and I will see you soon." Tamian shook hands with both him and Dante then jogged toward the door. Dante headed toward the morgue, and Gregor followed Joseph to get his woman. He was taking his mate home.

Forty

Gregor spent the rest of the day getting Tessa home and into his bed. He grabbed a spare comforter off one of the guest beds since Tessa had shredded his. He cleaned up the broken glass in his bathroom while Dante and Trevor worked fluidly to hook up the equipment and get Tessa settled. With her arms in splints, she couldn't easily lie on her side, so they brought in pillows from the other bedrooms and propped her up. Trevor had been unusually quiet on the ride to the cabin and hadn't said a word once they were inside.

"Trevor, I want to thank you for your help today." Gregor knew he could be intimidating, but there was no reason for Dante's assistant to fear him.

"I've seen her before, coming from Dane Abbott's apartment right before he disappeared." Trevor was staring at Tessa.

Gregor and Dante looked at each other. Dante was the one to speak up. "They are cousins." That was the truth, just not the whole truth.

Trevor finally looked at Gregor. "I'm just glad she's alive, you know? After seeing all the look-alikes come across our tables, well I'm glad to see her like this instead of... dead." The kid could be morbid, but he had a point.

"Trevor, please take the bus back to the hospital. I will remain here with Gregor and Tessa for a while." Dante was still adjusting monitors, fussing over Tessa's pillows, checking and rechecking her I.V.

"Do you need a ride later? I can always come back after my shift is over."

"It's very kind of you to offer, but I will have a ride. I, too, appreciate your assistance today, and once I can put all my focus back on the morgue, you will be getting a well-deserved vacation."

"Wow, that's not necessary, but thanks! Okay, then, I will just be going." Instead of leaving, Trevor walked closer to the bed and Tessa. He touched her arm with his fingertip and whispered, "I'm glad you're here and not there."

Dante walked Trevor to the door. Even though they were downstairs, Gregor's shifter ears picked up the conversation. "I really appreciate all you do, and I trust your judgment in keeping our family business private."

"Absolutely. Besides, who am I going to tell? The corpses? It's not like I have any friends."

"You do have friends, Trevor. Gregor and I are your friends, your family. You just have to let us in."

Gregor was shocked at the gentleness with which Dante handled his assistant. Normally his brother was not the touchy-feely type, but his softer side was showing itself more and more. It was possible Isabelle had something to do with it. Up until about a week ago, Gregor's life had consisted of patrolling for Unholy and running the prison. He hadn't thought of either in the last few days unless it was mentioned to him. Finding one's mate changed a Goyle.

Gregor lay down next to Tessa on the bed, careful to not disturb her healing bones. "Hey, Red. It's just you and me for a few minutes. I brought you home, to my home. I hope someday this is our home. I understand now why you said it wasn't safe, but Baby, we're Gargoyles. Our lives have never been truly safe and never will be. It won't matter if you and I are together or apart. Someone will be after one of us whether it's my crazy uncle, or Flanagan, or Unholy, or ex-lovers.

"We were designed for one another. If the fates deem us mates, who are we to argue? All I know is I want you with me, by my side as my partner in life, for eternity. I have spent the last five hundred years alone, and I am ready to fill my days with someone other than ugly inmates and ugly

267

brothers." Dante coughed downstairs. He was listening to Gregor talk to Tessa.

"Okay, maybe not ugly brothers, just ones who need to smile more often." That got an *hmph* from downstairs. "Like I told you before, I will give you all the time you need. Right now, I want you to concentrate on getting better, on waking up. Even if you decide to carry on with your life without me in it, I want you to open those pretty green eyes. I need to hear your sassy mouth telling me to fuck off. Tessa, I just need you." Gregor settled in beside her, closing his eyes, and concentrated on the sound of her breathing.

The sound of voices woke Gregor from a deep sleep. Having slept in a hospital chair the last few nights had been brutal. Glancing at the clock, he noticed the lateness of the day. Once he sat up, he could feel the pull of the moon. The shifter inside warred between the need to fly and to stay by Tessa's side. He brushed her hair away from her face and placed a soft kiss on her lips.

Tamian appeared in the door, "I thought I'd come give you a break. If you want to go talk to your Clan, I can sit with Andi." One of the monitors started beeping. Within seconds, both Dante and Isabelle appeared in the doorway.

"What happened?" Isabelle pressed a button, and the beeping stopped.

"St. Claire here called his sister *Andi*. She fucking hates that name, man," Gregor admonished him.

Tamian shrugged, "Hey, it's her name. Maybe when she wakes up she can legally change her name to Tessa since she's so fond of it. Out of all her aliases, she prefers that one."

Hmm, had Tessa not shared her choice of names with her brother? "She has a reason for choosing Tessa. Maybe one day she'll tell you why," Gregor told Tamian as Isabelle fussed over her cousin. Dante's eyes rarely left his own mate.

"Who all's downstairs?" Gregor stood and stretched. His large bedroom was getting crowded. As badly as he wanted to stay with his mate constantly, he needed to eat. He would only be a few steps away from her, and she would be in good hands while he took a break.

"Rafe and Kaya, Frey, Julian, Sixx, Jasper, and Dane." Dante rattled off the Clan who had come to check on him and Tessa.

"Tamian, please don't upset your sister again. I'm going downstairs for a little bit."

"Yes, Boss." Tamian gave him a smartass salute and settled into the chair next to the bed. Dante and Isabelle headed down the stairs, but Gregor stopped in the doorway to observe Tessa and her brother. Tamian gently took her hand in his and kissed her knuckles. He didn't say a word, so Gregor figured Tamian was attempting to mind speak with his sister.

Tamian was aware of Gregor standing at the door, but it didn't bother him. If the roles were reversed, Tamian doubted he would leave Andi's side for one second. As her clone, he needed the connection. Once he was old enough, Tamian had followed his sister all over the world, watching her back and basically just being near her. Andi. Shit. He would have to get used to calling her Tessa. He had felt a twinge of jealousy that Gregor knew the meaning behind Tessa's favored moniker when he didn't.

Ever since Tessa had figured out Gregor Stone was her mate, she had become obsessed with the man. Tamian eventually tired of listening in on her thoughts about *her warden* and started tuning her out. Now he would give anything for her to drone on and on about living happily ever after with the Gargoyle of her dreams. On the outside, she had rebuked their mating bond. On the inside though, her thoughts rarely strayed from the man, even when she had been dating Jacques.

"Tessa, it's me, Tam. I'm going to sit with you for a bit while Gregor gets something to eat."

"Awesome. Please do me a favor, and tell him to stop being so mopey, or I'm going to shoot him."

"Oh gods, you can hear me!"

"Of course I can, I just haven't been able to respond. I've heard everything everyone has said since I woke up. What's wrong with me?"

"This is great! At least I know you're in there. We don't know what's wrong. The MRI didn't show any blockage or swelling that would cause your continued condition. I guess since you can talk to me, you aren't actually in a coma. I should tell Dante and Isabelle so they can check you out."

"No, not yet. Just sit with me for a few minutes. The poking and prodding gets old."

"Of course. Do you need anything?"

"Yes, take these fucking splints off. They're driving me crazy. My skin is itching, and my claws are ready to rip through the bandages."

"You will just have to tough it out; I'm not taking them off. Don't you want your bones to heal properly?"

"Of course, but shouldn't they already be healed? We're fucking Gargoyles after all."

"Half Gargoyles, and that's a question for your doctor. Speaking of which..." Tamian didn't get a chance to finish his thought. A commotion downstairs had both him and Tessa thinking, *"Oh fuck."*

"I should probably go downstairs and play referee. Will you be okay until someone gets back?"

"Yep. Please don't let Dad kill my mate before we have a chance to actually become *mates."*

"*So you plan to go through with it?*" Tamian had no right to deny his sister her happiness, but the green-eyed monster was ever present.

"*I do. Before I was chased by a fucking lunatic, I had time to think about it. A purple duck made my decision for me.*"

"*A purple duck?*" His sister always had wild ideas and stories. This one he had to hear.

"*Yes, but that's a story for another time. I think you need to go rescue my mate and the King from our father.*"

"*Okay, I'll send Mom up as soon as the smoke clears.*"

"*Tamian, I love you. You know that, right?*"

His heart tightened in his chest. It was wrong, the feelings he had for his sister. He didn't understand them, never had. He was attracted to other women and had bedded plenty of them. It had always been a quick fuck, a means to an end. Emotions were never involved. He attributed his deep need for his sister to the clone bond. It was a burden he had to bear. For the rest of his life, he would endure it. Alone. "*I love you, too.*"

Tamian placed a kiss on his sister's forehead and made his way downstairs to intervene. He didn't need shifter hearing as the shouting could be heard in the next county over. He paused at the bottom of the steps, taking in the chaos.

Forty-One

The scene in Gregor's home warmed his heart. Kaya and Priscilla were working side by side in the kitchen preparing a meal. Gregor would later find out they had fixed enough food to freeze so he wouldn't have to cook for weeks. The men were refereeing an argument between Dane and Julian.

"I am telling you, she is not your mate!" Julian was in Dane's face, but the newbie wasn't backing down.

"Then why did I transition immediately after meeting with her?" Dane had his hands on his hips.

"I don't know. What I do know is Katherine Fox is *my* mate." Julian had vowed to stay away from the reporter, but Gregor knew once the mate bond hit, you couldn't let it go that easily.

Gregor's doorbell rang, and he left the arguing men to their own defenses. He opened the door, and his breath caught. Standing in front of him was a woman who was the spitting image of his own mate. Directly behind her was Xavier Montagnon, one of the Original Elders. The arguing in the room ceased as Rafael seethed, "What in the fuck are *you* doing here?"

Gregor felt the heat at his back as Rafael now stood behind him. He knew Elizabeth would not have aged, but she could pass for Tessa's twin. "I invited them, although when I did, I wasn't aware of exactly who Tessa's father is." He was speaking to Rafael but looking at Elizabeth.

"Do you mind letting us in? And while you're at it, stop staring at my mate." Xavier was not happy about the situation. That much was clear.

Gregor stepped back, opening the door wider. "Please, come in." When Rafe didn't move, Gregor nudged him with his shoulder. "I can explain."

"Yeah, this I'm ready to hear." Rafael backed up and allowed them to pass.

Most of the Clan had met Xavier at some point in their lives. They had not met Elizabeth. The mother of the first cloned baby who disappeared off the face of the earth was a legend. A gasp escaped Kaya and something inhuman came from Isabelle.

Dante's mate walked right up to Tessa's mother. "Hello Elizabeth. You're looking...young." She didn't bother with niceties. The sting of being kept away from her own mother with no knowledge of being a shifter was still not sitting well with her.

"Isabelle, I..." Elizabeth was cut off by Xavier.

"You can have your reunion later. Where is Tessa? I want to see my girl."

"She's upstairs resting." Gregor worked hard to calm himself. The conversation between Rafael and Xavier regarding human bonding came to mind.

"And you left her alone? In her condition?" Xavier was headed toward the staircase when Rafael stepped in front of him.

"Of course she isn't alone. Her brother is with her," Rafael confirmed angrily. He obviously hadn't forgotten the conversation either. Gregor knew his brother, and he was about two seconds away from phasing. Xavier may be Tessa's father, but he was in Rafael's territory now.

"Tamian's here?" Elizabeth's eyes lit up. "I thought he was in jail?"

"He was, undercover, until Tessa's accident. Now he's not." Rafael wasn't playing nice. Gregor needed to diffuse the situation before it escalated to a minor war. The men began arguing and the Clan circled, taking up for their King.

About that time, a loud whistle ceased the quarreling momentarily. From the staircase, Tamian called out to his parents, "Hello Mom, Dad."

Elizabeth ran to her son and wrapped her arms around him. The arguments continued but lessened as Elizabeth's crying could be heard by all.

Tamian pulled back from his mother's embrace. "Let's all have a seat and discuss why you were invited other than the obvious reason."

Neither Rafael nor Xavier moved to sit. Kaya closed the gap between her and Rafael, placing a hand on his arm. "My King."

Elizabeth eased in to Xavier's side and grabbed his hand. "Honey."

The instant change that came over both men was amazing. Kings may rule the world, but the Queens ruled the Kings. The Clan members stepped back, giving the couples room to sit on the opposing sofas. Frey took a spot directly behind Rafael and Kaya, standing sentry. The others moved off to the side of the room looking less menacing. Gregor stood in front of the fireplace between the two sofas, hopefully appearing neutral.

Gregor asked Isabelle to go sit with Tessa while he spoke with Xavier. Once he knew his mate was being looked after, he addressed the room.

"Tessa is not critical, she just needs time to recover from her injuries. Her doctor assured us she will wake up on her own, when she's ready. You both know how stubborn your daughter is. I think she's milking the attention." Gregor smiled at Elizabeth, trying to ease her anxiety.

"I feel it's best to lay all our cards on the table, however painful they may be. First, Gordon Flanagan may or may not be dead." Elizabeth closed her eyes and sighed. Xavier reached for her hand.

"Richard Merrick, the man who was chasing Tessa, has been identified as the Redhead Killer. If you weren't aware, women in New Atlanta who could pass for Tessa's sisters were being strangled. The last body had a message carved into her skin. This message was supposed to get Tessa's attention and flush her out of hiding. We haven't been able to ask Tessa how Merrick found her, but he did. When he began chasing Tessa, a helicopter joined in the pursuit. Tessa thought it was Flanagan, and Geoffrey later confirmed it.

"Now, we know how people can change their appearance, just like the decoy who lost his life at the warehouse a few weeks ago. The man most likely was Flanagan, but as of now, a body has not been recovered. We will not assume he is dead until we see a corpse. We've made that mistake before." Rafael opened his mouth to add something but Kaya squeezed his arm, effectively silencing him.

"For now, we are going to hope he is dead, and we have one less pain in our ass. Next, we need to discuss the fact we have been kept in the dark about mating with humans. Xavier, we know why this has been hidden from us. Jonas being ostracized was not our fault. Furthermore, we are not afraid of Alistair. As far as we're concerned, he can sit on his throne in Greece and rot. He has no authority over our Clan, and we will not put our lives on hold because one bigoted Gargoyle has a problem with our lifestyle. As you can see, Rafael and Kaya are mated. Kaya is our Queen, and now we have proof humans have carried Goyle babies to term with no trouble.

"I intend to live a long and happy life with your daughter. I would prefer to do that without our families at war. If what you feel about Alistair is true, we are going to need to work together on a united front, not opposing sides."

Xavier stood. "Rafael, I need to apologize for lying to you. Athena and I only want what's best for our children, and we agreed the longer you were kept in the dark, the longer you could avoid Alistair's misplaced ideas."

Rafael stood facing Xavier. "I guess this is why my mother refuses to take my calls."

Xavier nodded. He met the eyes of every member of the Clan. "I am apologizing to you all, to your King, your Clan. I have watched you rule, Rafael, and you are the best King I have ever known. I pledge my Clan's allegiance to yours." Xavier fisted his hand over his heart and bowed his head. Likewise, Rafael bowed his head to Xavier.

Gregor smiled internally. "Now, would you like to see your daughter?"

Elizabeth literally jumped up from the sofa. It was disconcerting how much she and Tessa looked alike. No wonder Flanagan had been able to find Tessa. "I need to warn you, she has both arms in splints. Her left leg is fragile, as the bone will take time to heal. She also has monitors connected to her. We believe she can hear us so please, talk to her."

"Oh, she can definitely hear you." Tamian appeared to be gloating.

"How do you know that, unless she spoke to you? Did she fucking talk to you and you're just now mentioning it?" Gregor was ready to throttle the man.

"She didn't speak out loud, no. But she did mind speak, and she has a message for you. She said to stop moping around, or she's going to shoot you."

Gregor threw his head back and howled. The others in the room probably figured he'd lost his mind, but he couldn't stop the laughter. "Of course she will." He shook his head, and his heart filled with hope for the first time in days.

Gregor asked that they not overwhelm Tessa since she was obviously aware of her surroundings. They agreed, and Elizabeth went in to see her first. Gregor stood outside the door listening. He should give her some privacy, but he didn't want to be far away in case she became agitated. After Xavier spent a few short minutes talking to his daughter, Elizabeth grabbed Gregor's hand and pulled him into the room with her. Even though Tamian had said Tessa could hear them, Elizabeth spoke as if she couldn't.

"I remember when she got this." She was running her fingers gingerly across Tessa's tattoo. Gregor had dressed Tessa in one of his button up shirts. It was the easiest thing to get on over the splints without too much trouble. "I knew then you two would eventually find your way to each other. I'm just glad the glass cut through the A and not the G."

"What are you talking about?" Gregor looked closer at the tattoo. When he took the time to analyze the ink, he finally figured out the swirls were more than just fancy lines. His initials, GAS, were flowing along her skin.

"Tessa has always known who you are, Gregor. While you may truly be a Di Pietro, to her you are a Stone. Her hardass." Elizabeth laughed as she stroked her daughter's hair. "Tessa, I know you can hear me, so you'll just have to forgive me for spilling your secrets." At that, the fingers on the hand Gregor was holding twitched.

Forty-Two

Gregor offered a spare bedroom to Xavier, but he declined. While Elizabeth wanted to stay, Xavier was still very protective and was ready to get her back to their home. Most of the Clan cleared out, giving Gregor his privacy. Rafael and Kaya stayed later than most, discussing Xavier and Alistair, and what that meant for the Gargoyles. Rafael planned to call a meeting of the Clans and inform them of human bonding, as well as the repercussions and possible war with Alistair.

Gregor had missed out on helping Jasper move. The Julian-Dane battle over Katherine Fox had continued then. More than once the other brothers had intervened. The two hadn't come to blows yet, but if they didn't settle who she was actually mated to soon, Rafael was afraid they would battle it out with their fists and claws.

"What's the deal with Tessa and her brother?" Kaya asked quietly as she sat sipping coffee.

"They're close. I'd say as close if not closer than twins because they come from the same DNA. I was right; they can hear each other's thoughts. He is very protective of her, has watched over her for years now," Gregor told her. Tamian was once again upstairs with his sister. Gregor had a feeling things were going to change for them as soon as she woke up.

Speaking of Tamian, he slowly descended the stairs and stepped into the living area. "She's asking for you. Now that I know she's going to be okay, I'm going to head on home. Promise me you'll take good care of her." His words sounded like a real goodbye, not just "I'll see you later".

"Of course I will, but you don't have to leave."

"Yeah, I do. She needs you, and you two need to start your life together without anyone hovering." Tamian clapped Gregor on the shoulder. "Rafael, Kaya, take care."

278

With that, Tamian walked out the front door without looking back.

"Why did that feel like goodbye?" Kaya was hugging herself.

"Because it was." Gregor didn't need to have Dante's psychic abilities to see the truth for what it was.

Rafael called for Priscilla who was still in the kitchen. Gregor would be searching for his utensils for weeks. "We will leave you to your mate. If you need anything at all, just call." Rafael pulled Gregor in for a brotherly hug.

"Thank you both, for everything." Gregor kissed Priscilla on the cheek and bowed his head to his Queen. Once the house was empty, Gregor took the stairs two at a time to get to Tessa.

"It's about time." Tessa smiled at Gregor.

"Holy shit, Baby! You're awake! Oh my gods, Tessa!" Gregor wanted to grab her up and twirl her around, but with her injuries, he didn't dare. "When Tamian said you were asking for me, I didn't know you were *really* asking for me."

"I was really asking for you. Can you get me some water? My throat feels like fourteen cats have been clawing around in there."

"Of course, hang on." Gregor grabbed a glass of water from the bathroom and helped her sip it. "I need to call Joseph and ask if it's okay to remove the I.V."

"Who's Joseph?" Tessa asked between sips of water.

"Your doctor. He operated on you after the wreck."

Tessa appeared confused. "But where's Jonas?"

"Jonas?"

"Yeah, my uncle. I know his voice as well as I know Tamian's. He was there the whole time, talking to me. I don't recall anyone else."

"Holy fucking shit." Gregor couldn't believe it. Now it all made sense. Joseph Mooneyham was Jonas Montague. That explained the recognition between him and Tamian.

"Tessa, I am pretty sure your uncle has been right here in New Atlanta for the last ten years posing as Joseph Mooneyham, Chief of Staff."

Tessa rolled her eyes. "Of course he has. That's why Caroline was able to get here so quickly when Dane transitioned. They've been hiding close by." She laughed until she started coughing.

"Easy, Baby. Don't overdo it. I just got you back." Gregor fussed over her pillows, and her shirt, and her hair.

"Stop fussing. Do me a favor and call Jonas. Ask him about the monitors and the I.V. and these fucking splints. I'm pretty sure my bones are healed by now. And get this fucking catheter out of me. Now."

Gregor laughed at her sass and leaned in to kiss her on the cheek. She surprised him by offering her lips. It was a swift brush of skin. "I would give you some tongue, but my mouth tastes like those fourteen cats have used it as their litter box."

Gregor went to the bathroom and came back with mouthwash. "Until we can get you up to brush your teeth." Tessa swished a little mouthwash around and spit it in the offered glass. While she was swishing he told her, "About the catheter, I'm not pulling it out. I'm not a doctor, and I don't want to hurt you. Let me call Joseph, I mean Jonas. If he can't come by here, I will get Isabelle on it."

Gregor made the phone calls, and Tessa rambled on about nothing. She was catching up on lost time using her voice. The doctor instructed Gregor to feed her broth until her stomach got used to something other than the fluids that had been flowing through her veins.

Even though the hour was late, Tessa had insisted all tubes and monitors be removed from her body. Dante and Isabelle arrived together. Working as a team, Isabelle removed one splint while Dante removed the other. Jonas had agreed to the splints on her arms coming off, as long as she promised not to put any weight on them or pick anything up for several days. Getting around required the use of crutches, so she would be immobile for a while longer. Gregor had to promise Tessa would not move herself. He had no problem with carrying his mate wherever she wanted to go.

Isabelle shooed Dante and Gregor from the room so she could remove the catheter. Tessa and Isabelle spoke privately while Gregor and Dante did the same downstairs. Gregor noticed Dante's mood was lighter than it had been in years. "What's up?"

"Isabelle asked me out to dinner."

"Do you think she is ready to move forward?" Gregor hoped so for his brother's sake.

"We shall see. It is, however, just dinner at Chez Vaison. A very public place where absolutely nothing other than conversation can happen."

"Truth, Brother. It's what happens after dinner that could be exciting." Gregor clapped him on the shoulder just as Isabelle came down the stairs, shaking her head.

"She's all yours. I don't know how you put up with her mouth."

Gregor laughed, thinking how much he loved Tessa's mouth and what she could do with it.

For the second time that day, Dante and Isabelle said goodbye, this time happy that Tessa was awake and on her way to a full recovery.

Gregor shut and locked the door and headed to his mate. He stopped just outside the bedroom and stared. Bruised, cut, and in desperate need of a shower, she was still the most beautiful woman in the world. She smiled at him and patted the bed beside her. Gregor sat down, scooting over until he was next to her good leg. She leaned up so he could slide his arm around her waist. When he did, she laid her head on his shoulder. Gregor's heart sped up. Having her back in his bed was a dream come true, even if they could do no more than cuddle.

Tessa gingerly placed a hand on his chest, letting her fingers trail swirls over his skin. "I need to ask you something."

Gregor momentarily tensed. He had no idea what was going through her pretty head, but he would tell her what she wanted to know. "Anything."

"Is Gordon dead?"

Gregor let out his breath. This he could deal with. "Honestly, we don't know. His helicopter was shot down, but only one body was recovered. That doesn't mean he got out alive. Doesn't mean he didn't. Now I have a question."

Tessa looked up at him. "Anything," she responded in kind.

"How did Merrick find you?"

Tessa frowned. "Who's Merrick?"

"The guy chasing you, the one driving the Mustang."

"Oh, him. I think it was dumb luck. I was standing in the food line at the festival, and he turned around, dumping his food on my shirt. When he went to apologize, he must have recognized me. If he was working for Gordon, he probably had a picture of my mother. Did he get away, too?"

"No, that fucker's dead."

Tessa thought on that a beat then asked, "What's up with Dante and Belle?"

Since the Clan already knew, he didn't see anything wrong in telling Tessa. "They're mates. I thought you might have figured that out already."

Tessa raised her head and looked at him, "No, but I'm glad it's your brother. She was really worried about who it might be. Although, I hope they never have kids."

"Why not?" Gregor's heart stopped. Where was she going with this? Did she not think the Gargoyles and half-bloods should have children?

282

"Have you seen those two? Neither one of them knows how to smile. Just think of the scowling ass babies they'd have."

Gregor started laughing. He couldn't help it. She did have a point, but hopefully now that Isabelle had asked Dante out, they would give each other something to smile about.

Tessa snuggled in closer then spoke to his chest, "When I left here Halloween morning, I wanted so badly to turn around and come right back. My heart felt like someone had reached into my chest and ripped it right out. I went to the fall festival and walked around, thinking. Do you really want children?"

Again, Gregor was leery of the subject. He didn't know if she wanted children, but if this was going to work, they had to be honest with each other. "I do. Do you not?" He closed his eyes, waiting on her answer.

"I wasn't sure I did until I observed the families at the festival, watching the parents interacting with the kids. And then there was this purple duck. That sealed the deal."

"A purple duck? I didn't know there was such a thing."

Tessa explained how she won the stuffed toy for the little girl whose mother didn't have the money or ability to win the toy for her daughter. "The joy that one insignificant toy brought to that child instilled the longing within me to see my own child happy. I want children. Your children."

Wetness was forming in Gregor's eyes. He didn't try to hide the emotions from his mate. Honesty came in many forms, and that included allowing your true feelings to shine, even in the form of tears. He pressed a kiss to the top of her head. She had just given him the world.

"Does this mean you're ready to make the bond official? Not now, but when you're healed?"

Tessa nodded, her own eyes shining with tears. "Yes, I am ready to be your mate."

Epilogue

When the world was falling apart, all because Tessa's uncle decided to clone her, the Di Pietro family began buying up real estate all over the world. The small Greek island of Atokos was one of those properties. Sixx had offered the island to Gregor and Tessa for a belated honeymoon. Once Tessa had healed, Gregor more or less turned the Pen over to Deacon. Wherever his mate went, Gregor followed.

Tessa produced Jonas' final journal that chronicled the lives of his seventeen children, showing humans could mate successfully with Gargoyles. As soon as Tessa gave the journal to Rafael, he had thrown his Queen over his shoulder and sequestered her to their bedroom for days. Needless to say, Dane Abbott became Chief of Police.

With the Stone Society owning Atokos Island, Gregor and Tessa had all the privacy they wanted. What started as a one week holiday turned into a month-long sex fest. When Sixx originally bought the island, he had razed the local hotel, and in its place built a huge mansion full of windows that overlooked the Ionian Sea. The only others on the island were the cooks and caretakers who kept out of site of the guests.

The weather was such that they could stay on the beach with no worry of rain. The temperatures were mild, and they rarely saw the inside of the mansion. The cabana by the sea boasted a kitchen, king-size bedroom, and bathroom. Gregor built a fire on the beach every night, not for heat, but just because Tessa wanted one.

Tessa was lying on a chaise, sunning her naked body. All of her scars had been removed with the exception of the one running through her ink. Gregor insisted she leave it. He wanted the reminder of how precious life was. He stood, admiring his nude mate, his cock standing at

284

attention. He had worn a hard-on since they arrived at the island. They had made love and fucked in every room of the mansion. The hot tub had to be cleaned daily.

When Gregor shaded Tessa's body, she asked, "Do you remember when we went cliff diving in Acapulco?"

"Yeah." Gregor bent down closer to his mate, his cock straining against his swim trunks. "What about it?" He got closer still and ran his nose up her inner thigh, stopping at the juncture between her legs. As long as he lived, he would never get enough of her scent, her taste.

"I want to go Gregor diving." She was grinning at him.

"Gregor diving?" He lifted his nose from her crotch. The mirrored aviators she wore concealed her eyes. He couldn't tell if she was yanking his chain.

"Yep, I want you to fly me above the water and let me dive off your shoulders."

Gregor gently slid the shades down her button nose, seeing the glint of mischievousness in her eyes. "You're serious."

"Of course I'm serious. You'll be able to see the water and know I'm not diving close to any rocks. The farther away from shore you fly, the deeper the water."

Gregor licked a trail up her torso, admiring the goose bumps that popped up. He sucked her left nipple. "What do I get in return?" He sucked her right nipple. Tessa squirmed in her chair.

"Anything you want," she responded in a husky voice.

Gregor liked that answer. Tessa was a wildcat in bed. They had experimented with just about every toy imaginable. They tied each other up, submitted to and dominated each other. Tessa was an expert when it came to dishing out just the right amount of pain. She was the perfect sexual partner. If she wanted plain vanilla, slow and gentle love making, she never hesitated telling him so.

Gregor was more than okay with being gentle when his mate needed it.

"Suit up." Gregor dug through the duffle bag sitting next to her chair and grabbed one of Tessa's many bathing suits, tossing it to her. There was no way she could jump into the sea without getting a saltwater douche. She grabbed his hand, and he pulled her to her feet. Even with her red hair, she tanned evenly without burning. Her toned, tan body was sexy as hell, especially now that she had another tattoo on the opposite hip as his initials. When Tamian had taken off, it nearly broke Tessa's heart. When she asked Gregor if he minded her getting ink to honor her brother, he was all for it. Gregor almost felt guilty for her brother running off. Almost.

The workers on the island had been hired specifically because of their knowledge of the Gargoyles. If they noticed Gregor flying with Tessa and her diving into the blue water, they wouldn't think anything about it, other than it might look fun. Once Tessa was wearing a swimsuit, Gregor unfurled his wings and wrapped his arms around Tessa's waist. He launched into the air, flying out over the water. When he thought he was high enough, she shook her head, "Higher." He flew higher yet, and when she told him to, he helped her climb onto his shoulders. His wings held him in place while Tessa dove from high above the sea into the crystal blue waters. He flew after her, landing almost as soon as she did.

Tessa kicked her legs and broke the surface of the water, laughing louder than he had ever heard. "Again!"

After the sun started going down and the moon was showing its face, Gregor grabbed her and pulled her body to his. Tessa wrapped her legs around his waist, her arms around his shoulders. The smile on her face could light up a small third world country. He vowed to keep her smile in place for an eternity.

Tessa ground her pussy against his ever present hard cock. It wouldn't be the first time they made love in the sea. It wouldn't be the last swimsuit Gregor shredded to get his mate skin to skin. She pressed their mouths together, twirling their tongues in a dance as hot as a Samba. Gregor shuffled them closer to shore so his feet could find purchase in the sand. Tessa had his swim trunks down his legs and his dick in her hand, ready to impale herself. Between kisses she asked, "How do you feel about the names Tabitha and Antonio?"

Gregor froze in the water. "Do you mean what I think you mean?" His heart stopped. Ever since Kaya had given birth to Sebastian, Gregor had been longing to have a child of his own, their own.

Tessa's bright green eyes glowed. "If you think I'm pregnant with twins, then you would be correct."

Gregor kissed Tessa with all the love he had in him. His mate carrying his babies in her stomach was the greatest gift she could give him.

Gregor latched his mouth onto her neck, sucking the blood to the surface, adding it to the other marks he had put on her body these last few days. Gregor smiled at his woman, "Hold on." When she was wrapped tightly around his body, he phased and used his wings to lift his woman into the now moonlit sky.

Gregor's wings flapped softly, keeping them hovering just below the clouds. "Have you heard of the mile high club?"

"Of course. What are you...?"

Gregor didn't give her a chance to finish her question. He crashed their mouths together as he thrust his cock into her warm, wet core. Gregor and Tessa made love in the evening sky over the sea, celebrating the two lives growing in her belly.

The Beast

By: Gregor Stone

The beast within
Wants nothing more
Than to take you now

The man without
Wants so much more
So I take it slow

The beast inside
Needs to claim you
Take what's his

The man I am
Needs to love you
Take my time

The beast is raging
Fuck her now!
I need it rough

The man is feeling
Across your skin
I need to touch

The beast is howling
I need to come
Down her throat

The man is quiet

She needs to come
I want her to float

The beast is furious
Can't stand it anymore
He starts to take over

Her beast heeds the call
She grabs on tight
My mate, my lover

Coming Soon:

Dante and Frey

Stone Society Books 3 and 4

If you liked Gregor, please leave a review where you bought the book.

About the Author

Faith Gibson lives outside Nashville, Tennessee with the love of her life, and her two-legged best friends. She began writing in high school and over the years, penned many stories, and poems. When her dreams continued to get crazier than the one before, she decided to keep a dream journal. Many of these night-time escapades have led to a line, a chapter, and even a complete story.

When Faith isn't penning her crazy ideas, she can be found playing trivia while enjoying craft beer, reading, or riding her Harley.

Connect with Faith via the following social media sites:

https://www.facebook.com/faithgibsonauthor

https://www.twitter.com/authorfgibson

http://tsu.co/AuthorFaithGibson

Sign up for her newsletter at:

http://www.faithgibsonauthor.com/newsletter.html

Send her an email: faithgibsonauthor@gmail.com

Other Works by Faith Gibson

The Stone Society Series

Rafael

A Kiss of Poetry

Poetry Anthology

The Sweet Things Series:

Candy Hearts – A Short Story

Troubled Hearts

Spirits Anthology

Voodoo Lovin' – A Short Story

41117077R00171

Made in the USA
Lexington, KY
29 April 2015